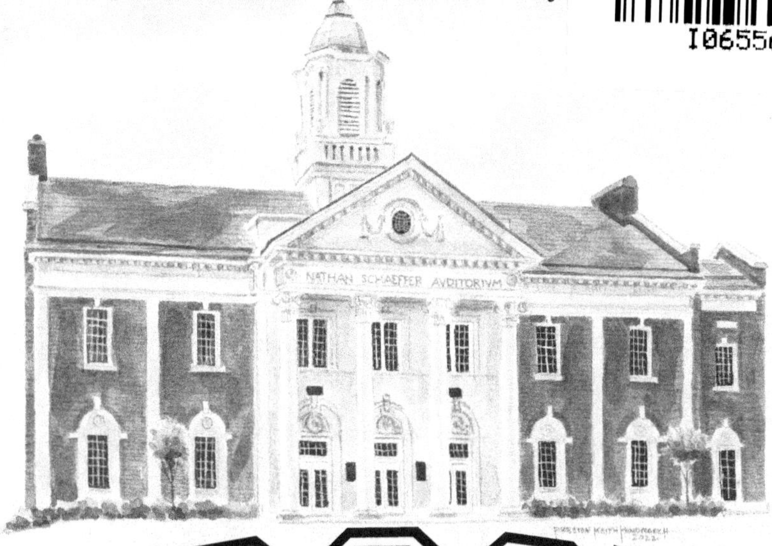

FROSH

A One-Year Memoir

John R. Scannell

Wutherwood Press

To so many women

To Richena Carol Hindmarch
my first crush, my first love,
who loved me unselfishly

To Professor Annette Monroe Mazzaferri Robertson
who helped the seventeen-year-old me
realize a world of possibilities

To Wendy
my wife, my best friend, my editor
who loved me enough to insist
I tell my stories

TABLE OF CONTENTS

Prologue
SPEAK ONLY GOOD OF THE DEAD
March 2018

Uncle Jack's death took us all by surprise. Perhaps me, most of all. But then, Uncle Jack was always something of a mystery to us all, and he was always full of surprises. Just thirteen months younger than my dad, we loved him to pieces—he was funny and thoughtful and generous—but he was always… well…something of a mystery.

For most of his adult life, Dad's brother had lived 3,000 miles away in the Pacific Northwest. His first professional position was, according to my father, "leading the ever-eccentric life of a high school English and Drama teacher." Then, when he became a national sales consultant with a big textbook publisher, he'd surprise us, showing up on our doorstep a half-dozen times every year. Because of his unannounced visits, Grandma characterized Uncle Jack as "the will-o'-the-wisp" for his sudden appearances. Dad called him "the family's goodwill ambassador who knows how to make an entrance."

Among the biggest surprises of all—and the one that caused the greatest consternation—was Uncle Jack's sudden marriage to an unknown woman, in distant Seattle, in a civil ceremony, without benefit of clergy, without telling anyone he was getting married, and without inviting anyone to the wedding. Of course, you'd think a fifty-five-year-old, never-married bachelor could do as he pleased, but my grandmother—his mother—would disagree.

Yep, his nuptials caused quite a stir in our family. Grandma was genuinely pissed (pardon the vernacular). Grandpa Timins had died four years earlier, and Grandma, who fell out of bed and broke her hip, was now living at Heart & Soul, an assisted living facility, when she got the news of Uncle Jack's marriage.

You should have heard Grandma.

"What's that dunderhead thinking?" she snarled when the news reached her ears. "He's certainly not behaving like the good Catholic gentleman I raised him to be. Married? Without a priest? It's positively disgraceful. Jack didn't even have the decency to introduce his fiancé to me before they got married. I never even knew he had a fiancé. What's this world coming to?"

I tried telling Grandma how things are in the 21st century, but it didn't matter. My grandma, born in 1919, didn't live in the 21st century, and I suspect she liked it that way.

A little more than a month after they married, Uncle Jack and the "unknown woman" we'd come to know as Vivian flew east for a visit. He decided he'd like to introduce his new wife to the whole family—on Grandma's birthday.

Uncle Jack suggested we all meet at Heart & Soul. As we drove to Grandma's assisted living facility, Dad said, "Well, this should be interesting."

Moments later, Mom replied, "Interesting? Could you be more specific?"

We met Uncle Jack and my new Aunt Vivian in Heart & Soul's parking lot, with the typical Timins' burst of enthusiastic hugs, kisses, and laughter.

Naturally, everyone congratulated the newlyweds.

"Welcome to the family, Vivian," Dad said, beaming at Vivian and his brother. "We are thrilled to meet the woman who could make my brother sit still and behave."

"Did you say sit still? Did you say behave?" Vivian asked with mock surprise. "I'm afraid you've mistaken me for some other woman."

After the laughter subsided, Dad turned to Uncle Jack with a big smile. "It's also good to see you, Brother Jack, as always." He threw his arm over his brother's shoulder. "Let's go in. Mom's waiting for us."

As we walked down the hall to the atrium commons, I warned my uncle. "Dad says things are about to get 'interesting,' Uncle Jack. Are you ready for this?"

"We'll see," Uncle Jack replied with an impish smile. He turned to look at his new wife, and nodded in Vivian's direction. "I brought my secret weapon."

Grandma was seated in her wheelchair in the commons area, and Uncle Jack went over and kissed her on the cheek. Grandma seemed surprised but pleased. Almost completely blind, Grandma thought it was my dad.

Then Uncle Jack said, "Hello Mom."

It took only the briefest of moments for Grandma to realize it was not my dad.

"John Robert Timins," Grandma began. Full names always presaged trouble. "Why wasn't I invited to your wedding?" she asked. Grandma seldom minced words. Whatever was on her mind came out of her mouth.

Uncle Jack attempted to introduce Vivian to Grandma, but Grandma, undeterred, interrupted him.

"I asked you a question, young man," she said sternly.

My dad stifled a laugh. When I heard "young man," I realized that some things never change—regardless of age.

Dad, Mom, and I were standing behind Grandma's wheelchair while Uncle Jack quickly grabbed two chairs and placed them directly opposite Grandma. Uncle Jack sat next to Vivian and began speaking slowly, with incredible kindness.

"No one was invited to the wedding, Mom. No one. Vivian and I decided to get married, that's all."

"This would've killed your father, Jack. Thank God he's in his grave."

Uncle Jack paused for a moment. He reached over and took one of Grandma's hands.

"I'm sorry, Mom. I really am. But it was partly out of consideration for you that Vivian and I decided to marry without any guests. If we'd invited anyone, rest assured that you would have been first on the list. But we didn't invite anyone."

Uncle Jack paused again.

"What would you have done if we'd sent you an invitation, Mom? You're in this wheelchair. You can't fly comfortably these days, and it's a long plane trip to Seattle. Besides, if we had invited you and all my east coast family and friends, each of them would have had to travel that same three thousand miles for the wedding—six thousand miles round trip. That's a lot of planning—and a lot of money, too. Come on, Mom. Airfare? Hotels? Rental cars? Meals? Vivian and I didn't want to put that pressure on anyone. As things worked out, no one had to spend any money to come to our wedding. And here we are. On your birthday."

Grandma immediately switched topics. "I hear you were married by a justice of the peace and not by a priest. At city hall." From Grandma's tone, I could tell that was the real issue.

"That's not true, Mom. One of Vivian's best childhood friends, Karen, married us—she's a clinical psychologist. And my best friend, Rick, stood up for me, and another of Vivian's lifelong friends, Carrie, stood up for her. We got married at our home—outside, in our back garden—with our three dogs and three cats in attendance. I bet you didn't have any dogs or cats at your wedding, did you? Well, we had a full half-dozen."

Grandma did her best to repress a smile. "No. We most certainly did not have any dogs or cats at our wedding."

We all laughed. Uncle Jack always had a way of finding Grandma's soft spot.

Uncle Jack squeezed his mom's hand. "I'm sorry if you felt hurt, Mom. It wasn't our intention to hurt anyone. I've loved Vivian since the night we met at Seattle Symphony's Benaroya Hall. I'm fifty-six, Mom, so I decided I wasn't going to waste one minute more not being married to her. I know you'll like her, because I love her." Uncle Jack rubbed the back of his mother's hand. "Vivian and I are as married as anyone can be."

Vivian, who had been sitting silently beside Uncle Jack, broke her silence. "I love your son, Mrs. Timins. That's why I insisted that we make this trip to see you as soon as possible. And may I say, it's a genuine pleasure to meet the mother of such a wonderful man."

Grandma leaned toward Vivian, nodding as a smile began to form. "Watch out for him," Grandma said, gesturing with her crooked index finger, "sometimes he's such a dunderhead."

"I know, Mrs. Timins. Boy, do I know. But his being a dunderhead is one of his most charming qualities."

Everyone laughed. My dad moved over to his brother and slapped him on the back. Vivian stood up and kissed Grandma on the cheek.

"Well," said Uncle Jack, "that's settled. Vivian married a dunderhead. Me!"

Grandma's face lit up, and she said, "Vivian, you can call me Vera." Then she turned to Uncle Jack. "I knew I'd like your wife, Jack. She sees you the same way I do. A dunderhead."

As the laughter erupted again, I realized that all the tension was gone, and everyone was happy. I shouldn't have been surprised that Uncle Jack had pulled another rabbit out of the hat. But I was.

The way he'd sidestepped the whole question of religion impressed me. It was a very practiced maneuver.

I'd known Uncle Jack my entire life, and marrying Aunt Vivian was only one of his many surprises. Decades ago, a few days before I was scheduled to begin my freshman year at college, Uncle Jack made one of his "will-o'-the wisp" appearances—a surprise visit—arriving unannounced, as if by magic, late on a Friday afternoon.

Dad, Mom, and I were lounging in the fully-screened gazebo my father had built in our side yard—built precisely because Pennsylvania was famous for hot, sultry, summer evenings like this one—when Dad spotted his brother standing at the gazebo door.

"Whoa! Who's that knockin' on my door?" Dad said. "Could it be our family's goodwill ambassador?"

"Body and soul, Brother Will," Uncle Jack's good moods were infectious. "I'm sorry. I should have phoned," he said, looking only slightly contrite.

"But you just couldn't resist making an entrance, could you, Brother Jack?" Dad teasingly remarked.

"Methinks thou dost speaketh true," Uncle Jack said, in his amusing British accent.

"Don't go all Shakespeare on me, Jack. Just get in here. You've already had a long day if you've come all the way from Seattle. Let me get you a cold one."

"Sounds like a plan," Uncle Jack said. He stepped inside the gazebo.

"Make sure that door is shut, Uncle Jack. No mosquitoes allowed."

"You tell him, Julie," Dad said, reaching into the cooler. He grabbed a beer, popped the cap, and handed the bottle to Uncle Jack. "Here on business?"

"Mostly." Uncle Jack took a big swig. "I've got a teacher in-service workshop on Monday in Upper Saddle River, New Jersey."

Then he turned to me.

"But I decided to come here first because I hear tell that someone is college bound, and that she desperately needs some money before she begins hitting the books."

He handed me a sealed envelope.

"There's some money in there. Just don't spend it all at one time, and for goodness sakes, don't give any to your dad."

I tore the envelope open and peeked. Let me just say there was a small stack of very large bills. "Wow, Uncle Jack. This is a wonderful surprise."

"Part of that is your high school graduation gift, Julie. The rest is 'just because.'" He gave me one of his goofy uncle smiles.

"I love you, Uncle Jack."

That evening, our conversations wandered all over the place, as family conversations do. We talked about my heading off to college, Dad's job, Mom's job, the Seattle weather—and then somehow we switched gears and started discussing the days of yore.

"Remember when we'd drink the last bits of wine from the small bottles Father Gaffney brought from the rectory? The ones he used to fill the cruets for Mass?" Dad asked.

"Oh, yeah," Uncle Jack said as he and Dad laughed.

Mom raised her eyebrows. "So that's why you loved being altar boys? I don't believe I've ever heard your wine-swilling story before."

"Well, dear Brother Jack here was the real altar boy," Dad said with a rueful smile. "I only became an altar boy because Dad wanted me to."

"And I became an altar boy because I really loved it—the ritual, the ceremony. Most of all, I loved the Latin Mass. Not only did I memorize all my Latin, I knew what it meant. Unlike your dad."

"He's right," my dad confessed. "I had no idea what I was saying when I recited the Latin prayers. Your uncle here, Mr. Know-It-All, ended up being the altar boy who helped other altar boys learn *their* Latin. Not to mention he was always volunteering for special masses—like funerals and weddings. Didn't you serve for the bishop at Confirmation?"

"Twice," Uncle Jack said proudly. "I didn't realize it at the time, but I think I loved serving at Mass because it was theatre."

He took a swig of his beer, and fell quiet.

"Yeah, Julie, your Uncle Jack actually wanted to go into the seminary right out of eighth grade. He told Mom and Dad that he wanted to be a priest."

"Really? This I gotta hear. The seminary? Why didn't you go, Uncle Jack?"

"Mom—your grandmother—said absolutely not. She told me that if I wanted to go into the seminary after high school, that would be just fine. But thirteen was just too young. That's what she said."

"So why didn't you go after high school?" I asked him.

When Uncle Jack didn't immediately reply, my dad sat forward and looked at his brother. Then Dad shot me one of those inscrutable dad smiles—the ones that say *I'm about to impart a closely-held secret.*

"That's easy," Dad explained. "He'd discovered girls. Isn't that right, Jack? Girls and the priesthood are oil and water, Julie."

"Is that right?" I asked, raising my eyebrows. I loved teasing him.

"I started dating a girl named Katie. Her first name was actually Richena, a female version of Richard, her dad's name. But we both preferred her middle name, Katherine. Katie and I started dating just after our sophomore year, when we were both rookie lifeguards at Heil Pool. I was smitten, Julie. Head over heels. After graduation, we were talking seriously about getting married. As you know, Catholic priests don't get married. That meant I could choose Katie or the seminary. I chose Katie."

"Julie, you would have loved your Uncle Jack's first girlfriend," Dad said. "Katie was a Methodist, and she loved nothing quite so much as eating hot dogs right in front of him on a Friday—always with a big grin. In those days, the Catholic Church said, 'Thou shalt not consume hot dogs, hamburgers, hoagies, or any meat on Fridays. Unless, of course, you want to go to Hell.'"

"Come on, Dad. Hell? For a hot dog?"

"Okay, Purgatory."

"I wasn't going to Hell or Purgatory," Uncle Jack flatly declared. "So, I didn't eat meat. I ate fish. I obeyed the rule…no hot dogs, no hamburgers, no hoagies for me. Unlike your dad."

"Are you saying my father ate hot dogs on a Friday?" I asked in mock horror.

"I'm afraid you'll have to ask your dad. I'm not going to rat him out."

"No need, Uncle Jack, I'm sure he ate plenty of hot dogs. So, why did the Catholic Church change the meatless Friday rule?" I asked.

Uncle Jack sighed. "Who knows? Sometime in the early 1980s the rule changed. One day we were all going to Hell for eating a hot dog on Friday, and then, the next Friday, we could go back for seconds. They changed the rules. Just like that." He snapped his fingers for emphasis.

"And Katie…you never married her?"

"Nope, never did. And it didn't have anything to do with hot dogs. I went off to my freshman year of college—just like you're doing now—and, well, let's just say my life changed in ways I could never have imagined."

"So what happened freshman year that was so unimaginable?"

He considered my question with a big, impish, Irish grin. "That's a long story, Julie. You're young. Someday I'll tell you."

When Uncle Jack retired in 2014, his visits became far less frequent. Making matters worse, Aunt Vivian died from cancer in 2016. When she died, my dad and I flew to Uncle Jack's side to...to what? Offer condolences? Tell him we loved him?

My dad said that all we really had to do was be there.

"There's nothing any of us can really say, is there, Julie? The love of his life is gone. He just needs to know that we are here to share his grief. That's all we can do."

A year later, Uncle Jack died in his sleep two days after Christmas and four days after his 70th birthday. Uncle Jack's brother-in-law, Chris, called to deliver the bad news.

Later that day, my dad phoned me.

"Does anyone know Uncle Jack's cause of death, Dad?"

"Not yet, Julie. Your mom thinks it's a broken heart. But I'm guessing he died from silliness denied. When Vivian died, my brother had no one to return his silliness."

It was true, Aunt Vivian and Uncle Jack's stock in trade was silly, light-hearted banter, loaded with silly puns. They were the Siamese Twins of Silliness—continually playing with words, dancing with language.

I truly enjoyed that about Aunt Vivian, and always looked forward to her "silly sensibility" whenever I'd fly to the West Coast to spend some time with her and Uncle Jack at *Wutherwood*.

Wutherwood was the name Aunt Vivian had bestowed on her one-acre property. After spending the entire 1980s living in England, she returned to the Pacific Northwest, purchased a home on a piece of land crowded with tall evergreen trees and blackberries, and named it *Wutherwood*—long before she and my Uncle Jack married.

I remember asking her about the name during my first visit the summer after they married. It was just us gals for a few days because Uncle Jack was out selling textbooks to English teachers somewhere in the United States.

"Every piece of property should have a name, don't you think?" She stopped for a moment and said the name softly, with reverence. "*Wutherwood.* I named our home after the wuthering sounds of the wind through the trees. It's a beautiful sound."

Aunt Vivian took me by the hand and said, "Come with me, Julie. I want to show you how *Wutherwood* can make you feel."

Aunt Vivian opened the front door, and as we stepped out onto the deck, her three dogs bounded outside with us. Everyone—canine and human—ambled along to the middle of the front yard.

"Look up," she said quietly. "Aren't the trees magnificent?"

I marveled at how Aunt Vivian's property—*Wutherwood*—was populated with tall, tall evergreen trees.

"We have thirty-five trees that brush the heavens, Julie. Cedar, fir, spruce, pine, hemlock. Thirty-five trees soaring over one hundred feet into the sky. If you ever tire of gazing at the sky—which I seldom do—we've got tons of juicy blackberries, crisp apples, sweet pears, and delicious plums."

She pointed out the blackberry bramble and each fruit tree as she mentioned it.

"We're forever picking up fallen fruit because the dogs go outside and gorge themselves on it."

I watched her three dogs running and playing in the upper yard, and asked, "Your dogs eat the fallen fruit?"

"Oh yeah, they most certainly do. And they eat way too much, way too often. No dog has ever known the meaning of *Enough!*"

We fell silent for a moment as a slight breeze blew through the branches.

I smiled at my aunt and softly said the word, "*Wutherwood.*"

Several weeks after Uncle Jack's death—and after several phone calls between my dad and Chris—Dad received a letter from Jennifer Achziger, Aunt
Vivian's niece. Jennifer had actually taken the time to write us a letter.

"Who writes letters anymore?" Dad asked.

"People write letters when it's really important, Dad—when phone calls,
emails, or text messages simply won't do."

During each of the six trips I'd made to the West Coast, I'd spent a lot of
time with Jennifer—she was clearly one of Aunt Vivian's favorite people. The
letter began by explaining that she had inherited *Wutherwood*.

> Someone has to look after the dogs and cats. Whoever gets that job needs to really
> know them, needs to be able to call them by name. After Aunt Vivian died, Uncle
> Jack asked me if I'd be interested in being that person. I said yes, but I never realized
> that I'd be doing it so soon. I'm so sorry he's gone. I know you are, too.

The letter offered a few details about Uncle Jack's passing.

> Uncle Jack died in his sleep. I'm sure you probably know that. A neighbor dropping
> by with a present found him a few days after Christmas and called the authorities.
> The coroner said there was nothing suspicious. Everything seemed quite normal—except
> the dogs and cats hadn't been fed, and the dogs hadn't been able to go out to go. I'll spare
> you the details about the terrible mess and the horrendous smell in the house. (I think
> I did a pretty good job of cleaning up.)
>
> He'd left a letter with my dad with his final instructions. His unassuming last
> sentence is actually a bit funny. "This is what I'd like, but I realize I'm in no position
> to make demands." So, per his instructions, Uncle Jack was cremated, and his ashes
> were scattered over the waters of Lake Washington, mingling with Aunt Vivian's.

Jennifer's last few sentences chummed the waters of our curiosity.

There are some things here you both will definitely want to have. I could send them, but I'd love it if you could come and spend some time with me at Wutherwood. Uncle Jack is one of my favorite topics.

Sufficiently intrigued, and wistful for the comforts of memory lane, Dad and I went.

Jennifer greeted us at the door with a broad grin. "Come in, you guys. I'm so glad you decided to come out."

"Can you blame us?" I asked. I pulled Jennifer's letter out of my purse. "Let me read exactly what you said. 'There are some things here you both will definitely want to have.' What you definitely have is my attention."

"And mine," Dad said.

"Good. Now that I have your attention, the first thing I want to show you is right here in the family room."

Jennifer walked to the bookcase next to the fireplace, opened one of the glass doors, and pulled down a small porcelain urn. She turned and faced Dad.

"Uncle Will, would you like to say something to your brother?"

"I thought his ashes were in Lake Washington." Dad was clearly surprised.

"Most of them. And most of Aunt Vivian's too. But Uncle Jack and Aunt Vivian have been reunited here in this urn. I keep their ashes in this bookcase because it also has the ashes of all the dogs and cats that have lived here over the past three decades."

My dad sat down and cradled the urn.

Jennifer returned to the bookcase and pulled down a second, identical urn. "I decided that we all would want a piece of each of them to help us remember. So, I bought two urns, and then I put ashes from Aunt Vivian and Uncle Jack in each. That one is yours. This one is mine."

Jennifer sat down next to me and started to cry, and then I joined her. My dad sat quietly with his urn and his memories.

After a few moments of sad reflection, Jennifer wiped her eyes and stood up. "But wait, there's more," she said with an enthusiastic glint in her eye. "Follow me to Uncle Jack's office,"

We walked to the rear bedroom—actually an office with a Murphy bed—and Jennifer pointed to six file boxes.

"Are these boxes filled with things my brother accumulated?"

"No," Jennifer said. "No, no, no. Not just accumulated. Uncle Jack did more than collect, he created, too. He's got poetry—lots of his own poetry—in that box." She pointed to the box labeled POETRY. "And some political satires in that box. Those two boxes over there have programs and Playbills from decades of theatre-going—plus Uncle Jack was writing his own play. It's in there. Who knew?" Then she pointed at the box atop the desk labeled FICTION. "That box has short stories and part of a novel. And this box," she said pulling the box off the desk chair, "has a very interesting book titled *Frosh: A One-Year Memoir*."

"I didn't think it was possible to have a one-year memoir," I said as I pulled off the lid to take a peek.

"I didn't either. And then I read Uncle Jack's *Frosh* and I changed my mind. You should read it. There's lots of things in there that explain a whole lot about Uncle Jack. *Frosh* is the reason I decided to write you a letter, Uncle Will. That, and his ashes. Your brother spent years writing up a storm."

"When did you discover all this?" my dad asked.

"Oh, I'd always seen these file boxes stacked in his office. Aunt Vivian said they were Uncle Jack's hobby. I remember Aunt Vivian laughing that Uncle Jack spent hours scribbling on note pads and pecking away at his typewriter. She said he'd grumble that, 'I can't feel like Hemingway if I don't type my stories.' And she'd shake her head and say, 'Well, why don't you be like Charles Dickens and write with a quill pen by oil lamp?'"

"She finally convinced him to use a computer sometime after they married. Aunt Vivian said it was a struggle to get your brother into the 21st century, Uncle Will."

My dad reached into the *Frosh* box and pulled out five or six chapters, each carefully paper-clipped, and each typewritten on some stiff paper.

"Dear God, Julie," Dad said, "he may have been using a computer lately, but he must have written some of this stuff ages ago. This is erasable bond paper. He probably typed these chapters on his Royal portable—the one he got when he went off to college. Erasable bond paper. Wow. Does anyone even manufacture this anymore?"

"I'm just happy these pages were never erased," I said.

My dad smiled and sighed, "Me, too. Time has a way of erasing most of us anyway."

"You'll want to see these two stapled pages. They were on top of *Frosh*. I don't know if Uncle Jack ever intended them as part of his book."

She shared what Uncle Jack had written. It was dated November 2016.

Who said life flows like a river? It wasn't me, and it wasn't a lot of people I've known. Now that Vivian is gone, life has felt more like a stagnant pond. She was my source of rain, and now it appears I've reached my season of drought. But perhaps that's just the way life is. Perhaps we all dry up sooner or later.

When I went off to college, that tranquil river—meandering everywhere and getting nowhere—became a raging torrent. Almost instantaneously, everything I was sure I knew about life and love and eternity, or thought I knew about life and love and eternity, turned itself upside down and into a question. My crazy college roommate taught me that life is about questions, not answers. Until I met him, I was sure it was all about the answers—and that I already had all the answers.

Well, I was wrong.

My basic problem was that I arrived at college believing that all I needed was more information. For years, I could hear my first-grade nun saying that "All you ever need to know is that God loves you. Nothing else is important." I believed that. After all, if a nun tells you something, it must be true.

When I considered the most important aspects of life, I was sure I had all the answers. I was seventeen-years-old and I knew that I knew everything that was worth knowing. Questions about God, and morality, and how one should conduct one's life, were not up for debate. These things had been decided long ago by the Catholic Church. Wiser heads had already plotted my path through life, into eternity, and into Heaven.

Then my collegiate freshman year caught me unawares. My freshman year set my feet on a different path; on a path away from the Church, but on a path of discovery that would lead me back to myself.

I just want the people I love to understand how everything that had already been decided in my life—the existence of God, the Trinity, the Catholic Church being the one true church—suddenly began to dissolve. Answers became questions. Undeniably settled questions became unsettled. Dogma became...well...undogged. I thought of calling my manuscript _The Great Unraveling_, but it took years before the unraveling reached the end of the spool. Then, one morning, I looked in the mirror and said, "I'm done."

College is where the unraveling began. College is where I first discovered that heresy and truth are not opposites. College is where I learned that God is not a requirement for leading a good life. I learned that most miracles are man-made. So, this manuscript is about losing something important, but gaining something important in return.

On a personal note, I am sorry to leave everyone behind. But that is the fate of every human being, isn't it? I remember the delightfully humorous epitaph George Bernard Shaw had chiseled on his tombstone: "I knew if I waited around long enough something like this would happen."

Well, my waiting is over. Now it's happened, and these few boxes of my writings are all I leave behind. I leave behind my thoughts—in letters, in stories, in essays, in drama, and sometimes even in poetry. All I ask is that whoever reads this, please read it with love...and, if necessary, with forgiveness.

De mortuis nil nisi bonum. "Speak only good of the dead."

John Robert "Jack" Timins
December 23, 1947— (Please fill in the date of my death, as I will probably be unavailable.) December 27, 2017.

"That's my handwriting," Jennifer said, pointing at the final date. I filled in the date for him," Jennifer said. "Uncle Jack was…as he expected…unavailable."

My dad, Jennifer, and I spent the next day sifting through all of Uncle Jack's papers. Jennifer had only known him from the time he met her Aunt Vivian, and she was dying to know more.

"Where should I begin?" Dad asked.

"Tell Jennifer why you thought Uncle Jack was eccentric."

"He was eccentric—but it was a good eccentric. If you're looking for eccentric, look no further than an English teacher who loves theatre more than anything. Your Uncle Jack was a theatre person…"

"And theatre people are eccentric…?" Jennifer asked.

"Always," Dad said with certainty. "That's what happens when the world of make-believe and the real world become inextricably intertwined. Did Uncle Jack ever talk to you in his fake British accent?"

"Yes, yes he did. He was such a goofball. Even when Aunt Vivian told him his fake accent was ghastly, he'd just keep on talking that way. Aunt Vivian could spot a fake British accent in a heartbeat," Jennifer said.

That light-hearted moment was exactly how we wanted to remember the much-loved man we'd lost.

For the next few days, while Jennifer was at work, my dad and I read *Frosh* together. No question, Uncle Jack had one hell of a year. *Frosh* depicts the period between his last week in high school and the end of his freshman year in college—a story that is, by turns, funny, delightful, ribald, enlightening, sad, and tragic—but always compelling.

Uncle Jack's story overflows with firsts. His first brush with atheism; his first foray into the world of acting; his first broken heart; his first genuine physical encounter with "the opposite sex;" his first encounter with genuine grief; and the first serious cracks in his impervious body of Catholic belief. I often found myself laughing out loud at something he said or did, or shrinking back when his pain seemed unbearable. Sometimes I felt like a voyeur as he explored new boundaries.

I would have loved to ask Uncle Jack if his one-year memoir was the God's-honest-truth, but I'm sure he would have smiled, and said something like, "It was an incredible year."

Indeed, it was incredible to think back across the decades to when I was a fledgling freshman asking him what was so unimaginable about his freshman year. *Someday I'll tell you.*

That "someday" has arrived. In Uncle Jack's one-year memoir—his silly, serious, soul-searching, heart-rending, and hilarious story—his voice lights up the narrative on every page. It's his most recent, delightful surprise.

Chapter 1
CHILDHOOD'S END

June 1965

Something was different this morning.

Even my 6:30 a.m. alarm sounded different. My new Philco clock/radio—a high school graduation gift from Aunt Marian and Uncle Ted—had replaced my old alarm clock, the one that had rousted me out of a sound sleep for the past four years. The difference? Instead of waking to a five-alarm fire, I rolled out of bed to the tuneful rhythms of *Sugar Pie, Honey Bunch*. Unfortunately, my brother Will, who had graduated from high school the previous year, had no more patience for waking to the Four Tops than he had to being unceremoniously awakened by a clanging cacophony.

He protested grumpily. "Jesus, Red. Not everyone has to get up at the crack of dawn. This is the second morning in a row I've had to tell you to turn down your damn radio."

"Sorry, Will. It won't happen again. Sorry."

Neither the Four Tops nor I would make my brother Will's top-ten hit list that morning.

I turned off the radio and quietly donned the same prescribed uniform I'd worn for all of my four years at Notre Dame High School—white shirt, striped tie, tan slacks, and a blue blazer. My girlfriend, Katie, always teased me.

"You never have to think about what to wear," she'd say.

That was true.

"That's one of the best things about Catholic school," I'd tell her.

"Maybe," she'd reply, "but the best thing about Catholic school is also the worst thing. Don't you see the problem, Red? Your God has no fashion sense at all. His taste in clothing is definitely limited and unimaginative. White shirts and blue blazers? Really? And His taste in women's fashion is even worse. How do you think Notre Dame's girls feel about those dark green jumpers? The ones that scream 'frumpy and dumpy.'"

"Listen, Katie," I would say in a playful voice, "if God had wanted us to wear anything but white shirts and blue blazers, He would have put specific instructions somewhere in the New Testament."

"So, you're saying that the New Testament prescribes this uniform? Well, thank God you look good in a blue blazer," she'd reply as she patted my cheek.

Dressed, I went downstairs to the kitchen. My mother sat at the kitchen table in her blue chenille bathrobe, drinking her coffee and smoking a cigarette. A pall of smoke drifted above the *Allentown Morning Call* spread out on the table.

"Any tests today?" she asked as I reached into the cupboard for cereal.

"Nope," I said cheerily. "None today. Today is just final classes. My trig final is tomorrow and then I say *sayonara* to Notre Dame."

"Well," Mom cast a glance at the clock above the refrigerator, "you better get a move on. Eat your Cheerios quickly because you're running a bit late. Lord knows, Mike is never late."

Before I could finish wolfing down my Cheerios floating on a sea of milk, a car's horn alerted me to Mike Flynn's arrival.

"There's my ride," I said.

I hopped up, kissed Mom on the cheek, and dashed through the dining room to collect my book bag for my last full day in high school.

As I skipped down the concrete stoop for the thousandth time to Mike's waiting car, a small voice in my head insisted that nothing had changed. *Not yet*, the voice whispered. *But everything is about to change.*

I can't say why everything felt different today—even the ride to school seemed somehow different. We rode in relative silence.

Twelve years of Catholic school are coming to an end, I reminded myself. *Tomorrow's trigonometry exam will be my final final. No more pencils, no more books. No more teachers' dirty looks.*

That little rhyme played repeatedly in my head—this time, in German—as I made my way to German class.

My last German class. Keine Bleistifte mehr, keine Bücher mehr. Catchy tune.

I consciously attached the word "last" to everything that happened for the next two days.

Deo gratias, I thought. *Thank God. Today will be my last lunch in Notre Dame's gender-segregated cafeteria.*

Our cafeteria monitor, a bitter, scowling nun named Sister Joachim, deliberately kept the sexes segregated whenever they ate beneath her watchful eye, even on this day—our last full day.

Talk about dirty looks. Sister Joachim's got the market cornered.

Every Notre Dame student understood that fear and suspicion fueled Sister Joachim's cold, cold heart. Sister Joachim taught Religion—*irony of ironies?*—and she constantly abjured us to "Always be vigilant. Sin is everywhere. The devil never takes a holiday."

Sister Joachim could be certain that the devil never ate lunch either—not in her cafeteria. Her infamous lunchroom policy banished Notre Dame's female students—ever clad in dark green jumpers over white blouses—to the tables on the west side of the lunchroom, while their blue-blazered, neck-tied, male counterparts were quarantined on the east side. Both sexes cast occasional glances across the chasm, praying that Sister Joachim would not notice. Looking at a member of the opposite sex was a sin, at least in Sister Joachim's book.

When either gender approached the row of garbage cans bisecting the lunchroom, only then were they close enough to one another to trade greetings. Unfortunately, Sister Joachim patrolled the garbage line—Notre Dame's version of *no man's land*. Few things escaped the notice of our official lunchroom Gestapo. There would be no sexual congress of any sort while she was on duty. No glances. No comments. And no touching—God forbid there should ever be any touching.

As students dropped their refuse into the trash, any exchange of any kind between members of the opposite sex—however innocent—provoked an instantaneous response.

"That will be enough, Mister," Sister Joachim would sternly say. "Move along."

"There will be no shenanigans, young lady."

She'd wag a bony, hortatory finger in the face of any student who even vaguely appeared to be "up to something"—which in Sister Joachim's suspicious mind was virtually everyone in the lunchroom. In Sister Joachim's universe, all students were always "up to something."

The only thing I was up to was studying for tomorrow's trig final. My final final. After that, graduation. Then a summer job as Heil Pool's new assistant manager, and sultry summer nights made bearable when shared with my girl-friend, Katie.

Next September, I'd be off to college, but that was three months distant.

Had Sister Joachim known all the details of what I was up to—*all* the details—she would have grabbed me by the scruff of my neck while declaring in her most annoying, nasal tones that I must "Beware! Beware, young man! Guard against impure thoughts! Spurn the near occasion of sin! The thought is father to the deed. We all know where that kind of thinking can lead, don't we?"

It was a rhetorical question. Sister never waited for anyone's response.

"It's the road to perdition!" she'd declare. "The road to perdition, young man!"

For Sister Joachim, every teenage road was "the road to perdition," but, honestly, with Sister Joachim fiercely blocking the way, finding the on-ramp to that road could prove difficult. I took comfort in knowing that, by noon tomorrow, the road to perdition would be wide open, and I'd have the pedal to the metal with Katie as my passenger. Had Sister Joachim discerned my inten-tions, she would have been furious. But if she had known that my girlfriend, Katie, was a Methodist…a non-Catholic, well…she'd have been apoplectic.

According to Sister Joachim, Methodists—and non-Catholics of any de-nomination—were among the myriad "near occasions of sin." Consort with them at your own risk.

I was not risk averse.

Father Bonaventure was standing at his classroom door welcoming each student as we arrived for our "last" German class. The blousy sleeves of his Franciscan friar's chocolate-brown habit had been rolled up above his pale hands and forearms, and he shook the hand of each senior who entered.

"You are sad, ja, to be leafing?" he asked in an amused tone of voice. "You do not vish to leaf your high school, ja? Or your childhood? Ja?" He pinched my cheek affectionately and looked me straight in the eye with a gentle smile. His teasing always amused us. This short, balding, bespectacled Franciscan priest, an escapee from Austria after Hitler's Anschluss, had earned our affection with his self-deprecating humor and kindness.

We all assumed our seats, recited the *Our Father* in German, and then Father Bonnie wished us well in his heavily-accented English. He blessed us—in German, of course—and we felt blessed.

"I haf vun last duty bevore you leaf," he said. "I must collect your textbooks. Ef you haf written in zee book, pleeze eraze eny marks remaining on der payches."

That's when I realized that I'd left my German book at home. I could picture it on the dining room table.

Good going, Jack.

Calling my mother and asking her to bring the book to school wasn't an option because Mom didn't drive. Once, a long time ago, she'd tried learning to drive, and the results were not pretty.

All of my friends' mothers drive, but not mine.

I raised my hand, and Father Bonnie nodded and asked, "Was ist los, Herr Timins?"

"I am afraid I left my book at home, Father."

"Dummkopf." Everyone laughed. Father Bonnie had called everyone a dummy at one time or another. Even himself.

"Ja, I'm a Dummkopf, Father. What should I do?"

"You vill haf to speek mit Sister Maria Paula about zee book, ja? You know her?"

Yeah, I knew her, and I wasn't thrilled about it. Sister Maria Paula had taught my older brother, Will, Spanish. His description of her temperament and teaching style was less than flattering. Of course, Will's indifferent study habits and equally mediocre grades in Spanish never endeared him to Sister Maria Paula, either. Neither belonged to a mutual admiration society.

"Can't I just bring the book to you, Father?"

"Nein. Sister Paula ist zee book Frau," Father Bonnie said. "You must gif zee book zu her."

When the dismissal bell rang, I decided to see if I could track down Sister Maria Paula during lunch. I inquired at the office, and they directed me to the basement bookroom—a long, narrow room situated next to the boiler room. The faint smell of oil flavored the air, and I found a perspiring Sister Paula shelving French books in this dimly lit space.

"Sister Paula?" I called from the doorway.

She didn't even look up. "I'm busy at the moment," she said.

"Sister," I said from the doorway, "Father Bonaventure said I needed to see you."

She continued shelving books without looking at me. "Why would he tell you that?"

"Because I left my German book at home this morning, I guess."

Her veil was pinned back exposing the white wimple that surrounded her face. Large safety pins kept her sleeves above the elbow. She stood up, and, as she turned toward me, she wiped a bead of sweat from her brow with her thumb.

"And why did you forget to bring your book today?"

These were the kinds of questions I've never understood. What answer was possible? Why did anyone ever forget anything? Carelessness? Stupidity? Cupidity? I was tempted to ask, "What kind of a stupid question is that, Sister?" but I felt certain I should resist that temptation for at least one more day.

"I don't know, Sister," I pleaded meekly. "I just forgot."

Just forgetting, just being fallible and human, were never good defenses with the IHMs—those nuns who belonged to the Order of the Immaculate Heart of Mary. Sister Joachim and Sister Maria Paula both belonged to the IHMs, and both took a dim view of any sort of human failing. Forgetting was a human failing. She wiped another stream of sweat from her cheek and stepped toward me.

"What's your name?" she asked.

"I'm Jack Timins, Sister."

She paused. "Are you Will's brother?"

I nodded. She gave me an appraising look as if to say, *You're just like your brother.* The truth was that I was not at all like my brother. Will had always bridled under the strict rules imposed by Catholic school, the same rules that never bothered me. I don't know why. Nor did I mind the studying necessary for good grades, or the carefully-practiced, obsequious behavior required to earn favor with the priests and nuns.

True, I minded the kind of stupid questions the nuns often asked, but I never minded out loud.

"Jesus, Red, you are such a goddamn brown-noser," Will would say whenever we brought our report cards home.

"Is that what I am? A brown-noser?"

"Hell, yeah. You kiss way too many asses, Red."

And you don't kiss nearly enough, I would have liked to say. But I never did. Will's educational waywardness, disappointing to many, came with a kind of confidence and self-assurance that I'd envied since first grade. Years later, Will would remind me that the only difference between an ass-kisser and a brown-noser was depth perception.

The truth is, I'd figured out how to make Catholic school work for me. I knew how to stay inside the lines. Will hated those lines and pushed the boundaries as often as he could without being expelled.

As I stood in the doorway of the oily bookroom, I wondered whether I should apologize for being Will's younger brother. The Catholic Church seemed to relish guilt by association.

Hmmmm, isn't Original Sin all about guilt by association?

I had no idea what I should say next to Sister Maria Paula, but I needn't have worried.

"Just what am I supposed to do about you forgetting your book?" Sister asked.

I looked at her earnestly. Earnest looks often worked. "Can I bring it tomorrow?"

"It's due today."

"I know. I'm sorry." I took a deep breath and tried to look even more earnest. "Can I return it tomorrow?" I repeated.

"Tomorrow, there will be a late fee for failing to return the book on time."

"What if I go home and get it right after school?" I asked.

"I won't be here past four o'clock today," Sister said.

"Alright. I'll have the book to you by four o'clock."

Sister Maria Paula turned to her right and picked up another French book to shelve. I took her silence for dismissal.

To return the book by four o'clock, I would have to race home right after class, pull the book from the dining room table, and dash back to have it in Sister Maria Paula's hand by 3:59:59. That was my plan. I wondered if I should have synchronized watches with Sister Paula as I made my way to the lunchroom to look for Mike Flynn.

I didn't know exactly how I'd execute my plan since I didn't have a car at school. I carpooled to school with Mike Flynn and Sterling Carter in Mike's dark-blue 1950 Packard. Now I hoped to find Mike, ask him if I could borrow his car, zoom home, retrieve the book, zoom back, and deliver the book to Sister Maria Paula by the 4:00 p.m. deadline.

As I entered the lunchroom from the main hall, Sister Joachim spotted me. She was the busiest of busy-bodies. She strode toward me and asked me where I'd been.

"I'm sorry, Sister Joachim. I'm looking for Mike Flynn."

I began moving past Sister Joachim, but she grabbed me by the wrist. "Mr. Timins, I asked you a question."

I stopped, head bowed, realizing the futility of not stopping to answer her question.

"Yes, Sister," I raised my head and smiled at her. "I wasn't in the lunchroom earlier because I went to see Sister Paula in the bookroom. I accidentally left my German book at home. She said I must return the book by 4:00 p.m. today or face a fine. I've got to ask Mike Flynn if I can borrow his car to drive home and retrieve my book." I looked at Sister Joachim's unblinking eyes for some sign of comprehension. Or compassion.

She released my wrist. "Why did you forget your German book, Mr. Timins?"

There was that inane, unanswerable question again. I could feel the pressure build behind my eyes. I was tempted to say, *You know, Sister, I have no idea whatsoever. No fucking idea. None. Maybe you can tell me why I would do something like that. Haven't you ever forgotten anything?*

But, once again, I resisted temptation.

Instead, I shrugged my shoulders. "I don't know, Sister. I guess...I guess I was in a hurry."

"Just like you are now?"

Why am I talking to Sister Joachim? I didn't have to come to lunch at all. It's not required. I don't have to account to her for any of my actions before arriving here.

"Yes, Sister. Just like now."

"I'm sure that if you slow down, Mr. Timins, you'll find that God will give you a clearer perspective. The Holy Spirit cannot help us when we are constantly rushing from one thing to the next."

This is how despair seeps into one's soul, I thought.

"Yes, Sister. I'll try to remember that."

"See that you do."

And then she turned away and walked swiftly toward a young man who'd had the misfortune of catching Sister Joachim's notice by lofting his empty milk container toward one of the galvanized garbage cans. He'd hit his target, but such behavior was clearly unacceptable.

Good, she's found fresher prey.

Notre Dame's students always knew when the nuns were finished with their moralizing or their scolding, because they simply turned away. That's how conversations ended with many of the nuns. Few students had enough nerve to say, *Hey, wait a minute. We're not done talking yet. I have something to say.* I never did. Even now, years later, I can't say if my silence—when accosted by nuns—was wisdom or cowardice.

My brother, Will, however, had that kind of nerve. He'd gone toe-to-toe with the IHMs, and it cost him dearly in the way they treated him. They labeled him belligerent, difficult, a smart-aleck. All because he defended himself.

Unfortunately for us students, all the IHM nuns shared living quarters in the same convent, so when one IHM nun declared a student "belligerent," that status was communicated to all the sister Sisters. I used to kid Will that his picture was probably posted on the IHM "Most Wanted / Least Wanted" bulletin board.

That was too bad. I came to realize that my older brother sincerely believed respect should be a two-way street, and he didn't respond kindly when respect was demanded without being shown. A *quid pro quo*. The nuns may have understood Latin, but *quid pro quo* wasn't in their vocabulary.

Just before the passing bell rang, I got the keys to Mike Flynn's car.

"It's going to need petrol," Mike said. "The Beast is a mighty thirsty machine."

I promised Mike that I'd put gas in the car and be back to Notre Dame by 4:00 p.m., if not before. I'd also managed to see Father John Joseph in the hall as I raced to my next class. I had Father John, another Franciscan friar, for Latin during the last period of the day.

"Father John, I need to skip Latin class today because I forgot to bring my German book in for Father Bonnie today. I need to get home and bring it to Sister Maria Paula by four o'clock."

Father John's response was remarkable only in its unremarkability. He didn't ask a single foolish, unfathomable question. Instead, he peered over his dark-rimmed glasses with a knowing look. "I understand," he said.

He patted me on the shoulder. "I was hoping to see all of you and say goodbye today. Latin IV is something special. You are among the best of the best."

I laughed. "No Father, I just think we are more like the last of the last. Fourteen kids studying a dead language for four years…"

"No, Jack. Fourteen scholars studying the words and ideas of dead men whose ideas are still alive." Father John never called me "Mr. Timins" the way the IHMs did with their *faux* respect. Genuine friendship and respect had permitted a level of informality. "We've spent a lot of hours with Caesar and Ovid and Cicero and Virgil…"

"*Arma virumque cano*," I recited.

Father John broke into a broad smile. "Of arms and the man I sing," he said. "Aren't Virgil's opening lines of the *Aeneid* wonderful? I am glad you committed them to memory."

I laughed again. "You do remember that you *made* us memorize them, don't you, Father?" I said with a teasing grin. "We never had a choice."

"Of course you did. And you said 'yes.' One day, you will be able to recite Virgil's lines to your grandchildren."

This is what keeps despair at bay, I thought. *Kindness. Understanding. Why couldn't all the teachers here be like Father John or Father Bonnie?*

"Father, I've gotta get to class. But I am asking permission to cut Latin so I can go home." The two of us, student and teacher, looked at one another. "May I?"

"Drive safely," said Father John.

When sixth period ended, I headed for Mike's huge Packard parked behind the gym. I had never driven Mike's car before, but I'd been a passenger for most of the school year once football season ended. During the fall, Sterling and I had used my dad's 1954, Mack-truck green Chevy, because football practice made it impractical for Mike to wait for us   often past six o'clock.

As I unlocked the car, I noticed the carefully-scrolled gold lettering on the front fender just ahead of the driver's door. *The Beast.* No truer words were ever written. The Beast guzzled gas, and I had promised to put gas in the tank because Mike was doing me a favor. After sixth period, I reached into my pants pockets and discovered one handkerchief—a Catholic school requirement—two paper clips, some lint, and sixty-four cents. That was all. Gas was twenty-eight cents a gallon for regular—it had been about three cents cheaper two years ago—so I could buy two gallons of gas and have eight cents left to squander.

When I ran in through the back door of my house, my mother shouted from the living room where she was knitting while watching her soap operas. "You're home early."

She knitted and chain smoked constantly. During TV shows. While bowling. Probably in her sleep.

My German book sat on the dining room table, precisely where I imagined it to be. I picked it up, took off the graffiti-covered book cover I'd made for it, and walked into the living room. Mom looked up from her knitting, a cigarette burning in the ash tray next to her.

"Mom, I just came home to get my German book. I forgot that we had to turn it in today. I borrowed Mike Flynn's car, and I have to get back to school and turn it in. Gotta go."

I kissed her on the cheek, and, as I ran out through the back door, I heard her shout, "Be home for supper."

It wasn't anywhere near four o'clock when I pulled Mike's Packard into the Notre Dame High School parking lot. It was 3:05. *Three-oh-five!* I felt elated. Grabbing my book, I made my way down to the bookroom. Sister Maria Paula was still sitting on her short metal stool, still sweltering in the early summer heat, three stacks of Spanish One books crowding her feet.

"I brought my German book just as I promised," I said proudly.

Sister Paula was clearly fed up with shelving books in this humid, dimly lit, musty-smelling room. "That will be twenty-five cents," she said without looking up.

I was speechless.

"What?" was all I could muster.

"The fine is twenty-five cents."

"But I went all the way home to get my book. I borrowed a friend's car to get this book to you by four o'clock."

Sister Paula did not turn to look at me.

"You said if I had the book to you by four o'clock, there wouldn't be any fine. It was due today. It's here today."

"Your book is late," Sister Paula said. She stood up. "The fine is twenty-five cents."

I stepped into the book room, doing my utmost to control my temper. "I used all my money to put gas in Mike Flynn's car. I don't have twenty-five cents."

"Then you'll have to pay your fine tomorrow."

I'll never see this woman—this nun—ever again, I thought. *I've delivered my goddamn German book just as I promised. She has no right to levy a fine.*

"But that's not fair," I said. "You said if I delivered the book to you before four o'clock, there wouldn't be a fine."

"No. I only said I would be here until four o'clock. I never said anything about the fine."

I held out my German book. "It's right here, and it's on time," I said struggling to sound calm. I probably sounded pissed.

What should I do now?

I stepped forward and placed my German book atop the pile of Spanish books and walked out the door. "It's right there," I said over my shoulder.

As I went to find Mike Flynn in the library, I assured myself that this whole silly episode was finished. God was in His Heaven, Sister Maria Paula had my German II text, and all was right with the world. Well, almost.

As Mike, Sterling, and I drove home that day, we were listening to the Beatles, who wanted to hold our hands.

I interrupted the song. "Thanks, again, Mike. For letting me use your car today."

"So you got the book to Sister Paula and everything is copacetic, right?" Mike asked.

"Yep," I said, "everything is copacetic."

As I knotted my necktie in the mirror, I knew that only my Trig final stood between me and graduation.

So this is it, I thought. *My last day of high school. My last exam. My last day as a Notre Dame Crusader.* Then it hit me—*my last day in Catholic school.*

I was fifteenth in my class—a notable fall from my first semester freshman year at Notre Dame when I was first in my class—and I would be graduating in a few days and be the first member of my family to attend college.

One last test—my final final. Then, I'm a college freshman—well, almost.

A blaring horn—Mike Flynn's *The Beast*—woke me from my last day's reverie. I threw my jacket over my shoulder and kissed my mother good-bye.

"Do well on your exam," Mom said. Words said by every mother sending her child off to take a test.

"I will, Mom. It's only trig—and I have an 'A' in that class. I should be home before noon."

I felt light-headed—even a bit giddy. I leapt off the front stoop and then bounded down the ten concrete steps to the sidewalk. It was an old habit. My friend, Sterling, had the Packard's passenger door open. I could hear the lyrics of *Mrs. Brown, You've Got a Lovely Daughter* echoing from the cavern of the car. We always listened to WAEB on the way to school.

Today, Sterling was bowing like a footman. "Your chariot awaits, m'lord."

I think I looked puzzled.

"Get in, stupid, we've got a final to take before we say farewell and Godspeed to Our Lady."

I climbed into the backseat.

"Hey, Mike…it's the last day!"

"*Deo gratias*," Mike said.

"Damn right, thank God," said Sterling. "We've been waiting for this day…"

"Since the day we were born," quipped Mike.

"Maybe longer," said Sterling.

"It doesn't make any difference how long any of us have waited," I said with absolute certainty, "because after today I am done. We're done. Finished."

Some seniors were already done with their diocesan finals, others had two tests scheduled for today, but after those, they would be done, too.

"Today is the day every senior dreams about, isn't it?" I asked.

"Really?" Sterling quipped. "I never dream of trig finals."

"Me, neither," Mike replied. "I never dream of cleaning out my locker, either. By the way, that's what I'll be doing after the trig test today."

We continued to kid each other and joke about the coming class trip to Washington, D.C., as we drove to school. Three boys—Sterling, Mike, and I—had been classmates for twelve years, and we'd been born on December 24th, 20th, and 23rd. When anyone asked Mike when his birthday was, he would blow on his fingernails and shine them on his shirt. Then with mock braggadocio, he'd declare that "Jesus was almost born on my birthday."

Today was the last day that we would arrive at the schoolhouse door together. Today would be the last day that we sang silly lyrics to silly songs as we drove to school. Today's conversation—one of thousands of conversations over the years—deflected the sense that somehow we had reached childhood's end.

Roger Miller was singing *King of the Road* as Mike killed the radio and we all climbed out of the car. "I'll be seeing you later this morning in our pre-post-high school world," Mike announced.

"What world is that?" I asked.

"You know," said Mike. "It's the world where we are done. All-but-graduated…but not yet graduated. We won't be 'post-high school' until Friday, two days hence." Mike saw little comprehension in our faces, and simply waved good-bye with his empty book bag.

Sterling shut his car door, shaking his head as he watched Mike walk off. As we walked to our exam room, Sterling started laughing. "You know he's probably right. Mike, I mean. I don't know what the hell a pre-post-high school world is, but he's probably right. He always is."

My trig teacher was Sister Amelia, a large nun—some might say rotund—with thick glasses and a gentle, forgiving nature. Perhaps she wasn't the greatest trig teacher ever—some cast doubts on her trig acumen—but she willingly helped struggling students without exposing them to the withering verbal assaults that too often accompanied the typical stumbles along the learning path. She never stabbed students with hurtful comments.

"How can you be so stupid?"

"God gave you a brain, didn't he?"

"It's a wonder you can tie your shoes."

Many of the IHMs did, but never Sister Amy. She was ever the carrot, never the stick. Sister Amy was "the exception that proves the rule," Mike once explained when I wondered aloud how she could be so nice and still be a member of the IHMs. Put more charitably, she was the only IHM nun whom I felt was worthy of my respect. I looked forward to seeing her one last time. Maybe I could persuade the class to sing "Once in Love with Amy" the way we had last December before Christmas break. Generously, Sister Amy had declared a "homework holiday" for the entire Christmas holiday and one of the boys spontaneously began singing. Everyone joined in. She cried and told us to "get out of here, and have a Merry Christmas."

Our final exam was in Room 23, at the south end of the main hall, and

Sterling and I walked in about ten minutes before the test was scheduled to begin. Other classmates had already found their seats and were talking about graduation. I fished around in my book bag for my three No. 2 pencils—the answers must be recorded on bubble sheets using ONLY No. 2 pencils—and I also found some scratch paper for figuring out problems. Mike and I had once debated whether it might be a sin to use a No. 3 or No. 4 pencil.

"Using anything but a No. 2 pencil is an act of disobedience," I had asserted.

Mike's only response to my assertion was the patented Mike Flynn moment of silence. His head and shoulders drew back for a moment; one hand touched his chin and the other was slightly raised as if to make a point; a stern but quizzical look crossed his face; his head tilted slightly to the side. Invariably, the silence was broken with "Dummkopf" and a pantomimed triple slap—with sound effects, of course. It was Mike's way of saying, "A sin? Are you kidding?"

Mike might be right, I thought, *but I'm not going to risk it.* With No. 2 pencils in hand, I was ready. *Bring on the test.*

Then, in walked Sister Maria Paula. The class rose in unison as she hastened to the desk in the front of the room, her arms loaded with both the test booklets and the answer sheets. As she unloaded the papers on the desk, she said, "You may be seated."

We all resumed our seats in silence. Then it dawned on me. Sister Amelia taught five trig classes and only one of those classes could meet in her classroom for the final. This was one of the non-Sister Amelia exam rooms.

Clearly, Sister Maria Paula was the test monitor for Room 23. She looked considerably better this morning than she had late yesterday afternoon when she was dripping with sweat, and I hoped she would simply conduct herself as a fresh-as-a-daisy exam monitor rather than as the erstwhile sweaty and unreasonable Book Frau.

The passing bell rang signaling the beginning of the exam period. Like every class for four years, we began by reciting the *Our Father.* As soon as the prayer concluded, Sister Paula immediately read the scripted instructions that preceded all standardized diocesan exams. We all knew the answer sheets and exam booklets would be handed out when Sister said, "At the end of the allotted time period, any student still working on the test will be instructed to put down his No. 2 pencil and hand in both the answer sheet and the test booklet. Are there any questions?"

There never were any questions. Not from seniors who had performed the annual diocesan exam ritual for four years. Since there were no questions, the row monitors—the students sitting in each of the front row desks—began passing out the answer sheets and test booklets. Andy D'Agostino was the monitor in my row—my seat was the fifth in that row—and as he handed me the test papers, Sister Maria Paula called out to Andy from the front of the room.

"Mr. D'Agostino."

He turned to face Sister Maria Paula. "Yes, Sister?"

"Mr. D'Agostino, please don't give Mr. Timins his test papers."

What the hell? I thought.

The answer sheet and test booklet were already on my desk in front of me, and now Sister Maria Paula wanted Andy to do her dirty work, but there was no way that I was going to hand my papers back to Andy—the incredibly brilliant, but socially awkward, Andy D'Agostino. A stiff wind could have blown over his slight frame.

"I'm not giving back these papers, Andy," I whispered. "Sorry. Just finish the row and head back to your seat."

Andy looked back and forth between Sister Maria Paula and me. Back and forth. It became clear that the rest of the class had stopped whatever they were doing. They were watching us, too.

Go back to your seat, Andy, I thought. *Don't put yourself in the middle of this.*

The look on Andy's face alternated between fear and resignation. Unable to comply with Sister's request, he quickly walked back to the front, sliding into his seat. Sister Maria Paula carefully watched Andy, and soon realized that he couldn't comply.

She moved swiftly down the aisle to my seat. She wasn't tall, but she had the advantage when I was seated. "You haven't paid your fine, Mr. Timins."

"This test doesn't have anything to do with that, Sister. Besides, I returned my German book before four o'clock yesterday—before you even left school—so it was on time. There shouldn't be any fine."

She responded as if I hadn't said anything at all. "The fine is twenty-five cents." She reached across my desk and picked up my answer sheet. "When you've paid the fine, you may take your test," she said as she moved back to the front of the room.

"That's not fair," I said from my seat. I couldn't believe how angry I was. And embarrassed.

"Twenty-five cents, Mr. Timins, if you wish to take this test."

All eyes kept moving between Sister Maria Paula and me, wondering what was going on, and what would happen next.

"The rest of you had best get back to taking your test," Sister ordered. "The clock is ticking."

What am I supposed to do now? God damn it! What am I supposed to do?

My mind was a blank. No solution presented itself. I looked at the diocesan test booklet—Sister had taken only my answer sheet—and I realized I could take the test using only the diocesan "Do Not Write In This Booklet" test booklet. I began circling answers in it, and my actions caught Sister Maria Paula's notice. She confiscated my test booklet as well.

"Twenty-five cents," she said.

Checkmate, I thought.

Angry and red-faced, I stood up and walked to the classroom door in the back of the room, cast a look back at Sister Maria Paula, and stepped out into the hallway. If I had learned anything from my twelve years in Catholic school, it was this: hallways are a *no man's land* when classes are in session. Anyone in the hallway must have a hall pass signed by a teacher or the principal. Violating the hall pass rule resulted in detention—at the very least. I now stood in the hall—just outside the classroom—without a hall pass on my very last day at Notre Dame. An F on my trig exam would adversely affect my grade.

It's only twenty-five cents, I thought. *But that's not why I'm so pissed off. It's just not right.*

I sighed.

It doesn't make any difference who's right. She's holding all the cards, and, if I want to take that test, I'd better get to it.

I reached into the pocket of my beige chinos and found eighty-five cents. I took a quarter and walked back into the classroom. As quickly as I could, I walked to the teacher's desk where Sister Maria Paula was seated. She stood up as I approached. I reached out and placed the quarter in the open palm of her left hand.

"There," I said. I think I was scowling. "Are you happy now?"

I snatched my answer sheet and test booklet—the one in which I'd begun circling the answers—and returned to my desk.

Almost as soon as I resumed my seat, I heard the faint tinkling of a coin hitting the linoleum floor. But I didn't care. The clock was running and I had a test to take.

"Mr. Timins," Sister Maria Paula called in a stern voice. "Mr. Timins, please come up here and pick up that coin."

I looked up.

Unbelievable. I shook my head. *God Almighty, I don't believe this.*

I looked back down at my test. Then my anger spoke for me. "You dropped it, you pick it up."

"Mr. Timins," Sister Maria Paula said pointedly, "if you expect to take this test, you'll pick up that coin and hand it to me…respectfully."

Once again, everyone had ceased doing trigonometry. As my dad often said about such moments, "You could hear a pin drop," or in this case, a quarter. Moments of real drama in Catholic school were few, and most battles were already decided because students were powerless and teachers were almighty. Unfortunately, many teachers also thought they were infallible.

I surrendered, pushing myself out of my desk. I swiftly made my way toward Sister Maria Paula. The quarter, resting on the floor inches from her desk chair, showed George Washington in profile.

Heads, she wins, I thought.

In one quick motion I bent over and snatched up the quarter. I looked directly at Sister Maria Paula and, for the second time, placed the coin in the palm of her left hand. This time I folded her fingers around the coin, giving her a fist full of quarter.

"Hold on to it this time," I said. "Please." We glared at one another.

It's your last day. Your last test. Let it go, I reminded myself as I returned to my desk. I saw that everyone was still watching the drama unfold. But as far as I was concerned, it was over. This time I hoped to finish my test in peace.

It was a premature hope.

"Mr. Timins, I don't think I like your tone," Sister Maria Paula said from the front of the room.

What does she expect me to say to that? I wondered. *Should I say, "Tough shit? That's not my problem?" Answers like that could get me expelled, even on my last day. Ignore her,* I told myself. *Just ignore her. She's got your money. Just finish the test and go home.*

"Mr. Timins, I said I don't think I like your tone," she repeated.

The whole class was paying close attention to our verbal tennis.

What the hell. She'll keep serving until I return volley.

I put down my No. 2 pencil, leaned forward in my desk, and shot her a look of pure disgust. My anger and frustration shaped itself into one simple phrase: "You son-of-a-bitch."

I'd actually said what I was thinking. *Oh, Jesus, I actually said that out loud.*

The entire room inhaled and held its collective breath.

Until that moment—that very unfortunate moment—the class had probably been rooting for me. But when I'd uttered the words "son-of-a-bitch"... at a nun...in a Catholic school...out loud...in front of witnesses...I knew I'd transgressed some clearly defined, bright line. In instances like this, the truth hardly even mattered. Even if everyone in the world knew Sister Maria Paula to be the most outrageous son-of-a-bitch, in a clerical order filled with sons-of-bitches, everyone knew the eleventh commandment was "Thou shalt not call an IHM nun a son-of-a-bitch." Not out loud anyway. All my classmates knew it, too, and their silent support for my struggle had dissolved the moment I'd said it.

I knew what they were thinking.

We were with you, Jack. She was treating you like crap and you had our full, if silent, support. And then you called her a son-of-a-bitch. Wow! You may be right, but...sorry, man...you are on your own.

I waited for Sister Maria Paula to make the next move. I'd run out of moves. As I sat mulling my fate, I imagined banner headlines in the *Notre Dame Crusader* declaring my expulsion:

> *Catholic School Boy*
> *Loses Battle of Wills*
> *To IHM Nun*

> *SOB Nun Bests*
> *Stupid Student*

Headline editors love alliteration.

Sister Maria Paula arrived at my desk, just as I'd anticipated. I could not bring myself to look up at her. The other test-taking students were doing a pretty good job of pretending to ignore the final moments of our confrontation. Calling a nun "a son-of-a-bitch" would probably earn me a hard slap across the face. Maybe two. That was the predictable *modus operandi* for an IHM. After the slap, the nun's voice would turn venomous and cold. Words like "bold," "brazen," "impertinent," and "insolent" would be sandwiched between "never in all my years" and "I can hardly believe."

None of that happened.

Sister Maria Paula did nothing more than touch my elbow and quietly say, "Mr. Timins, you will remain after class."

That was it. She didn't rail at me for my insolent remark. She didn't slap me or take my test. She returned to the front of the room as beads of sweat rolled down my cheeks. Now I had to pull myself together and finish my trig exam. It was a slog, my concentration continually being overwhelmed by the words, "remain after class."

Few students handed their work in early this day. That was unusual—most students finished most tests early—but the histrionics in today's test room were hardly conducive to solving trig problems. I was still laboring to finish the last test item when Sister announced that everyone must put down their No. 2 pencils. I did as I was told. The row monitors collected all the answer sheets and all the test booklets, and Sister dismissed the class just as the passing bell sounded.

Sterling stopped momentarily by my desk as he made his way to the door. "Good luck, Red," he whispered. "You're gonna need it."

I sat still, trying to avoid the eyes of my classmates as they filed out in silence. What did I see in their faces?

Good going, asshole? You're a dead man? Good luck?

I'd sit tight. I knew better than to test her patience again.

Once Sister had counted the answer sheets, wrapped them all with a rubber band, and placed them all in a large manila envelope, she walked down the aisle to my desk. I'd been waiting quietly, but not calmly, trying to anticipate what she might say, trying to imagine what the possible consequences might be. For my part, I stared at the desktop where someone had long ago inscribed "God who?" with a sharp stylus.

"Mr. Timins, thank you for remaining after class."

Like I had a choice, I thought. I wouldn't let any vagabond words slip out again.

Sister Maria Paula pushed a student desk in front of mine and slipped into it. We were now eye to eye, except I kept my eyes downcast. I was not about to offer anything by way of defiance or explanation. I'd explained myself to Sister Paula, and my explanation had been plainly ignored. Besides, I was powerless in these circumstances.

"Please look at me, Mr. Timins." It sounded like a request not a demand, so I looked up. "What kind of student are you, Mr. Timins?" she asked.

I wasn't sure how to answer that question. "I don't know what you mean, Sister."

"Are you a good student? What kinds of grades do you typically get? In trigonometry, for example."

"I had an 'A' until today. God knows how I did on the test."

"And German?"

"I probably have an 'A' there, too. But Father Bonnie is an amazingly generous grader."

"So, you are generally an 'A' student?"

I had no idea where this was going. I nodded. "Yes. Generally."

"Do you plan to attend college?"

"Yes, sister. I've been accepted at Kutztown State. I'll start my freshman year this September."

Sister Maria Paula looked intently at me. "People who attend Kutztown usually become teachers, don't they?"

"Yes. That's what I'd like to do." I was attempting to figure out what was going on here. The normal paradigm of sin and punishment—my sin, of course, was my blatant disrespect in calling her a son-of-a-bitch—was not playing out in its usual fashion. Sister Maria Paula's congenial demeanor made me terribly nervous.

Was she planning to punish me?

I feared she was up to something, but admittedly, paranoia is the normal state of affairs in Catholic school.

"Good," she said. "We need good teachers, Mr. Timins. And good teachers are only good teachers when they've learned how to keep their tempers."

She stopped to see if what she was saying registered with me. "Mr. Timins, your temper is going to get you into trouble unless you learn to control it."

She pushed herself out of the desk, brushing chalk dust off the front of her habit. I didn't move. She walked back to the front of the room to retrieve the manila envelope.

As she walked back toward me, she said, "You're not the first student to call me a son-of-a-bitch." She bent over and looked me directly in the eye. "You're just the first student to ever say it out loud."

That comment struck me as funny, but laughing would probably not have helped my cause. Her comment felt like a cue for an apology.

"I'm sorry, Sister," I said. "I really am."

"Yes, I am sure you are." She appeared to be formulating what to say next. "Please walk with me to the office. I have to drop off these answer sheets."

We walked slowly down the hall. "You graduate on Friday, June 11th, don't you?"

"Yes. This Friday." I didn't like her referencing my graduation when she still might contemplate yanking it out from underneath me. "You're going to let me graduate, aren't you?" I could hear the pitiful pleading tone rising in my own voice.

She glanced sideways at me, knowing she held all the power. She could show mercy. "I'm not that awful, Mr. Timins. You've earned the right to graduate, but I believe your conduct today should be punished."

I knew we'd get to 'the punishment' sooner or later, I thought. *I'm not about to engage in a debate I can't win.*

"No seniors will be here next week—except for you. All the underclassmen will still be attending class and taking their final exams. I want you to come to school each day next week. Think of it as an extended detention."

I attempted to absorb what Sister Maria Paula had just said.

She wants to punish me after I've graduated? The question puzzled me. *Exactly how does that work?*

Then I realized the true import of what she was saying. "How can I do that, Sister? My senior class trip is next Monday and Tuesday. I'm going to Washington, D.C."

We paused outside the office door. Sister made her position abundantly clear. "You can't go to Washington, D.C., and be here. You'll have to choose."

I felt my anger rising again. I was tempted to play the only political trump card I had. My father was the president of the Notre Dame Guild, Notre Dame's chief fundraising organization. Each summer the Guild ran the enormously profitable carnival, and they hosted weekly Bingo on Sunday evenings. The profits totaled tens of thousands of dollars, dollars that Notre Dame relied upon to help keep Catholic education afloat.

My older brother, Will, the bane of many of the IHMs who knew him, once said that I could never be expelled "because Dad is the president of the Guild. You could stab Sister Joachim during lunch hour and the principal would ask how she managed to run into your knife. Dad is our golden ticket."

Will may have been right, but I resisted playing the political card. However, Sister Maria Paula was treading on ground where she had no right to go. She's the one who had upped the ante.

I took a deep breath. "Sister," I said, "I'll only ever have one high school senior class trip in my life." I measured my words, seeking to speak calmly. "My mother and father have already paid for this trip, and unless you are willing to ask Father Strassner for a refund, I plan to go."

Father Strassner, Notre Dame's principal, collaborated with my dad on all the big fundraisers conducted by the Notre Dame Guild.

"Are you willing to ask for a refund?"

She was taken aback by the question. "You should have thought of that before you decided to be so insolent today." Once again, her response was non-responsive.

I wondered if there was some negotiating room. Surely Sister Maria Paula could see that her own conduct could also be called into question. Exacting an unnecessary fine? Withholding a final exam that she had no right to withhold?

"I'll tell you what I think, Sister. I think Father Strassner would take a dim view of my conduct today. So would my parents. Even I'm not happy with me. So far, I haven't said anything to my parents or Father Strassner about our... our disagreement yesterday in the book room. I thought I could take care of it without involving them." I tugged at my necktie. "But let me ask you. How would Father Strassner feel about *your* conduct today?" The look on her face confirmed my suspicion. She was searching for a response when I interrupted.

"Let me propose a solution. I'll come to your class next Wednesday and Thursday—Thursday is the last day, right?—and we'll call it even. I'll go on my class trip on Monday and Tuesday, and then you'll have your pound of flesh." Unspoken was, *Or we can go plead our cases before Father Strassner.*

Sister had no stomach for that. I watched her struggle briefly with what she should say next.

"I'll see you next Wednesday," she said as she opened the office door.

I never did tell my parents about the episode with Sister Maria Paula. I told my brother Will who laughed and said, "I told you she was a piece of work. She was just as much a pain in the ass for a whole year of Spanish as she was with you. You only had to deal with her for two days. She just can't help herself."

I also told my girlfriend, Katie, but begged her to not tell her parents, Dick and Dot. They thought I walked on water. Even though they weren't Catholic, I feared I'd quickly submerge if they heard their daughter's boyfriend had called a nun a son-of-a-bitch.

I also concluded that Sister Maria Paula never said anything about my "son-of-a-bitch" remark to Father Strassner or any of her IHM colleagues. If Father Strassner had known, he would have said something to my dad, and my dad would undoubtedly have said something to me. But the topic never came up.

Even my classmates remained mum on the subject...until our D.C. class trip. They all wanted to know what Sister Maria Paula said to me after class. Everyone's comment expressed some level of disbelief.

"I can't believe she didn't smack you."

"I can't believe she didn't have you expelled."

"I can't believe she didn't lower the boom on ya!"

Denny Feeley teasingly suggested that I'd paid off Sister Maria Paula. "It's a shake-down, right? Am I right? How much money does she want?"

Barbara Bendl offered an alternative possibility. "I bet he's got to clean the convent every week for a month."

Other suggestions, some of them lewd, were all turned aside.

Jim Welsh summed it up. "Here's the truth. There is no sin without punishment. So, what's your punishment?"

Sterling jumped in at this point. "Listen, everyone, all you need to do is walk up to Sister Maria Paula and ask. 'Hey Sister, what's Timins's punishment for calling you a son-of-a-bitch?' I'm sure she'll tell you." Everyone laughed.

I could only smile. Everyone wanted to know how I was being punished, but I remained silent.

Only my two closest friends, Mike and Sterling, knew about my two-day "intensive detention." I'd explained Sister Paula's intended punishment to them while we were on our class trip.

Mike gripped me by the shoulders in mock sternness and looked me straight in the eye. "Never forget. A dirty mind is a great comfort in times of stress," Mike said.

Everyone else thought I had made a clean escape—but they couldn't figure out how.

After two wonderful days on the Washington, D.C., class trip, I reported to Sister Maria Paula's classroom on Wednesday. My parents thought I was helping organize the bookroom.

Back home, my brother Will hadn't been fooled for a moment. "You might fool Mom and Dad with that bullshit about helping in the bookroom, but remember that Sister Maria Paula and I were never bosom buddies. Just tell me what the hell's going on."

So, I told Will what the hell was going on, feeling a mixture of guilt and pride in actually calling a nun a son-of-a-bitch.

"Jesus Christ, Red. You actually called her a son-of-a-bitch? Way to go. It's about damn time."

He looked me in the eye, suspecting I was pulling his leg. "You really said that? Really?"

"Really," I replied, enjoying my brother's adulation. When we stopped laughing about it, I shrugged and said, "That's why I have to go to school for two days next week."

"Mom and Dad don't know what you said to Sister Paula?"

"Apparently not," I said.

"And you're still going to serve detention?"

"I really don't have a choice."

"Come on, Jack. Hell, you've already graduated. You're a college freshman.

In a college without nuns. You do have a choice."

"Yes, and I've made it."

"Why? Why the hell are you going? You're out. She can't do shit."

I understood Will's point, but I felt that Sister Paula and I had struck a bargain to keep a mutually-shared secret.

So, on the morning after my D.C. trip, off to school I went. I sat in the back of the room as instructed. Occasionally, an underclassman wandered by and asked what I was doing there, but I had orders not to speak. I sat mute. I was expected to sit up straight—no slouching—have my feet flat on the floor, and my hands folded in front of me. I had nothing to read.

"What am I expected to do?" I asked Sister Maria Paula as the day began.

"Nothing. I don't expect you to do anything. Perhaps you should pray for forgiveness."

Yeah, right. Forgiveness? Mine or yours? All this over twenty-five cents, I thought, *which I didn't owe.*

I guess every student ever harassed by any nun anywhere in the known world questions the demeanor and behavior of the nun standing before him.

You're supposed to represent God, I could hear myself say. *Or at the very least be God-like in your dealings with other human souls—like me. Be all-loving—not all-appalling.*

I sat with my hands folded, my feet flat on the floor, and thought about going off to college next September. I thought about my assistant manager's job at Heil pool this summer. Most of all, I thought about my girlfriend, Katie.

Admittedly, it was hard to daydream of Katie and maintain the strict Catholic posture that Sister Paula demanded—but I did the best I could. As soon as the school day ended, I would be hopping into my '54 Chevy to tool over to see her. I whiled away my idle hours with Jewel Akens singing in my head.

> *Let me tell ya 'bout the birds and the bees*
> *And the flowers and the trees*
> *And the moon up above,*
> *And a thing called "love."*

With any luck, a few hours from now, Katie might find herself in the arms of a newly-minted college freshman, and we both might find ourselves on that fabled road to perdition. Perhaps then I would have a genuine reason to pray for forgiveness.

Maybe even go to Confession.

Chapter 2
A TOE IN THE ADULT WORLD

Summer 1965

It was Monday, September 6, 1965. Not just any Monday. It was Labor Day—the holiday every kid universally dreads. Labor Day might mean a day off for working-class adults, but it's always the official end of swimming season, at least at Easton's municipal pools.

To school kids, the end of swimming season equaled the end of summer. "Back to pencils, back to books, back to teachers' dirty looks." Reason enough to hate Labor Day.

For me, this Labor Day meant that I'd be heading off to college in two days—leaving home for the first time—and leaving my girlfriend Katie behind as well. I'd also be saying good-bye to my dog, Impy, who'd arrived as a puppy the day after I had my tonsils removed when I was eleven-years-old. He slept every night on my bed. He'd trotted beside me as I delivered the morning newspaper for three years—fair weather or foul. He was my dog buddy. A sense of loss gnawed at me like never before.

This Labor Day also ended my first summer as Heil Pool's assistant manager. I said good-bye to the lifeguard staff and shook hands with my head lifeguard, Tom Detweiler. Tom was my age and, on Wednesday, we'd be heading off together to Kutztown State College to begin our freshman year.

"Summer's over, boss," Tom said with a broad grin. "Time for the next chapter. Time to be a frosh," he said exuberantly

"Yep. One chapter closes and another begins," I said.

The closing chapter had begun earlier this year during spring break when Mr. Schneider, Easton's Parks & Recreation supervisor, called me at home. I thought he was calling just like the previous year when he asked me if I'd like to be head lifeguard at Heil Pool. I had said, yes, of course.

But that wasn't the reason for his call. "I want you to be the assistant manager this season," Mr. Schneider said. He always got right to the point. "Over the winter, you obtained certification as a swimming instructor, and it looks like you'll be graduating in the top ten percent of your class."

I thought, *assistant manager? Really? Yes! Yes! Yes!*

What I said was, "It's only spring break, Mr. Schneider, but I'm pretty sure the bottom's not going to drop out of my grades." I wanted to sound calm, but I was doing handstands and backflips in my head. I'd expected to be head lifeguard again—not assistant manager. I was only seventeen.

"I know it's a big step up, Jack," he explained, "but we've been watching you work the past few years, and you've always taken the initiative. You're good with kids and adults, and you could probably use the money for college."

In the back of my mind, I could hear my mother prompting me, *Say thank you, Jack.*

"Mr. Schneider, I'd love being assistant manager. Thank you. Thanks for putting your trust in me."

Then, for a split second, I stopped doing mental handstands and backflips and realized the level of responsibility I was being given. I could hear the uncertainty creep into my voice. "I'm sure I'm going need some time to…"

Mr. Schneider interrupted. "Don't worry about any of the details, Jack. We'll work those out in early May. You just keep your eye on the ball and get ready for college—it's Kutztown State, right?"

"Yeah," I said. "Kutztown. The week after Labor Day."

There was a moment of quiet on both ends of the phone.

"Good," Mr. Schneider said. "I've got you down as assistant manager. Tank is our new manager this year. He did a great job last year. You'll be stepping into his shoes."

Tim "Tank" Gladwell, last year's assistant manager, would make a great manager. He looked every inch the defensive tackle that he played for the University of Delaware. We always teased him about playing for a team whose mascot was a Fighting Blue Hen—which we renamed The Big Blue Chicken.

"Expect a call in early May."

"Early May. I'll talk to you then." I hung up.

I'd decided that Notre Dame's spring break would be the best time to fig-ure out what I'd need when I went off to college in the fall. Clothes? Money? Suddenly, the money issue seemed a bit less daunting.

I was dying to tell someone my good news. *I'll tell Mom.*

My mother was across the street at Mrs. Ortelli's, having her usual mid-morning cigarette and cup of coffee. I dashed across the street and ran up the concrete stoop to the front porch and shouted through the screen door. "Hey, Mrs. O, can I come in?"

"Is that you Jacky?" I heard her shout from her kitchen. She didn't wait for an answer. "Come on in. Door's open."

I ran straight to the kitchen and witnessed a familiar tableau. My mom and Mrs. O were on either side of the table, sitting on red-vinyl, chrome-legged kitchen chairs while a cloud of cigarette smoke drifted and swirled lazily in the sunlight from the west window. Mom's pack of Salems sat in the middle of the table.

The whole scene was a study in relaxation. Housewives all across America re-enacted daily rituals just like this, taking breaks between vacuuming, wash-ing clothes, grocery shopping, and making meals. Once upon a time, every-body knew that being a housewife was a full-time job. A worthy job.

"Want a cup of coffee, Jacky?" Mrs. O asked me.

"No thanks, Mrs. O." I turned quickly to my mother. "Mom, you'll never guess who just called."

My mother pulled an ashtray toward her, stubbed out her cigarette, and then looked up at me.

"Well, I can see you're excited." She paused as she pulled another cigarette from her pack of Salems and lit it. "So, who called?"

"Mr. Schneider—head of Easton's Recreation Department. He asked me if I wanted to be assistant manager at the pool this summer. Not head life-guard…assistant manager."

Mrs. O immediately tossed in her two cents before taking a drag on her cigarette. "You said yes, right?"

"Yes. I said yes." I was shaking my head vigorously.

"Good," Mom said smiling. "Your father will be glad to hear that." She took a puff on her cigarette and exhaled a stream of pale smoke. "Have you told Katie, yet? I bet she'll be thrilled to hear your news."

"You're right, Mom. Gotta go." As I headed back to the front door, I shouted back, "See ya, Mrs. O. Gotta tell my girlfriend."

Back home, I immediately called my girlfriend, Katie, a senior at Easton High School. She was on spring break, too, and she had agreed to help her mom clean out their garage.

"How goes the garage cleaning?" I asked.

"There's stuff in our garage that no one has seen in years. It may just be a rumor of stuff, but you never know. Dad keeps saying that one of these days he'll actually park his car in the garage, but Mom says that's just silly talk. Why don't you come over and help? You know the way, don't you?"

"Yes. I think I do, babe. I'll be over as fast as my legs can carry me."

That meant walking or biking the four miles. I usually walked because I could thumb a ride part of the way. Easton was a small town and most people knew one another, by sight if not by name. And if I walked or thumbed my way over, Katie would usually drive me home—always with the possibility of a brief, amorous detour beneath the elms that lined her long driveway.

My girlfriend's given first name was Richena, named after her father whose name was Richard. No one I knew used her given name, and no one called her father by his given name, Richard, either. Her dad answered to Dick or to Whitey. His snow-white hair had earned him that nickname when he was only a twenty-four-year-old sergeant in the U.S. Army driving trucks across Nazi-occupied France.

Katie never really liked her name—Richena—but she wasn't terribly fond of the nicknames that others hung on her, either. Of all possible nicknames, she hated "Ricky" the most. Her grandmother had settled on Katie—a delightfully playful and feminine version of her middle name, Katherine—so I asked Katie if I could use that name, too.

"Only if I can call you Red."

"Katie, you may call me Red forever and ever and ever," I said. Then I kissed her. Kissing Katie occupied a large share of my time when we were together, and crowded my thoughts when we were apart.

Looking back, I can see that the summer of 1965 was a time in my life when our differences didn't seem to make a difference. I attended Notre Dame High School, the local Catholic high school, and Katie attended Easton High School, the local public high school. My classes put me on the college prep track, and Katie's took her down the secretarial track. She'd become wonder-fully proficient in shorthand and typing—skills that I totally lacked—but skills that she hoped would land her a job even before she graduated.

They did. On the first day of spring break, she'd received notification that Mack Printing had hired her—beginning on July 1st.

"It's a real job," she said as we cleaned out the garage. "Not part-time, assis-tant manager, summertime work," she teased. "My college boy won't be getting a real job for at least another four years."

I could hear the pride in her voice when she called me a "college boy." I was her college boy.

"That's right. That's right. But may I remind you that as long as I'm in school, I will never be drafted? And Kutztown State is a whole lot closer—and safer—than any place the U.S. Army is likely to send me."

I always dragged the draft into these "real job" conversations.

"I could get a real job soldiering in Germany—you know, keep the com-mies on their side of the Rhine River. Or I could go to Korea. Or Vietnam."

"Okay. Okay. Go to Kutztown. Please, go to Kutztown. I know I'd like that better."

"Me, too," I said, and then I kissed her. "Besides, Kutztown is only forty miles away. I'll be home most weekends."

What is it about the best laid plans?

I proudly announced my new job at the dinner table that night.

"I'm going to be the assistant manager at Heil Pool this summer!" My ex-citement was evident. Everyone who lived on Easton's south side swam at Heil Pool during the summer.

No one seemed surprised. To use my dad's expression, I had "risen through the ranks." First as a lifeguard in the summer of '63, then as head lifeguard in '64, and now as assistant manager in '65. Did I mention that I was only sev-enteen years old?

"It appears you've had a meteoric rise," my mother said. Hyperbole had always been her *forte* when praising me—something that always annoyed my brothers. "You should tell your brother Will the good news. He's working a double shift today."

"You're right," I agreed. "I'll tell Will whenever he gets home."

I turned to my father. "The really cool part of this new job is that I am on salary."

My dad beamed when he heard my news. Smiling a bit enigmatically, Dad shook his head and asked me if I knew what the definition of "salary" was.

"Sure," I said. "It means I'm no longer an hourly worker."

"That's true," said Dad. "But it means a lot more than that." He paused as I buttered a piece of bread. "Son, you'll soon find out that 'salary' means you have the privilege of working overtime for free."

I would find out what that meant quite a few times during the summer of 1965. Before Labor Day, I would also find out the meaning of "The buck stops here."

My conscience, fearfully formed and instilled by the good nuns and priests through twelve years of Catholic School, had inhibited me from pursuing far more inviting carnal pleasures. My longtime girlfriend, Katie—a product of the non-parochial public schools—had shown enormous patience with my in-transigent fear of sin.

"I'm a Methodist," she'd say coyly. "Does it make a difference if you sin with a Methodist?"

I'd met Katie at Heil Pool during the summer of '63 when we were both fledgling lifeguards. She had been hired as a lifeguard for Eddyside, but guarding swimmers who are frolicking in the Delaware's murky river waters is more nerve-wracking than watching swimmers in the crystal-clear, filtered waters of Heil Pool. Somehow, she had finagled a transfer to Heil Pool, and that's when we met. The summer of '63—the one before we began our junior year—was our Summer of Love, at least as far as I understood it and permitted it. Katie was my first love, and I was determined not to "spoil it."

That didn't prevent me from asking Katie to join me in the garage storage area beneath the locker rooms. It didn't prevent her either. Everything the pool needed to function was stored down here. Lifeguard dressing rooms with secure lockers. Picnic tables. 50-meter and 25-meter nylon lines with buoys for swim meets. Starting blocks. Extra life buoys. Oxygen tanks and masks. Gas masks for chlorine leaks. Flashlights. First aid kits. Mops, buckets, brooms, and cleansers for maintaining the changing rooms, the bathrooms, and the concrete decks. And toilet paper.

Best of all, the garage provided a dark, cool retreat for extended making out. But that was as far as I would go. I might entertain lascivious thoughts about Katie, but I would not cross the frontier separating thought and action. Sex could only be my daydream, not my reality.

More than once, I'd poured out my soul to my best friend Sterling, hoping to find someone who might comfort and advise me in my sexual struggles. Someone who might give me advice about dealing with the conflicting demands of human nature and the edicts of the Catholic Church. For a while, Sterling and I commiserated with one another, but then just before graduation, I realized that Sterling had capitulated, surrendered to his human inclinations.

"That's a sin, you know," I said.

"You are exactly right," he replied. "It is a sin." There was a twinkle in his eye. "That's why we Catholics have Confession."

"Aren't you at all ashamed?" I asked.

For a brief moment, Sterling acted as if he was actually mulling over my question.

"Nope."

"Well, I can't do anything like that with Katie," I said. "I may have dirty thoughts from time to time, but that's all."

"You can tell me all about your dirty thoughts," said Sterling, teasing, the twinkle returning to his eye, "but I have to tell you, Red, dirty deeds are way more fun than dirty thoughts. Way more fun." He loved teasing me.

Once, when I asked if Sterling thought sex was dirty, he smiled and said, "Only if you do it right."

By the end of our junior year, I'd given Katie my high school class ring—and she'd given me hers—a status that my older brother Will used to call "engaged to be engaged." And we had a second "Summer of Love" in '64—the one when I'd been promoted to Head Lifeguard—with the same restraints and restrictions that had always prevailed. Mostly.

Whatever our relationship status, things changed after graduation because Katie dove into the workforce full-time while I worked as Heil Pool's assistant manager.

We both knew I'd be off to college two days after Labor Day.

As a fledgling assistant manager, I had hoped for an uneventful summer. Uneventful, however, seldom meant problem-free. When Heil's doors opened on Memorial Day—the official beginning of summer—I reminded myself that this would be the last time the locker rooms would be pristine until Labor Day. Keeping dressing rooms clean was an endless battle. My two previous years working at Heil pool had schooled me in how dirty and slovenly people could be; the messes they could make; the messes they could so blithely ignore and leave behind.

Over the years, when I had grumbled to my mother about the thoughtless slobs…aka, Heil's customers…she'd console me. "It's not everyone, Jack. You know that, don't you? But there are always the few who seem to make life difficult for everyone else."

I often wondered if "the few" had morphed into "the many."

As assistant manager, I made it my job to field complaints about the filth of the dressing rooms, or the epidemic of cigarette butts in the grass. I told my staff to send concerned or irate pool patrons directly to me.

"The buck really does stop here," I told them. "Dealing with complaints shouldn't be your job."

My job included daily cleanliness checks of dressing rooms and bathrooms, and I exhorted my staff *ad nauseum* to continually police people's litter and cigarette butts. None of us liked it, but it needed to be done. I cannot say how often I repeated, "It's the job."

As I said, my fondest hope was for an uneventful summer. No drownings. No heart attacks. No fist fights. No problems that required outside intervention from medical personnel or police. Dirty dressing rooms, scattered cigarette butts, stubbed toes, scraped knees, sunburn—and the occasional floating turd—constituted the uneventful norm that the pool staff and I dealt with every day.

As a novice assistant manager, I also hoped to avoid dissatisfaction among the ranks. Along with our new manager, Tank, my responsibilities included scheduling the ten lifeguards hired by the City of Easton to ensure the safety of the swimmers and maintain the cleanliness of the pool and its grounds. I also assumed the scheduling of activities at the pool—like swim lessons and community dances. Tank had his hands full, coaching the Heil Park Swim Team.

I should have realized that my hope for an uneventful summer was doomed from the beginning.

In mid-May, with our Memorial Day opening looming, I joined Tank, and we walked around the grounds to see what needed to be done over the next few weekends. We needed to prepare the pool and facilities for the coming season.

The city had begun mowing the grass in early April, and all the benches scattered around the pool area had been freshly painted. The lifeguard stations—elevated chairs giving the lifeguards an unobstructed view of the swimmers and the pool area—had all been refurbished. Brand new life rings, decorated with broad red stripes and carefully printed with "Heil Pool," hung from the each of the four chairs. Mr. Haley, who ran the concession stand, was already taking inventory and making sure his equipment was ready to pop popcorn and grill hot dogs and hamburgers.

The pool itself was 50 meters long, with two 25-meter legs extending out from each end, and a separate, foot-deep "baby pool" between those two legs. From the air, Heil Pool looked like a capital E—undoubtedly for the City of Easton. To ready the pool for opening day, it had been scrubbed, cleaned, and refilled with fresh city water, kept sparkling by three large diatomaceous earth filters. On this May day, the water glistened in the noonday sun. After Tank and I checked out the filters and the chlorine injection station, we went into the garage beneath the dressing rooms and the concession stand.

"What's that smell?" Tank asked as soon as we had lifted the garage door.

"I don't know, but it's pretty awful," I said. We both walked further in, but the rank odor intensified with every step.

I tapped Tank on the shoulder. "Let's get back outside. That smell is making me sick."

We swiftly left the garage, happy to be outside taking deep breaths of the warm, fresh, spring air.

"Jesus," Tank said, inhaling deeply. "I feel sick, too." He bent over, hands on knees, fighting nausea. "Something's dead in there," he said. "I know that smell. That's the smell of putrefaction. Whatever we smelled is rotting."

Tank was still bent over, breathing deeply.

"You learn that word in Sister Clare's class?" I asked Tank. "Putrefaction?"

Tank looked up. We smiled at each other. We'd both had Sister Clare for senior English at Notre Dame High School.

"Yeah," Tank nodded. "Putrefaction was just one of many." He pronounced the word again, tasting it, savoring it. "Putrefaction. Never thought I'd ever have any use for that word."

We both paused, savoring the fresh air, wondering what we needed to do next.

"Okay," I said to Tank, "I've got an idea. Behind the starting blocks, there's a wooden trunk with a couple of gas masks. They store them here in case we ever have a chlorine gas leak in the filter room. I don't think the box is locked—it never has been. You stay here. I'm going in for those masks. We're not going back into the garage until we can breathe without puking."

"Really?" Tank asked.

"I should be in and out in less than a minute. I plan to hold my breath."

"You sure?" Tank asked.

"About what? Holding my breath? Or not sucking in putrefied air?"

Tank was staring at me. "You're the assistant. I can't ask you to do this."

"You're not asking. I'm volunteering."

"Great, let's go in together," Tank said.

So, in we went. We looked at one another, took a deep breath, and dashed to the back of the garage about 25 yards away. We tossed open the lid of the trunk and found the two carbon-filtered gas masks. They were right where I had remembered. We each grabbed one and raced outside, finally able to take a deep breath.

"Okay, we are about to test the efficacy of these filters," Tank said.

"First it was 'putrefaction' and now it's 'efficacy?'"

"You know how it is. It's the only way anyone will believe I'm going to college," Tank laughed. He was right. His blonde crewcut and freckled baby-face made him look about twelve. Only his broad shoulders and hulking phy-sique—he had been a defensive tackle on Notre Dame's football team and now he played defense for the Fighting Blue Hens of the University of Delaware—betrayed him.

"Are we ready?"

Tank shook his head yes, and I said, "If you feel sick, get out."

We both pulled the gas masks on and pulled them tight around our faces. We looked like something from one of our favorite science fiction movies. Giving each other a thumbs up, we went back in. We found the concession supply section and began looking around for anything that looked like it might be rotten.

Tim tapped me on the shoulder and pointed to a large box labeled Toilet Paper. A ragged hole had been chewed from the outside and rodent droppings were scattered everywhere around the ragged opening. Except for that hole, the box was unopened, the clear packing tape still unbroken. I used my penknife to cut the tape and ripped open the top of the box. There was no doubt, this was the source of the smell. A half-dozen dead rats, rotting and putrefied, had nested inside the box. They had chewed roll after roll of toilet paper, defecating everywhere. Somehow, they had died.

It remained a mystery until Mr. Haley explained he had scattered rat poi-son in the garage area sometime in March. "I always do that right around the beginning of spring. To kill any varmints who've decided to take refuge in the storage area over the winter."

We assured him that his rat poison had worked as advertised.

Tim and I pulled the rat-infested box out of the garage and dragged it to the far side of the pool grounds and over the grassy embankment. We stopped beneath one of the tin-roofed pavilions where picnickers would gather lat-er that summer. The pavilions offered us large concrete pads in the open air. Fortunately, the picnic tables that typically filled the pavilions during swim season remained in storage.

I retrieved a five-gallon gas can from the garage and returned to the pavil-ion to soak the putrid box. Tank lit the match. Only after the putrid rats and box were fully ablaze did we remove our gas masks. As black smoke swirled upward, we shared sarcastic comments about an early cookout.

Then Tank turned to me and commented, "It's always a pleasure watching putrefied rodents incinerate in the pyre's efficacious flames."

I looked at Tank and said, "Couldn't you just say, 'It was fun burning up the rotten rats?'"

"Don't worry, Jack, you'll be talking just like me by the time you begin your junior year in college."

"If I didn't know your girlfriend, Tank, I'd think you were dating Merriam-Webster's daughter."

Day one for the new assistant manager commenced with an unexpected olfactory adventure.

Happily, the paying customers would not arrive for another two weeks. Ignorance is bliss.

Chapter 3
"...AND THEN THAT HAPPENED."
Summer 1965

Summer and sun beckoned.

The rats were gone, the garage cleared and cleaned. The dressing rooms were ready. The pool water sparkled brilliantly beneath a cloudless blue sky. The water was the proper pH, what Tank liked to call "BP" water—Before Pee. All this for the annual Memorial Day weekend opening. At Heil Pool, summer officially commenced a full three weeks earlier than the calendar's summer solstice. People arrived *en masse* as they did every year when eighty-degree temperatures tempted the pale-skinned droves to seek the refreshing waters of Heil Pool.

By two o'clock, hundreds of kids and adults were splashing in the pool, reclining on blankets, eating sandwiches, playing cards, smoking cigarettes, and slathering themselves with suntan lotion. Heil Pool was open for business. The air was alive with laughter, conversation, and tweeting whistles.

Above the general hubbub, guards yelled a whole variety of commands: "Slow down," "No running," "Get that baseball bat out of the water." I spent most of my time circulating among my lifeguards, making sure that they felt comfortable and confident. Virtually every south side family—mostly blue-collar and middle-class—had season passes, and today would be the first of many days at the pool soaking up the summer sun.

Among the surprise patrons that day was my girlfriend, Katie. Mr. Sawyer, who ran the ticket office, had paged me over the pool's PA system to come to the ticket office. Usually he said why, but not this time.

"This young woman says she thinks she can get in for nothing," said Mr.

Sawyer, gesturing at a smiling brunette in a yellow summer dress. His smile said all I needed to know. "Just who does she think she is?"

"I'm the assistant manager's best girl," Katie said coyly, as she sashayed over to me and kissed me warmly. The already hot day grew hotter. "I thought I ought to check up on him."

"I think we'd better let her in for free," I said to Mr. Sawyer.

"Whatever you say, chief."

As we stood outside the office on the upper deck, overlooking the pool with its hundreds of animated patrons, I swung my arm like Moses parting the Red Sea. "Behold," I said.

"Is this all yours?" Katie asked.

"Only for the summer," I said. "Then I have to give it back to the City of Easton."

As we stood there, comfortable in the love we felt for one another, Katie pointed to the high dive.

"Is that Ronnie Cooper?"

"Who else? Every year. Same time. Same station," I replied.

Over the years, certain individuals became fixtures at Heil Pool. People like Ronnie Cooper. He was probably in his early twenties. Without question, he was a narcissist—a bronzed, blond, well-built, broad-shouldered narcissist—who loved to dive. Heil's diving well offered three boards: two one-meter boards and one three-meter high dive. Ronnie preferred demonstrating his gymnastic diving skills from the three-meter board. Whenever Ronnie came to Heil, there was the mandatory Ronnie Cooper Diving Exhibition for anyone who happened to be enjoying the sunshine.

My dad referred to Coop as "a character"—a rather vague description— but my sense of it was that Coop was a bit eccentric. Coop's attention was always on himself. He posed. He strutted self-consciously. He walked as if people were always watching...and truth be told, people were always watching. His array of dives off the three-meter board included a beautiful swan dive, an inward swan dive, a backward swan dive, a one-and-a-half in both the pike and tuck positions, a two-and-a-half, inward versions of the same, and reverse dives—called gainers.

Coop loved an audience, and he certainly had one on Memorial Day. Late in the afternoon, he decided it was time to perform a one-and-a-half reverse dive—the diver, eyes forward, springing off the end of the board and then flipping backward one and a half times. If everything goes well, the diver slips vertically into the water, hands-first with fingers pointed, with nary a splash. If it doesn't go well, he hits his head or shoulder on the board as he begins his backward flip.

This time, things did not go well.

Katie and I were near the baby pool when Ronnie smashed the back of his head on the end of the three-meter board. A kind of collective "Oh!" caught our attention and then a flurry of shouts and screams and whistles indicated that something was going on in the diving well. People were running in that direction. I joined them.

I turned to Katie. "Can you call the Emergency Squad?"

"I can do better than that, Jack. I'll run across the street and get them."

Tom Detweiler, the lifeguard on duty, had immediately gone into the water, and now he cradled Coop's head and shoulders, keeping him above water while moving toward the ladder. I shouldered people aside to get to the water's edge. There was that ever-present press of humanity that always gathers to watch an accident. Coop appeared to be conscious but weak and disoriented. Already a red plume spread from the back of Coop's head, a growing dark smudge in the crystal-clear water of the diving well.

As Tom and Coop reached the ladder, Mrs. Black, one of the swim team moms and a registered nurse, arrived with clean towels and years of head trauma expertise. Four people helped Tom lift Coop out of the water and laid him on the dry towels at the water's edge. Then Mrs. Black took over. Katie arrived moments later with the medics from the Easton Emergency Squad in tow. They'd carefully driven their ambulance across the pool deck avoiding all the curious onlookers. They joined Mrs. Black, who was bending over Coop. It was clear that the ambulance medics knew Mrs. Black, and they deferred to her. She continued to give instructions; in almost no time, Coop was on a gurney, head swaddled in blood-soaked towels, riding off to Easton Hospital with Mrs. Black by his side.

The ambulance left with siren screaming.

When everything had settled down to a dull roar, Katie and I walked to the pool office.

"Oh, Katie, you saved the day. Thanks for getting the emergency squad." I said as I wrapped my arms around her. "I was hoping for an uneventful day."

She cupped my face in her hands—kissed me warmly—and said, "I think you're going to be busy for quite a while. I'd best be going." She grabbed her purse. "Thanks for getting me in for free," she said with an impish tilt of her head. She gave me a peck on my cheek, and sauntered out the door while blowing me a kiss.

"Uneventful" would have to wait until next summer.

Yes. Memorial Day was memorable.

Heil Pool sat on the high ground overlooking the Lehigh River as it lazily flowed northeast toward the Delaware River. For decades, the land beneath the pool had been a landfill—the Easton dump. Until the pool was built in 1960, south side Easton had a dump but no swimming pool. Immediately south of the pool was Heil Park, a large baseball diamond that alternated between Little League games and neighborhood kids playing pick-up games. It was the only south side playfield that had lights for night games.

Outside the pool fence, two houses flanked the pool. One was tucked between the baseball field and the pool, and it was a house where, according to my mother, "No sane person could live during the summer. Not with all those kids screaming and carrying on—on both sides." Its owner seldom appeared during the daylight hours.

The other house—owned by a Mrs. Pachiolli—stood just north of the pool. Mrs. Pachiolli patrolled her backyard during the summer swim season, yelling at kids to "Get away from my goddamn fence." She was tired of footballs, whiffle balls, beach balls, and other flying objects landing in her yard, and even more tired when kids tried to climb her eight-foot, chain-link fence to retrieve their items without asking.

Still, I had enlisted Mrs. Pachiolli's help in keeping an eye on the pool after hours—at night and in the morning—by getting her a season pass to the pool as well as the occasional burger from the concession stand.

Late one July night, Mrs. Pachiolli called my house, waking my mother and father from a sound sleep. Phone calls around 1:00 a.m. are both infrequent and seldom good news. My mother answered the phone, then walked down the hall to wake me. She shook me hard.

"Wake up, Jack, wake up! Jesus, Mary, and Joseph, you sleep like the dead. There's a woman asking for you. Sounds urgent. Something about the pool. Take the call downstairs."

I scooted downstairs and picked up the receiver. "Hello," I said. I felt very groggy.

Without any introduction, an excited, woman's voice whispered, "Someone's in the pool."

"What pool?" I asked, trying to make sense of what I'd heard.

"What pool do you think? Heil Pool," said the woman. "Someone's here. And they're in the water."

Suddenly, I realized who was on the other end of the phone. "Mrs. Pachiolli?"

"I think they're all guys, but I can't tell for sure."

My head was clearing. "How many are there?"

"I don't know." She sounded annoyed. "It's dark. But they're swimming around and making noise. Somebody threw something off the high dive. The splash woke me up."

I paused, collecting my thoughts.

"You better get up here pronto," she said. "Or I'm calling the cops." She hung up.

I never got the chance to say thanks. I pulled on some sweats, tied my sneakers, and told my parents where I was going.

"Be safe," Mom said as I dashed downstairs.

Who the hell knew that this would be a twenty-four hour a day job? It was like my dad said: "I have the privilege of working overtime for free." I should be calling the cops. Instead, I'm driving to the pool in the middle of the night. I could get my ass kicked.

I called my head lifeguard, Tom Detweiler.

No sense getting my ass kicked solo.

Tom lived two blocks away, and I could use the help. Tom's mother answered the phone.

"Mrs. Detweiler, I'm really sorry about calling so late, but I need Tom's help at the pool."

"At one o'clock in the morning?"

"I'm really sorry. It's a long story…"

"I'll get him," was her curt reply. Tom's mother was a patient woman.

My mind raced, formulating my plan of action as I waited for Tom to get to the phone.

Turn off my headlights and park across the street from the pool. Unlock the front door and go in through the locker rooms…quietly. Unlock the office and switch on the pool lights—the underwater lights and the deck lights. If things get bad, we'll lock ourselves up in the office and call the police from there. Oh, yeah. Don't get beat up.

A sleepy voice said, "Hey, what's up?"

"Tom," I said. "Sorry to wake you. Look, Mrs. Pachiolli just called me. She said some people are swimming in the pool. I'm heading up there and wondered if you'd like to go with me."

He paused. "Is that because you don't want to be alone when you get the shit kicked outta you?" Tom asked.

"Kinda," I said.

"Okay, pick me up in five," Tom said, then hung up.

I grabbed the car keys and made my way through the darkness to our '54 Chevy parked beneath the cherry tree in the backyard. It was a hot, sultry night. A perfect night to climb over Heil Pool's chain link fence for a nice cool swim.

Tom was sitting on his front porch in a t-shirt and shorts when I pulled up. As he climbed in the car, he asked, "Why didn't you just call the cops?"

"I don't know. I probably should have. Maybe I still will."

I explained my plan as we drove the half-mile. Tom kept asking, "You sure this is a good idea?"

"No. I'm not sure, but I want to find out who's there."

"You probably shoulda called the cops."

"Yeah," I nodded. "Probably."

"Okay, but we better be quiet," Tom said.

"I'm not the one who's talking," I said. It's really annoying when someone else is right—out loud.

I killed the Chevy's engine and turned off my headlights as we drifted to a stop across the street from the pool. As we crossed to the front door, we heard whooping and laughter from the pool.

Mrs. Pachiolli was right.

"Sounds like a bunch of guys," Tom whispered as we unlocked the front door.

I could hear our mothers' warnings: "Be safe."

Mrs. Pachiolli was probably watching from her window and wondering, *What the hell is going on?*

We made our way through the pitch-black corridor, past the men's dressing room, and out onto the deck overlooking the pool. The voices were louder now. Clearly masculine.

"Who the hell are they?" I whispered.

"We're gonna find out in a moment," whispered Tom. "We probably shoulda called the cops. Hope you brought your brass knuckles."

Once in the office, I flicked six switches and Heil Pool suddenly burst with light above and below the water. Bravely, I stepped outside my office. Tom stood behind me in the office doorway. I shouted to several shadowy, swim-suited figures by the diving well. "What the hell are you guys doing here? Who are you?"

A deep male voice boomed from the freshly illuminated high dive. "Timins? Is that you?"

I knew that voice. It sounded amazingly familiar. "Who's asking?" I yelled.

"It's me," said a shouted reply. "Bill Metz."

"Officer Metz?" I called out. The reality dawned on me.

"Yeah," came the reply.

"What are you doing here?"

"Swimming," shouted Officer Metz. The others with him began laughing, and I started walking down the steps toward the diving well. The way was well lit.

"Jesus H. Christ," shouted Tom in amazement. "It's the cops."

"I was about to call the cops," I shouted in their direction. Suddenly, the laughter was loud and raucous.

"No need to do that," said Officer Metz. "All the cops are here."

Indeed, all the cops were here—all the cops who finished their shift at midnight, anyway. I counted six in all.

Officer Metz did a cannonball off the high dive, swam to the ladder, and pulled himself up. Broad-shouldered, his crew cut gone gray, his face and arms were tan and weathered but the rest of his body was a study in white. He brushed the water from his face as he walked toward his towel draped over the lifeguard chair.

"Hey, man, I'm sorry we got you out of bed. We just wanted someplace to cool off. The humidity's awful today, and we didn't think we'd be bothering anybody if we came up here." He pointed up toward the office. Tom still stood in the doorway. "I see you brought back up."

"Yeah, I didn't know what I'd find when I came in here. That's Tom Detweiler. All the way here, he kept telling me I shoulda called the cops."

"Smart man," Officer Metz said as he patted his face with a towel labeled Property of Lafayette College. "Aren't you glad you didn't?" He stepped next to me. "Detweiler?" he asked. "His old man is with the state police, right?"

"You know him?"

"Course we do. We work with the state police all the time." He looked up to where Tom was standing in the office door. "Hey, Tommy," he shouted, "maybe your dad could have some of his friends swing by for a dip."

His shouting brought a response from the darkness. From somewhere in her backyard, Mrs. Pachiolli's voice made its way to where Officer Metz and I stood talking.

"Metzie? Is that you?"

All either of us could see was the glowing tip of her cigarette.

"That's Mrs. Pachiolli," I said. "She's the one who called me."

"Mrs. Pachiolli? Michael's mom?"

"Who's Michael?" I asked.

"Mike Pachiolli. He's a justice of the peace...down on Berwick Street—right across from Shull Junior High. He takes care of a lot of traffic court stuff for us."

Jesus, it's turned into old home week.

Officer Metz started walking toward the lit cigarette. As he approached her backyard fence, I could hear the teasing tone in his voice, "So, Mrs. Pachiolli, you squealed on us."

"Damn right I did, ya big galoot," she said. "How the hell was I to know it was you? What would you have done if I called the cops?"

"I'd probably arrest myself," Officer Metz said. "And throw myself on the mercy of the court."

"Uh-huh," she said. "No mercy for you, buster. You guys woke me out of a sound sleep."

Moments later, Tom joined me down on the pool deck. "All's well that ends well?" Tom asked.

"So it would seem, Tom."

I turned to Officer Metz.

"Listen," I found myself saying, "if you guys want to swim after you get off your shift, call me, okay? It's probably not a good idea for you to be climbing over the fence and going for a late-night swim. I think they call that trespassing. And I'll be damned if I know what to do when it's the cops who are trespassing."

My comments were interrupted by Tony Calandra, youngest member of this rogue police sextet. "Mind if we swim a little longer?" asked Tony. The other four policemen flashed Tom and me hopeful looks.

It's nice seeing policemen looking so contrite, I thought.

I looked at Tom as if to ask, *Do you mind?*

Tom shrugged.

"Fine by me." I pointed at Tom. "I've got my best lifeguard here. So, I guess we're open for business until you guys decide to go home."

They all left about 2:30 a.m.—through the front door. I had to dissuade Officer Metz from leaving the way he came in.

"Climbing over the fence is the fun part," he said.

I said I'd have to call the cops if he didn't comply.

I never knew if that was the one and only night the cops came for a moonlight swim. That summer produced its share of uncomfortable, sultry nights— the kind of nights that required air-conditioning or a cool pool to provide some relief. So maybe they popped in now and again for a quick swim. If they did, I never again got a call from Mrs. Pachiolli. And why should I? Mrs. Pachiolli didn't have to go further than her backyard to call the cops.

One afternoon, soon after the midnight swim incident—which was never officially reported to anyone, as far as I know—Officer Metz arrived at the pool and walked into my office.

"Can't stay but a moment," he said, "but I just want to say thanks."

I laughed. "Glad I could help you guys cool off after a full day chasing bad guys."

"Brought you something, Timins," he said. "I think you'll be able to use it."

Officer Metz placed a silver deputy's badge on the desk. In bold, circular, metallic relief it said, EASTON POLICE.

"Is this real?"

"You bet it is. And it's yours for as long as you're Heil's assistant manager. Tank got his last year."

"Does this mean I can arrest you the next time you jump the fence?"

Officer Metz scratched his head. "I suppose so." Then he smiled. "But we're the only ones with guns."

"Good point," I said.

Officer Metz turned the badge over, revealing the silver pin. "Pin it inside your wallet. It'll be safe there."

"Thanks for this. I really hope I never have to use it."

Officer Metz stood up. "I know how you feel, Timins. Every cop feels the same way. We feel that way every day we go to work." He looked wistful for a moment. "Gotta get back to work." He stopped briefly and stared at the pool. "Water sure looks great."

Out he walked. Neither of us could predict he would be back around the end of July, protecting everyone from "the bad guys"—and ironically, protecting one of "the bad guys" from himself.

I had been concerned about the July Fourth holiday because, for some reason, too many otherwise-reasonable customers wanted to smuggle alcohol onto pool grounds. Holidays, the theory went, were more enjoyable if one was boozed and buzzed. Fortunately, this past July 4th was remarkably booze and buzz free.

Later in July, however, on an especially sultry, non-holiday weekend, I had my don't-count-your-chickens moment. It was a hot, hazy, crowded Saturday at the pool. Late in the day, dark cumuli were building in the distance over the meandering Lehigh River. One didn't need a degree in meteorology to understand that, at some point, those clouds would follow the river's northeasterly path and arrive over the pool. Summer squalls, especially late in the afternoon on sultry days, were quite common, and the lifeguards were tasked with keeping a close eye on thunder and lightning.

"Electrocuted swimmers tend to be unhappy customers," I told my guards at orientation.

Low rumblings off in the distance were usually the first warning, and when the hollow sound of empty barrels came rolling up the valley, lifeguard whistles rang out their shrill warning. The guards jumped down from their chairs, and continued whistling while waving everyone out of the pool as the skies continued to darken.

People scrambled out of the water as best they could—they could see the ominous weather approaching, too. Some parents came to the pool's edge and urged their children to get out of the water; some politely, some less so. Others scooped up blankets, towels, paperback books, and anything else they had brought, to keep their belongings out of the downpour that the western sky promised would come.

After a few chaotic minutes, the pool was empty. Everyone had moved away from the water and toward higher ground, crowding for cover around the bathhouse.

All, except one.

One man still waded chest-deep in the middle of the pool, oblivious to the whistles, shouts, and the mass exodus of hundreds of swimmers. It wasn't so much that he refused to get out of the water, it was as if no one could get his attention.

Three lifeguards, Sheila, Tom, and Rick, stood at the edge of the pool, doing their best to get him out of the water.

"If I hit him with a rock, do you think he'd notice?" Rick asked.

"I'm not sure he's sober," said Sheila. "Look at him."

They all looked.

"He looks out of it."

Simultaneously all three blew their whistles at Mr. Oblivious—a name that stuck whenever any staff discussed this incident later. Mr. Oblivious was a rather large, slightly balding man, with a paunchy midsection and excessively hairy chest. He kept walking along the center black stripe on the pool bottom, deaf to the pleas of the lifeguards. He wasn't getting out of the water. The sky continued to grow darker as the squall approached. Patrons watched a gray curtain of rain falling and advancing from the west. The occasional bolt of lightning punctuated the dark clouds—followed quickly by the threatening crack of thunder—and we all knew any sober person would be alerted to the danger and exit the pool.

Except this one, lone, pool patron. He just kept walking in the chest-deep water.

"Doesn't he see the storm?" Sheila asked.

"If he can't hear our whistles, he's really tuned out," Tom said. Tom took off his flip-flop and hurled it at Mr. Oblivious. It sailed the twenty feet and hit Mr. Oblivious on the right shoulder. Mr. Oblivious grabbed the floating flip-flop and looked up. He looked puzzled.

"Sir," Tom shouted. "You have to get out of the water."

Mr. Oblivious looked at Tom, then looked at the flip-flop. He tossed the flip-flop aside. "Why?"

"Because there's a storm coming, sir," Tom said. Thunder rumbled as if to confirm his point. "It's dangerous to stay in the water when there's lightning. Just look." Tom pointed to the west where the darkening clouds gathered closer and closer to the pool.

"There's no lightning," said Mr. Oblivious defiantly, still not looking at the approaching storm. "Show me the lightning."

Another shard of lightning lit the western sky, and thunder crashed more loudly than before.

"There," said Tom. "There's your lightning."

Unsurprisingly, Mr. Oblivious had not seen it. Tom's shoulders slumped.

"Shit. How do you show somebody the lightning?" Tom asked rhetorically. "If I were Thor, I'd whistle a bolt right over this idiot's head."

"Be better than a flip-flop," Sheila said.

Tom renewed his efforts. "Sir, trust me. There's lots of lightning. You've got to get out of the pool."

He refused.

Wow, I thought, *stupidity's gonna kill this guy.*

I had watched the pool's evacuation from the office and then hung back as my lifeguards attempted to get Mr. Oblivious out of the water. Suddenly, I realized this might just be the kind of situation Officer Metz meant when he had handed me the deputy's badge and said, "I think you'll be able to use this."

I joined my guards, poolside. They admitted being out of ideas. They had done everything they could short of jumping into the water. But their training had not trained them for the amazingly stupid exception, and this guy was the amazingly stupid exception.

I took the reins. "Sir, you must get out. For your own safety," I said, saturating my voice with as much authority as possible.

No response. *Maybe it's because I'm not wearing a uniform.*

Reluctantly, I told Tom to call the police. "Tell 'em it's really urgent."

Tom raced up the steps to the office.

Time for my ace card, I thought.

Pulling out my wallet, I held up my new deputy's badge so the man might see it. No response. I took a deep breath and then surprised myself by saying, "I'm authorized to arrest you if you fail to get out of the water."

The man looked up. The sky grew ever darker and the lightning more frequent. No one could miss the roll of thunder. I could hear the iconic and ironic Academy Award winning score of *Exodus* playing in my head. Heil Pool wasn't the Red Sea, but danger is still danger.

"Did you hear me, sir?" I asked.

"So come in and arrest me," Mr. Oblivious said, still walking.

Everywhere on the upper deck, pool patrons were witnessing the unfolding drama. I understood it would be rank stupidity to join this man in the pool—the lightning was getting closer. And even if I could get to him, what then? And what if the man decided to fight?

I was weighing only bad options when the arrival of two uniformed policemen—with Officer Metz leading the way—heightened the drama.

The two officers joined me and my staff at poolside.

"He won't get out of the pool," I explained. No explanation was needed.

Officer Metz pulled out his policeman's whistle and let everyone in two counties know who has the lungs with the biggest vital capacity. My ears rang, but Officer Metz had gotten the attention of the pigheaded swimmer.

"Get over here," shouted Officer Metz. "Now."

There was no denying the sound of authority. Metz sounded like God talking.

Mr. Oblivious made his way to the edge of the pool.

"Now get out of the water until the lightning has passed," Officer Metz commanded.

The man placed his hands, palms down, on the pool edge to push himself out of the water, but then paused. He appeared to be mulling something over.

"Get out now," commanded Officer Metz.

Whatever Mr. Oblivious had been mulling, whatever he thought he ought to do, he made the wrong decision just as the downpour began.

Mr. Oblivious pushed himself out of the water in one remarkably swift and easy motion. I detected an uneasy sway—perhaps Mr. Oblivious was a bit tipsy—but then, without warning, he swung and knocked off Officer Metz's cap. Bursting forward, he shouldered Officer Metz out of the way, then knocked down his partner who was blocking the pool steps. Mr. Oblivious bounded up the steps, two at a time, before disappearing into the men's dressing room corridor.

Pretty good for a drunk guy.

I stood there dumbfounded. The rain was coming down in torrents.

Apparently, police learn to react instinctively when people behave badly. While I gawked in astonishment, Officer Metz scrambled up the stairs in hot pursuit, just a few yards behind Mr. Oblivious. Just as quickly, his partner picked himself off the pool deck and was only a few feet behind him. Onlookers huddling under cover on the upper deck, safely sheltered from the pelting rain, just stood and stared. The chase was on.

Pool patrons ran to peer through the fence as the drama played out just beyond the pool's front door. Mr. Oblivious, barefoot and obviously inebriated, ran out the entrance and across the grass to the Heil Pool sign which was planted like a large grave marker in front of the pool's entrance. The flag pole stood next to it.

With both arms extended on the chiseled stone sign, Mr. Oblivious steadied himself, while the two policemen approached him from either side. It was clear to everyone—except Mr. Oblivious—that escape was impossible.

I had run through the dressing room corridor and stood at the pool's front entrance. It was almost as if Mr. Oblivious was playing a game with the police—the way a child plays "Catch me if you can" in the living room or the backyard.

As Officer Metz closed in, Mr. Oblivious pushed back from the stone sign and knocked Metz's partner over for the second time. The grass was slippery, and Officer Metz had shoes with better traction. He quickly caught up to Mr. Oblivious and tackled him just as the grass gave way to the pool's macadam driveway. Mr. Oblivious fell face first into the macadam, and Officer Metz rolled him over and sprayed his eyes with some kind of burning substance.

Immediately, Mr. Oblivious began screaming in pain. His eyes were on fire. Officer Metz slapped a handcuff on one wrist and then rolled him over to cuff both hands behind his back. His eyes burning, his chin split open, and his cheek and chest bleeding from the tackle, Mr. Oblivious was led to the police car that sat only feet away. The rain increased in intensity, and a bolt of lightning flashed directly overhead.

That's when the hearts of every onlooker collectively broke.

As the thunder quieted, everyone heard a pitiful little voice.

"Daddy."

Everyone turned. A little girl—four, maybe five years old—cried from the embrace of her mother's arms. She reached out toward the fence, having seen her father brought down by the two policemen. The little girl couldn't possibly understand that the police were just trying to save this man from himself.

"Daddy, they hurt Daddy," she screamed.

Once the crowd's attention turned to the little girl's cries of misery, the mother hurried away from the fence. In a few moments, still holding her daughter, she dashed past me into the pouring rain. She stopped, pleading with Officer Metz. As the rain danced noisily on the macadam, I could see the tears streaming down her face. Officer Metz opened the squad car's backdoor, and she and her daughter joined the handcuffed Mr. Oblivious in the backseat.

Officer Metz joined me back at the pool's entrance. Finally under cover and out of the rain, he shook the water from his cap. That struck me as funny because the officer was already soaked to the bone. He smelled of wet leather.

I shook my head. "Thanks. Good Lord, you're soaked. I feel as if I owe you guys an apology. I never expected anything like this."

"Glad I could help," he responded.

"You know I showed him that badge you gave me—and he ignored it completely."

"The bad guys always do," Officer Metz conceded. "He ignored our badges, too. That's why we call them bad guys." He put his sodden cap back on. "Listen, I'm going need a statement from you, okay? Swing by the station when you get off today."

As the patrol car slowly exited the driveway, I could see the woman in the backseat carefully wiping her husband's swollen eyes.

Whenever I remember that day, I wonder if there might have been another way—a better way—to handle the problem. And then I ask myself if there is ever a "better way" to deal with the amazingly stupid exception.

Chapter 4

CONFESSION IS GOOD FOR THE SOUL

Summer 1965

Throughout the summer of 1965, I spent my evenings at Katie's house when I wasn't managing Heil Pool. Along with her younger brother, Preston, we'd listen to *The Beach Boys* latest albums, *Summer Days* or *Shut Down*. Katie would cuddle up with me on the sofa, while her brother sat on the floor actively ignoring the two of us making out.

On especially hot and sultry Pennsylvania evenings, we'd cool off beneath the stars in their small, round, above-ground pool in the side yard. The water might be warm, but it was cooler than the humid night air alive with mosquitos and fireflies.

Sometimes we'd walk up her long driveway and visit her grandmother who lived about a hundred yards away. Grandma would offer us iced tea and conversation, both laced with a gentle understanding. College-educated and a retired teacher, Katie's grandmother thought it was terrific that her granddaughter's boyfriend planned to be a teacher.

"What would you like to teach?" she'd ask, and Katie would always jump in and declare that "Jack is going to be a high school English teacher."

Her grandmother would smile at both of us, then look directly at Katie and ask, "How long has Jack been a mute."

"Oh, Grandma, I'm sorry. I'm sorry, Jack. I know you can speak for yourself. I'm just so excited that he's heading off to college, Grandma. The man I love is going to be a teacher."

Our conversations frequently turned to my reasons for choosing to be a teacher. And I'd tell her about Miss Manzolillo. Throughout twelve years of Catholic school, my English teachers were all nuns—except for Miss Manzolillo—my ninth-grade teacher. Her energy and love of language proved infectious—to me, anyway.

"She'd urge us all 'To step into the book. You'll find worlds you cannot find anywhere else.' Sometimes she'd walk around the room and ask, 'What are you reading this week?' I began reading because I didn't want to disappoint her when she asked me what I was reading. Not reading something was no longer an option. So, I just started reading all kinds of things.

"One thing that Miss Manzolillo did—the thing I really loved—was she'd read to us. It's been ages since anyone read to me. Every morning she'd step around her desk and say 'I read this last night. You're going to love it.' And then she'd read to us. Sometimes what she read would take a minute or two, sometimes it would take the entire class period—like the time she read Flannery O'Connor's *A Good Man Is Hard to Find*. You know that story, don't you, Grandma?"

I turned to Katie and explained it was a short story that ends with the murder of an entire family.

"We all wanted to know who this guy Flannery O'Connor was. What kind of guy would write a story like that?"

"Yeah," Katie chimed in. "What kind of guy would write a story like that?"

I gave Katie the same dubious look Miss Manzolillo had given us. "Flannery O'Connor isn't a guy—she's a woman. Yeah, a woman. That fact took us all by surprise."

"Did you like everything Miss Manzolillo read to you?" Grandma asked.

"No," I said, "not all of it. But we knew she loved it. She used to tell us that we should find what we loved to read. She'd say, 'Not every book is everyone's cup of tea. Find what you like. If you don't like what you're reading, put it down and find something else. There are simply too many good things to read.'"

"She's right," Grandma said as she sipped her tea. "If I read everything I'd like to read, I'd have to live forever to do it. There are so many good things to read."

"Better yet, Miss Manzolillo helped me learn to like things I didn't think I'd like," I said.

Grandma flashed me her "Like what?" look.

"Well, I remember when we were beginning Shakespeare's *Romeo and*

Juliet. I was pretty sure it was going to be uninteresting."

"Red means 'boring,' Grandma," Katie said.

"I thought that's what Jack meant," Grandma said gently. She patted Katie's hand. "Let him tell his story."

I continued. "Like always, she assured us we were going to love it. 'It's a love story,' she said, 'but you probably know that already. It's also a love story that ends badly.' Then she paused in front of our classmate Sam Farwell, and spoke with incredible tenderness. 'I'm sure some of you already have had a love story end badly, haven't you?' Everyone turned to look at Sam Farwell whose girlfriend, Denise, had died of leukemia a few weeks after school began. Her death devastated Sam. We all sat in respectful silence for what seemed like forever—until Miss Manzolillo leapt back in. '*Romeo and Juliet* may have been written 370 years ago, but Shakespeare understood love and loss. That's one of many reasons we still read Shakespeare.'"

I began tearing up right there in front of Katie's grandmother. I confess. I'm a crier, prone to involuntary bouts of crying when feelings of happiness or sadness overwhelm my nervous system. Crying is one of the things Katie said she loved about me. She also loved that I would blush—turning a vivid red when I said or thought something sexual. Katie called it my "naughty response."

Katie watched my tears welling up and pulled me close. As she kissed my cheek, I smiled and shook my head. "I don't think I'll ever forget Miss Manzolillo's kindness to Sam. No one our age is supposed to die."

"You're right, Jack" Grandma said. "But it happens. Sometimes young people die. It seems so unfair. My youngest brother died of polio back in…let me see…in 1920 when he was fourteen." Grandma smiled at the memory of her lost brother. "That's forty-five years ago."

"I never knew that, Grandma," Katie said.

"Katie, there are some memories that are my own private memories. I've tucked them away until the right moment arrives. And I think that moment just arrived. Jack, I really do understand Sam Farwell's sense of sadness and loss. I haven't thought about my brother in ages—but tonight…tonight it feels like he's sitting right here with us."

Grandma took a deep breath and said, "So what other wonderful things did your Miss Manzolillo have to say about *Romeo and Juliet*?"

I began laughing. "Well, Grandma, the next thing she said took us all by surprise. I couldn't believe I was hearing this from one of my teachers."

"Well, for goodness' sake, Jack," Grandma said, "don't keep us in suspense."

"You're right, Grandma. Here's what she said. 'You realize, of course, that Shakespeare also understood teenage boys. Act 1, scene one, will really get your attention when you realize Shakespeare opens his five-act love story with two horny teenagers standing on a street corner talking dirty.'"

Grandma put a hand to her mouth as a huge smile blossomed across her face.

"That's what she told us, Grandma, and most of the boys laughed—including me. She didn't talk like any English teacher I'd ever had before. I'd only ever had nuns as my English teachers, and I can't imagine hearing a nun say something like 'two horny teenagers standing on a street corner talking dirty.' After the laughter died down, Miss Manzolillo reiterated what she'd said. 'Yes, really. Two horny teenage boys, talking dirty. Some things never change.' I remember the girls laughing at that remark."

"So, I assume you enjoyed *Romeo and Juliet*?" Grandma asked.

"Yeah, I did. Somehow, Miss Manzolillo made *Romeo and Juliet* feel like it was 1961 instead of 1591."

"That's why they call it literature," Grandma said wistfully. "It's timeless." She paused for a moment and looked longingly at Katie and me as if she were remembering something both wonderful and awful. "It's as timeless as the excitement of first love."

I began to blush. Shakespeare would have understood.

"That's wonderful that you love to read, Jack," Katie's grandmother told me with quiet satisfaction. "All the best people love to read. Mark Twain once said that 'the man who does not read has no advantage over the man who cannot read.' Keep on reading. And Katie," Grandma said gesturing at me, "I hope you hold this reader close to your heart."

"I will Grandma. I promise." Katie squeezed my hand and put her head on my shoulder. The warm night instantly became warmer. I could feel the warmth of both their smiles—and my blushing warmed my face even more.

Right on cue, Grandma broke the silence. "So, Jack, what are you reading this week?"

It took me a moment to gather myself. "I'm very happy you asked," I replied with mock formality. "Right now, I'm reading a book of short stories by

James Thurber, *The Secret Life of Walter Mitty.*"

In a lifetime of summers, the summer of '65 was my favorite. I was in love—"from the tips of your toes to the top of your head," my mother would tell me—and my girlfriend's grandmother proved to be a kindred spirit. We talked books and plays that summer—and Katie's new job provoked a whole new array of conversational topics: the world of work, office politics, the internal power structure, lazy colleagues, and the behavior of bad bosses. During the latter conversations, I learned that the words "boss" and "asshole" could be *bona fide* synonyms.

So that's how my summer unfolded. At the pool. At Katie's. At her grandmother's.

Katie's mom and dad trusted me with their daughter, and my mom and dad reciprocated. Katie was Methodist and I was Catholic—and the rules for making out were more liberal for Methodists than they were for Catholics. I knew lots of guys who bragged about "how far they'd gone," but I vowed I'd never allow things "to get out of hand." That's how several of my religion teachers—all nuns except for one priest—had expressed it. "Never let things get out of hand." Those comments always underscored their mini-sermons exhorting us to remember our bodies were sacred. A simple translation was "Don't have sex. No touching that arouses you and no intercourse." Kissing was a gray area—except for French kissing. That was colored bright red.

Then one evening it happened. I don't know what hormone kicked in, but my libido went into overdrive. Since graduation our kisses had grown more ardent, and there was nothing I wanted more than to touch Katie. I already knew she would never object—never say "Stop! What are you doing?" That's because she'd know what I was doing and so would I…sort of.

But no sooner had I done "it" than a wave of guilt swept over me. All the "thou shalt nots" drilled into me across a dozen years of Catholic school, all the dire warnings of dying in the state of mortal sin and being dragged into Hell, mortified me.

To say my reaction ruined the moment would be an understatement. Imagine the plight of Adam in the Garden of Eden. It would be like Adam saying, "One minute I was enjoying myself. My girlfriend and I were eating an apple, and one thing led to another. You know how that is. And then next thing we know we were being thrown out on our asses. Naked as jaybirds. The end. Pardon my language."

It's funny how guilt makes your insides crumble. The moment I felt her breast beneath her blouse, I pulled back immediately, precipitously. I felt as if I'd violated her, though I don't believe she felt violated at all. I was the only one standing at the intersection of Guilt and Sin with red lights flashing in every direction. Katie was, figuratively, at a completely different intersection, and all the lights were green. In fact, she was solicitous, asking me if I was alright. Was I hurt? She was both surprised and dismayed by my response—because I acted as if touching her were somehow an unpleasant or painful experience.

It wasn't.

Besides guilt, I felt enormously confused. For the first time, it occurred to me that God, the one who created human beings, had decided that human beings shouldn't act like human beings. Why else would I feel dirty or sinful for doing what my own body was instructing me to do? A whole posse of nuns and priests had warned me that the chemical urges that surge through my bloodstream must be staunchly resisted. These eminently human feelings were forbidden—unless one were married.

That's why I went to Confession.

Some confessions are easy, and some are difficult. Lately, all my confessors had been Franciscan friars—the same priests who were my instructors at Notre Dame High School—and I'd seldom had anything real to confess. No robberies. No assaults. No murders. And no touching of any young women—girlfriend or otherwise. Among my sins, there was nothing that anyone would find shocking.

Confession for me was more of a cleaning and dusting—light housework. My sins had a more cerebral cast—that is, I *thought* about doing many of the things I was forbidden to do. Until now, it had never gone beyond thinking. However, as I said, thinking about doing, and doing, were equivalent evils in the Catholic lexicon of sin.

As my brother once said, "You're too damn good, Jack. You ought to try sinning a little. I mean, really sinning. You know that? I have no idea why you ever go to Confession."

Will knew whereof he spoke. He'd had a succession of girlfriends who adored him. Our neighbor across the street had anointed Will with a catalogue of nicknames—the Make-Out King, the Grape-Arbor Lover—and I believe my brother reveled in his reputation. I can't say if any of his many conquests "put out" for him—that was the slang we used in 1965—but they certainly craved his company.

Me? I felt lucky just to have Katie kiss me.

Probably the worst thing I remember confessing—other than enjoying libidinous, lascivious thoughts—was lying to my mom and dad about where I'd been after I'd been making out with Katie in the Chevy.

And then I touched Katie.

I was an amorous young man, who would have loved not feeling guilty or ashamed about touching the woman I loved. My brother, and several of my friends, assured me that I shouldn't feel guilty or ashamed, but to no avail. As my brother would say from time to time, "Red, you're too damn Catholic."

It wasn't until many years later, when I began traveling nationally, that I really comprehended what it meant to be in the grip of deeply buried feelings.

I'd taught for about fifteen years right out of college, including a short detour to graduate school. Then, after I left teaching, I traveled for a textbook publisher as a national consultant. For more than two-and-a-half decades, I flew millions of miles—four point seven million miles, to be exact.

I occasionally hated flying because it was time-consuming, tedious, or crowded. But I was seldom afraid. There were times, however, when I'd be seated next to a white-knuckle flyer—someone whose fear of flying was palpable. White-knuckle flyers constantly worried that the plane would somehow crash. Despite all the statistical data proving the safety of flying, their imaginations crippled them with thoughts of their own horrible deaths in the plane's crumpled fuselage.

While I never had any fear of flying, I met plenty of people who would have preferred walking the three thousand miles across the country rather than taking the plane. White-knuckle flyers only flew when they had no choice.

Just as white-knuckle flyers could never escape their fear, I could never escape my guilt or shame. Our fears were ingrained—an integral part of who we were. That's why I never once said, "Don't be afraid," to a fearful flyer. Telling them to not feel what they were feeling—feeling fear in spite of themselves—was wasted breath.

I distinctly remember the day I touched Katie. I would have liked to excuse myself by claiming I was in the throes of hormonal powers beyond my control. I was. Or that Katie didn't mind. She didn't. Or that we were in love. We were.

But all I could hear were a cacophony of voices—the voices of the nuns at St. Joseph's Elementary School and Notre Dame High School—who had earnestly exhorted me that the devil never sleeps, and assured me that such touching would send one's immortal soul swiftly to Hell.

Unfortunately, my own unshakable guilt and shame overpowered any pleasure I might have enjoyed, and spoke to me in capital letters, despite Katie's best efforts to assuage my guilt.

"You mustn't feel that way, Red," she said. "What you did is perfectly natural."

But I did feel "that way." I felt guilty. I felt ashamed. After twelve years of Catholic school, guilt and shame were autonomic responses, like breathing.

I went to Confession.

Protestants always seem either amused or confused by the Catholic sacrament of Confession. If the topic ever came up among Katie's friends, Katie would raise her eyebrows, flash me a dubious look, and then tell everyone in a teasing tone, "Jack thinks Confession is his get-out-of-jail-free card."

That comment irked me precisely because there was some truth to it.

Soon after I began dating Katie, I found I was at war with myself. To sin or not to sin, that was the question. Well, it wasn't really a question—it was an ongoing battle—with myself. I don't know if such emotional turbulence was normal for all teenagers, but I always foundered on the rocky shoals between duty and desire. I suspect that a decade of moral instruction in Catholic School contributed mightily to the conflict.

For two years, Katie and I kissed. Sometimes modestly, sometimes fervently. But when we graduated from high school, we found we had become freshmen in the adult world—we weren't "just kids" anymore. Katie ventured into the adult work-a-day world and I took my new assistant manager's job until I'd go off to college later that summer. Something important had changed—and that included our kisses.

Now, I found myself kissing an adult woman who ardently kissed me in return, her kisses laden with unspoken promises and worlds of possibility—kisses that tickled those twin opposing responses, pleasure and guilt. Suddenly, kissing felt like sitting down to dinner and having only a small salad with no entrée. No dessert. Like many a teenage boy, I was unaccustomed to leaving the table hungry. For two years, on my self-imposed kisses-only diet, the excruciating tension between what I wanted to do, and what I was forbidden to do, never disappeared. While the Baltimore Catechism whispered warnings in my ear, counseling caution, a bio-chemical tsunami threatened to drown me.

As the summer of '65 rolled into July, many of my evenings ended with a delightful-but-frustrating make-out session with Katie. As I drove home, I'd hear the voices of all the nuns who had ever addressed the topic of sexual desire in the most oblique language. "You must never desecrate a holy vessel." Nuns, of course, women who had taken a vow of chastity, seemed to me ill-equipped to lecture hormone-fueled teens in matters of sex. In fact, their solutions could be summed up in one word: Don't.

Don't kiss. Don't pet. Don't copulate. And don't even *think* about kissing, petting, or copulating. (I don't think I ever heard a nun say "copulate," except in my imagination. Fornicate? Yes, but never copulate.) In the Catholic Church, any of those deeds themselves were mortal sins, but so were the thoughts that preceded the deeds. Since Catholics made little or no distinction between thought and deed—the thought was not, as the saying goes, "the father to the deed"—it was its twin brother.

In the secular world, I could not be prosecuted for what I thought, but in the spiritual world of the Catholic Church—where all sin was duly recorded—I could be condemned eternally for my thoughts. Unapologetically.

For almost seventeen years, I never gave much thought to matters of sex. But first-love, high school graduation, and the knowledge that I would be going away to school, changed that. I'd had a girlfriend for two years, but now I thought about Katie all the time. Each time she and I spoke, face-to-face or over the phone, I would breathlessly tell her how I felt about her. Invariably I'd blurt out, "I love you so very much."

I was ecstatic to hear her own breathless reciprocation. "I love you, too, Red."

Our "thinking-about-you" thoughts supplemented our daily telephone calls and our almost daily visits—at the pool, in her home, in the car, along the tree-shaded lane near her grandmother's—everywhere and anywhere. Admittedly, the feelings that coursed through my entire body when I was with her—often unannounced but never unwelcome—were new and unmanageable.

I went to Confession.

The priest I chose as my confessor was the assistant pastor at our church, and he was relatively new. Since I no longer served as an altar boy at St. Joseph's, I really didn't know what kind of man Father Boylan was. As I entered the dark confessional, I told myself that he was just another priest—one among many—who had the power to forgive sins.

That was my first mistake.

I knelt down and waited for the small confessional door to open. When it did, I began as I always had. "Bless me father for I have sinned. It has been six weeks since my last Confession."

"Father," I said, struggling to find the right words, "Father, I touched a young woman this week."

"How many times?" he asked.

"Just once," I stammered.

"Was she clothed?"

"Yes, Father. She was fully clothed."

"Is she your girlfriend?"

"Yes, Father. We've been going out now for almost two years."

"And this is the first time you've touched her?"

"Yes, Father."

I wasn't sure what to expect next. I assumed that any priest who has listened to hundreds, maybe thousands, of confessions would know what to tell me. That was my second mistake.

I could see the priest's face through the screen. He appeared to be grimacing. "Well, then, this young woman has become a near occasion of sin for you."

I could feel my stomach tighten. "What are you saying, Father? It was the first time. The only time that I..."

My confessor interrupted me. "You need to break up with your girlfriend."

I was at a loss for words. *Am I hearing what I think I'm hearing?* I'd never disobeyed a priest—not really. *What can I say to him?* My mind sought an answer that simply wasn't there. I think my silence aggravated him, because when he next spoke, he growled, "Did you hear what I said?"

"Yes, Father. I heard what you said."

"Good. Now tell me what I told you to do."

I thought, *What should I tell him? I can't break up with Katie. I love her.* I heard myself say, "You said I have to break up with my girlfriend."

"That's correct. If you don't agree to do so, I cannot grant you absolution from your sins. Your girlfriend has clearly become a near occasion of sin for you, and when I tell you to 'Go and sin no more,' that's unlikely if you return to the girl you've sinned with."

Again, I fell silent—feeling totally defeated.

"Do you understand?"

My words came out in a whisper. "I understand, Father."

"So, you must tell me here and now that you will break up with your girlfriend."

My mind was empty, devoid of words. I felt trapped, feeling a growing anger. I wanted to stand up in the gloomy confessional and say, *God damn it, Father, I'm out of here. I'll find a different priest who will give me absolution.* But I knew that wasn't an option. And lying to your priest in Confession was equally unthinkable. God—in the unfathomable person of Father Boylan—was listening. God was waiting for my answer—and even if I decided to lie, God would know what was in my heart. Lying was not an option. Surrender was my only option.

"Okay, Father, I'll break up with her."

That was my third mistake.

"Good," he said to me. "You'll be much happier without her." He began giving me absolution.

Much happier without her? I thought. *Is he kidding? Is he that heartless and obtuse?* I wondered if such thoughts about my confessor were sinful.

I tried to imagine how I could actually do what I had just promised the priest I'd do. If I understood correctly, I was supposed to tell the girl who loved me—and whom I loved—that we were through because I'd fondled her fully-clothed breast through her blouse without benefit of matrimony.

I knew one thing for certain. I'd never step into a confessional with Father Boylan again. His indifference to human feelings, and his ignorance of the consequences of his confessional commands, staggered me. It was as if he had no comprehension of what it was to be human.

I left the confessional scared, confused, and defeated—the exact opposite of how one should feel after being unburdened of one's sins.

That night I told my brother, Will, about my confession as we sat together on the front stoop. It was a warm, humid night. Will listened to me, frequently nodding or shaking his head. Then he told me what he thought.

"You're not really breaking up with Katie, are you? You guys are crazy for each other. You love her, don't you? Right? You're not gonna break up because some priest, who wouldn't know what to do with a beautiful woman if he found one in his bed, tells you that you have to break up? Who the hell does he think he is? Jesus, Red, what are you gonna say to her? 'Sorry, Katie, Father Boylan says you can't be my girlfriend anymore?' That's nuts. You're crazy if you do that."

"I told him I would," I said sullenly.

"Okay, sure. You told him. Just put that in the Lies I've Told column for your next confession," Will said. "Don't do it, Red. If you ask me, Boylan's stepped way over the line. You know what he's telling you, don't you? He's telling you to hurt someone you love. That's what he's telling you. Breaking someone's heart has got to be a sin, doesn't it? Where does he get off telling you that you have to hurt someone you love to get absolution? What gives him the right? I've confessed to way worse than you, and no priest ever told me to stay away from any of my girlfriends."

The next day I went to see Katie. We were walking up the long driveway toward her grandmother's house, and I told her exactly what the priest told me to do—I didn't hold back anything.

"What does that mean, Red? Aren't we together anymore?"

I didn't know how to answer her.

"Well, are we or aren't we?"

I heard the anger in her voice. "I don't know," I said. I was stunned at how lame my answer sounded.

"Well," she said in an unusually quiet voice, "you damn well better figure it out because what you did—touching me—it didn't bother me one bit. Besides, I was completely dressed for God's sake. You touched my blouse not my skin. You want the truth? I liked it. I did. I'm still trying to figure out why it's taken you so long to get that far. But I don't see how it can be a sin if I wanted you to do what you did. I have to say, Catholics have some screwy ideas about sex. Does the Catholic Church think it's a sin to be human, too?"

I searched for something to say—but found nothing.

"Maybe the priest is right. Maybe we should break up until you can figure out how *I* feel about *you* touching *me*."

Katie pulled off the senior class ring that I'd given her when we decided to go steady. "Here," she grabbed my hand and shoved the ring deep into my palm. "Here, better take this. I wouldn't want you to burn in Hell. I wouldn't want to be your near occasion of sin." Her voice began to crack. I knew the tears would follow.

I stood there. Silent. Ashamed. *I've betrayed her*, I thought.

She turned away and made a beeline for her grandmother's front door. She called to me over her shoulder.

"Don't follow me, Red, you're not welcome here. Not today." She stopped at the front door and turned toward me. Her face was filled with sadness. "Go home and figure out what it means when someone tells you they love you. Go home and figure out if you really mean it when you say you love me."

She disappeared into the house.

I walked back to my Chevy, climbed in, and drove home.

Will spotted me from the kitchen window as I drove down our back alley. He bounded out the back door and trotted across the lawn to my rolled down window. "Slide over," he said. "I'm driving. I want to hear all about what just happened."

He backed the car into the alley, stopped for a moment to light a cigarette, put the car into first gear, and headed toward Morgan Hill.

"I see you have your class ring back."

"Yeah."

"You did what Father Boylan told you to do?" he asked as he shifted into second.

"Yeah, I did."

"That means you're off the hook, Red, right? You broke up. You really did it, right?"

"Yeah, I did just what he told me to do."

Will took a long drag and shifted into high gear.

"Here's the thing, Red. You did exactly what you said you were gonna do. You did exactly what you needed to do, so you could feel that you weren't lying to Father Boylan. You followed the letter of the law."

"I suppose."

"Nope. Nope," Will shook his head and waved his cigarette at me. "You don't have to suppose. You did exactly what was required. So, you want the good news or the bad news?"

"There's good news?" I asked.

"Oh yeah," Will said. "You followed the letter of the law."

"And the bad news?"

"Come on. You know the bad news. You hurt someone you say you love—someone you say you love a whole lot. You followed the letter of the law."

"Okay," I said unsure of why the good news was good news. "Why is that good news?"

"I gotta hand it to you, Red, for someone so smart, sometimes you're really stupid." He paused at a stop sign and looked at me intently. "You told that asshole, Father Boylan, the truth. You broke up with Katie. You shouldn't have listened to him—and he should never have told you to do what you did—but okay. Now that's done."

"Yeah," I said without enthusiasm. "That's done."

"Now, if you're smart—and you're the guy going off to college in September, so I'm guessing you're smart—you'll go back over to Katie's and apologize for being a first-class asshole."

My face betrayed my fear of facing Katie.

"You hurt her because Father Boylan said you had to. Now that you've done what you said you'd do, now do what you need to do. Go tell her you're sorry…"

"I *am* sorry," I said interrupting him.

"But before you say you're sorry, you better know what you're sorry for. Are you sorry for touching her? Or for being stupid enough to listen to Father Boylan? For breaking her heart?"

"I guess I better think about that," I replied.

"I guess you'd better. But don't think too long. Broken hearts are time sensitive—especially when the girl is your first love. Don't forget, Red, first loves only come once in a lifetime. You can't throw them away because some priest doesn't understand what he can't understand."

We headed home.

"If I were you," Will said as he turned down our alley, "I'd be thinking about your apology while you're driving over to see her. Now seems like a good time to do that," he said, as he pulled on the parking brake.

Will opened his door and I slid behind the wheel.

"Thanks, Will," I said.

Will stood for a moment beside the car. "We all do stupid things, Red. Sometimes we hurt people when we do those stupid things. But when I do something stupid, I try to make sure it's my stupid idea and not somebody else's. I know you love Katie, and I'm pretty sure she loves you, too. Let her know how you really feel. Let her know that no priest can tell you who to love or how to love. It's none of his damn business."

As I slowly drove the four miles from my house to hers, I thought about my apology. Contrary to the way I normally made my way to Katie's, I took my time. I waited as long as possible at stop lights. I delayed at stop signs. I used every moment to practice what I wanted to say. I needed the right words in the right order—words with lots of love and, hopefully, a touch of magic. Words that could rescue us both from despair.

I'd already broken her heart once today, and I didn't want my apology to be part two of Red's Heartbreak Special. I wanted Katie to know how much I loved her. I wanted her to know how foolish I was for hurting her—needlessly and cruelly hurting her—when all she'd ever done was share her love with me.

I paused the Chevy at the head of her driveway before turning right. "What-ifs" plagued me, and I felt ashamed. *Grow up*, I told myself. *Katie deserves better.* Moving slowly down the long, narrow driveway, I saw Katie and her grandmother sitting together on her grandmother's deck. The raised deck looked up the driveway and north toward the distant horizon.

They both saw my car at the same time, and I watched Grandma pat Katie on her hand, stand up, and wave to me. I began reciting my prepared apology in my head as I pulled off the driveway and parked next to her grandmother's Buick. I killed the ignition and stepped from the car.

I stood next to the car and took a deep breath. I felt terribly alone. As I walked to the front door, all I could hear in my head was, *God, I'm scared.*

Katie met me at the front door. We stood looking at one another. Silently looking at one another. The tears began forming in her eyes and mine. Not a word was spoken. Not one. We let our faces and our hearts and our arms speak for us. Mine said, *I'm sorry.* Hers said, *You're forgiven.* Our lips were otherwise engaged—for quite a long time. Talking was simply not possible as we kissed… and kissed…and…

Will was happy to see me when I returned home.

"So, she still loves you?"

"I'm pretty sure," I said jokingly.

"Only pretty sure?" Will asked. "Maybe you need to apologize every night for the rest of the summer. Maybe then, you'll be more than pretty sure."

Will was right about a lot of things. First love only comes along once in a lifetime. The novelty of the experience is accompanied by joy and confusion.

Katie and I spent the rest of the summer of '65 without ever looking back.

I became a little more Methodist and a little less Catholic, much to Katie's delight. I also took my brother's advice and tried "sinning a little."

That day, when I broke up with my first love, was the day I discovered how important love and trust really are. That was the day that I trusted my brother's wisdom, and I trusted Katie's heart.

I was rewarded on both counts.

Chapter 5
RULE 1: NOBODY DROWNS

Summer 1965

During my career at Heil Pool—can a summer job ever be a career?—I had encountered every possible kind of person.

Bushel-loads of rambunctious, energetic kids arrived every day. I had to continually remind my lifeguards—and myself—that these kids weren't being rambunctious and energetic to aggravate the lifeguards. These were kids… having fun in the way kids knew how. I was certain that my mother's shoulder-shrugging comment applied. "Kids will be kids."

Kids or not, the pool staff had to be ready for a wide variety of potential problems. For instance, despite the fact that we were a *swimming* pool, not everyone knew how to swim. The staff's biggest fear was the *faux* swimmer—kids who thought they could swim, but couldn't.

I recall two five-year-old kids who dove off one of the diving boards when I was a rookie lifeguard. The diving well was fifteen feet deep at its deepest point, and younger, unproven swimmers had to demonstrate they could swim before they were given permission to use the diving boards. Whenever youngsters with unknown or dubious swimming abilities pleaded for diving privileges, the diving-well lifeguard would ask the guard on "walking duty"—there were four guards in elevated chairs and one guard on walking duty—to take the kids to shallower water for a quick test. This system worked flawlessly, in theory anyway. Reality, however, especially on crowded days, invariably interfered with the theoretical.

The diving-well lifeguard chair was situated about six feet above the water so the lifeguard could easily survey all three diving boards. I enjoyed watching the procession of divers launch themselves into space, some gracefully, some comically, some painfully. The diving lifeguard's primary duty was simple: Nobody drowns. They might crack their heads on the diving board, or lose a key portion of a swimsuit as one young lady once did, but nobody drowns. In addition, the diving guard's duties encompassed issues of fairness as divers lined up to use the boards—"Wait your turn," "No butting into line"—and safety—"Can you swim?"

On this very busy day, as head lifeguard, I occupied that diving-well chair. A tow-headed youngster, who had been patiently waiting in line, scooted along the sandpaper top of the nearest one-meter diving board and jumped into the water. He didn't dive. He jumped. That wasn't unusual; kids loved to jump. They especially loved doing cannonballs and spraying everyone within a fifteen-foot radius. Not everyone liked being cannon-balled, but if one wanted to stay dry, one avoided the diving well area.

This youngster, so small and light that he hardly made the board bounce at all, made nary a ripple when he jumped in. For a second or two, he bobbed just below the surface, and then a large burst of bubbles streamed to the surface. No air means no buoyancy. He sank like a rock to the bottom.

I rose from my chair, ready to dive in, when a second youngster, tanned and in bright red trunks, zoomed along the same diving board, following his friend into the deep. He frantically breast-stroked his way to his friend on the bottom. I decided there was no more time to wait when a second barrage of bubbles streamed to the surface. I jumped, hands flat on my sides, feet first, toes pointed. Almost immediately I touched bottom. In the crystal-clear water, I saw the two youngsters entangled a few feet away. I reached them, easily wrapped my arms around them, coiled my legs, and pushed off the bottom. We broke the surface and I pushed them poolside with a giant scissor kick. The two youngsters struggled to take deep breaths, but otherwise they seemed alright.

"You lied to me," the tow-headed youngster said accusingly between coughs and wheezes. He'd been the first off the board.

"What do you mean he lied to you?" I asked.

"He said that if I jumped off the board and started drowning, he'd save me."

All I could do was shake my head. "He said he'd save you?" I asked the blonde-haired boy how old he was.

"Five," he said proudly. "Older than him," he said gesturing at his contemporary who had failed to save him.

"Can you swim?" I asked.

"Not yet, but I'm learning."

Not if you drown, I thought. There were things you must never say out loud—not to a five-year-old with everyone standing around.

Tank, the pool's assistant manager that year, had listened to this exchange because a gathering crowd had alerted him that something required his attention. Towering over the boys, he said, "Hey guys, come on up to the office with me. Okay."

They obediently followed Tank to the office. The pool's PA system summoned the mom who'd brought them both to the pool. When she heard what had happened, she was appalled by the behavior of her son.

"What if you had drowned," she said, clearly angry. Moms could always say what I couldn't.

Tank tried to mediate the situation. *There was no way a five-year-old could respond to that question,* Tank thought, but to no avail.

"I can't believe you did that," she said. "Stand up, we are going home." She turned to the second youngster who had attempted his rescue. "Wait'll I tell your mother about this." Both youngsters started crying.

"Stop that crying right now," she said, "or I'll really give you something to cry about."

Words to live by, Tank thought. She left, telling Tank that she was sorry that he'd been forced to deal with her son's reckless behavior.

Almost all lifeguards, at one time or another, face unusual or unexpected situations that challenge the "Nobody Drowns" rule. One of my lifeguards, Herbie, once watched a young lady experience a grand mal seizure as she went off the diving board. Twisting and contorting herself in mid-air, Herbie wasted no time swimming to her aid. Herbie wasn't sure what was going on, but it was clear that the girl was in crisis as she sank in the clear water. Nobody drowns.

Tom Detweiler was watching a young boy move from the really shallow area of the pool to a steadily deeper part of the pool. That twenty-five-meter section went from eighteen inches to a depth of about four feet if one crossed all six swimming lane lines. Nothing seemed terribly amiss to Tom, but there was just something that made him feel uneasy. Tom, a competitive swimmer whose specialty was the butterfly, couldn't remember a time when he couldn't swim. His lithe six-foot-two frame made him a dolphin in the water.

"Learned to swim in the womb," he'd always say with a grin, particularly when his mother was around. But he also understood kids who had never learned. He knew there were those who were fearful, and those who were fool-hardy. He was here for both. Lifeguards also knew that many non-swimming kids loved challenging themselves.

"Guess how far I walked out today?" one bragged to a friend. "I got to the fifth line!" Guards watched little kids challenge deeper waters all the time, before turning back to shallow waters and safety.

Sitting in his chair, Tom watched this particular boy walk into deeper and deeper water. Curiously, this boy's arms were spread out from his side as if he were an airplane. Tom remained vigilant.

He's in past his waist. Now the water's chest high. Okay, he's up to his chin. Are you gonna keep going, kid? Tom asked himself. *Yep, you're gonna keep going. How tall are you?*

Tom guessed he couldn't be more than four feet tall. The water was now just beneath the boy's nose and a step or two later, only the boy's brown hair floated above the surface.

The boy stood on line six—a line at the four-foot level that gave short non-swimmers bragging rights. His arms straight out to the side. He was not moving.

What's going on, kid? You planning on drowning quietly? Tom asked himself. *Come on, move for me. Show me you're okay.*

When the alarm sounded in Tom's head, he jumped from his chair and easily made his way to the stationary boy who remained still and unmoving, completely below the waterline.

Tom grabbed him beneath his armpits and hoisted him above the water. There is a noise that people make when they are searching for that deep draft of air, when they've been deprived of oxygen and breathe as if their lives depended on it. It is a strange, high-pitched sound, strained and hollow. That's the sound this young man made as he struggled for air.

Tom carried him a few feet to the edge of the pool and sat him down. "What the heck?!"

Between coughs and wheezing breaths, the youngster managed to thank Tom. "Thanks, mister. Thanks. I'm glad you got to me. I was drowning."

Sometimes there is just nothing you can say. "Maybe you should just stay in the shallow area of the pool until you know how to swim," Tom said. Nobody drowns.

Heil was a family pool, and the majority of the regular pool patrons were kids—both the swimming and the non-swimming varieties. Some parents would bring their kids to the pool and spread out a blanket and spend most of the day enjoying the sunshine. Most kids never understood why their parents weren't just dying to jump into the pool with a gang of tag-playing, cannon-balling, chicken-fighting, and—yes—urinating youngsters. Adults were happy with the peace and quiet of the hazy sunshine, the grass, and a trashy novel. I'm certain many parents were grateful for the active, and truly inexpensive babysitting service that Heil Pool provided. Parents came to relax and have my staff watch their children.

It's also true that most pool patrons were season ticket holders. Membership at Heil Pool was both cheap and convenient. At the pool's entrance, season pass holders handed over their passes to Mr. Sawyer, and he'd place them in an alphabetized file box. Those same patrons retrieved their passes from Mr. Sawyer as they departed. There were no picture IDs on season passes, but Heil Pool had Mr. Sawyer, and that made picture IDs completely unnecessary. Mr. Sawyer knew every season ticket holder by name and by sight, so on days when someone had forgotten to bring their season pass, he'd let them in. Heil was not only a family pool, it was a family affair.

Unfortunately, families occasionally have their problems, and some even have problem children.

On one particular day, a woman in yellow sunglasses and a floppy polka-dot hat came up the steps to my office. The office door was always open.

"Excuse me, Mr. Timins?" said the woman looking in my doorway. She was a woman I'd often seen, but her name was a mystery. Mr. Sawyer surely knew it.

"Yes? Come in, please. What can I do for you…Mrs?…Mrs…?"

The woman stepped inside, then looked out the door. "Mrs. Renaldi."

"I'm sorry, Mrs. Renaldi. I should know who you are. You bring your kids almost every day."

"That's okay," she said. She kept looking back toward the pool. "I have to keep an eye on my blanket." She sighed and then turned back to me. She appeared troubled, searching for the right words.

"I don't want to make trouble…and I don't want to accuse anyone…"

I joined her at the door because she clearly wanted to keep an eye on her blanket while conducting a *sotto voce* conversation.

"What is it?" Mrs. Renaldi.

She hesitated, gave me a pained look, and then spoke in a whisper. "I think someone is stealing."

It wouldn't be the first time, I thought.

This kind of problem always made me angry and sad. "Do you know who this someone might be?"

She nodded. "Not by name," she said. "But I can point him out to you."

"Let's take a walk down to your blanket," I said. "Tell me who and what you saw."

As we walked out into the sunshine, she said, "I'm sorry."

"You don't have to apologize, Mrs. Renaldi. I appreciate it when patrons bring problems to my attention. If someone is stealing, I want to know about it."

As we walked down the stairs, she discretely pointed out the young man whom she suspected. Crewcut and tan, he was in the pool, goofing around with a couple of other kids his age. I guessed he was about eight or nine. I'd seen him here at the pool from time to time, but I hadn't a clue about his name.

"About two hours ago, I saw him reaching under a blanket, pulling out a wallet. I didn't think anything of it at the time. My kids are always coming to my blanket, for popcorn and hot dog money and such. I thought it was his mother's blanket. Then ten minutes ago, I saw him at another blanket over there." She pointed to an area beneath some maple trees. "That's when it occurred to me what he might be doing." She looked pained. "I hope I'm not jumping to conclusions."

"Don't worry, I'll see what I can find out. Thanks."

I decided to sit on a bench and watch the youngster Mrs. Renaldi had pointed out. Apparently, he was playing tag with a couple of other kids. Nothing unusual. After ten minutes, he hopped out of the pool, and went to his towel that was laid out by the kiddie's pool. He picked up his towel and walked around the pool back toward me. Along the way he seemed to be eyeing a variety of blankets, but perhaps I was just primed to be suspicious. He paused to look around. He had put his towel over his head and stood in the grass looking back and forth. I wondered if he was being careful, calculating the odds, surveying the area to see if any grown-ups might be watching.

I also wondered if I was really seeing what I thought I was seeing. I recalled what my dad had once told me. *If you are a hammer, everything looks like a nail.* Put another way, *Is he really a thief? Or am I imagining that he's a thief sizing up his next victim?*

Sure, I didn't want this to go wrong, but I also didn't want someone pilfering from my pool patrons. I decided to talk to the young man, so I fell in step with him as he walked up the steps to the concession stand.

"Hi," I said. "I watched you and your friends playing tag. Are you having a good time?"

"Yeah." The kid pulled the towel around his shoulders. "I guess."

"I see you here a lot. Do you have a season pass?"

"Yeah."

"What's your name?"

"Jake. Why?"

"Jake, I think I found your season pass on the ground. I've got it in the office."

"The guy out front has it," Jake replied.

"Well, let's go to my office anyway."

A reluctant Jake walked into the manager's office and stood next to my desk. I stood in the doorway. "Jake, how much money do you have on you?"

"Why?" Jake wasn't sure where this was headed.

"Just curious."

"A couple of bucks, maybe."

"Could you empty your pockets for me, Jake?"

I was fairly certain that Jake knew he was trapped, but he'd have to fight his way out of the office, and he wasn't old enough to know he should demand a lawyer. Jake pulled the soggy cash from his pockets and spread it out on the desk. Sixteen dollars and seventeen cents. Three fives, a one, and a dime, a nickel, and two pennies.

"That's more than a couple of bucks, Jake."

"It's mine," Jake said defensively. "It's my money. My mom gave it to me."

"Good. Let's call your mom and find out."

"She's not home. She's at work," Jake said nervously.

"Okay, but I want to call your mom anyway," I said. "You shouldn't be coming up here with so much money. I wouldn't want to see you get robbed. You know, Jake, people have been known to steal money here at the pool."

"I didn't steal it. It's my money." Jake was clearly agitated.

"That's what you said. And I never said you stole it. I just want to check with your mom…"

I hadn't finished my sentence when Jake decided to make his break. "Fuck you," Jake screamed, as he dashed past me and ran out the door.

I followed him through the men's locker room as far as the front door. Mr. Sawyer, sitting in his niche with his file box full of season passes, watched as Jake dashed down the street. Jake hadn't asked for his season pass back.

We both quietly watched Jake run across the street and take the shortcut through Hays Cemetery.

"What's up, chief?" Mr. Sawyer asked.

I handed Mr. Sawyer the sixteen dollars and seventeen cents.

"This money is all wet," Mr. Sawyer said.

I explained what had just happened.

"You know, chief, someone should wash that boy's mouth out with soap."

"Probably. I want you to hang onto that money…and hold onto Jake's season pass, too. He can't come back until we've had a chance to meet with his mom."

"Gotcha, chief." Mr. Sawyer always addressed me as "chief" after I became the assistant manager. "You know, you're gonna see Mrs. Malcolm real soon. There's no dad in the picture, chief, and Jake is a real handful. I think Heil Pool is her full-time, baby-sitting service."

Mr. Sawyer's prophecy was fulfilled the very next day about an hour after the pool opened. Mrs. Malcolm had dropped off her son just as she normally did. However, as she was driving away, Mr. Sawyer told Jake that his season pass was suspended, and that he couldn't get back into the pool until his mother had met with the manager.

Jake ran back home—he lived on Wilkes-Barre Street more than a mile away—and whatever he said to his mom lit a fire under her. She instantly channeled her inner Mama Bear.

Mr. Sawyer gave me a heads up as Mrs. Malcolm parked her car and stumped around to the pool office. Jake joined her, and her scowl broadcast the depth and breadth of her aggravation.

I welcomed them both into my office and closed the door because the noise generated by hundreds of screaming, splashing kids could make conversation difficult. Mrs. Malcolm settled into the chair beside my desk, while Jake pulled a stool from the corner and sat immediately next to her.

I'd just begun to ask, "What can I do for you?" when she cut me off.

"Why did you steal my son's season pass, yesterday?"

"Is that what your son told you?"

She didn't back down at all, but repeated her question.

"I didn't steal it," I said. "It's out front with Mr. Sawyer."

I had side-stepped her question, wondering what I should say next. I couldn't be sure what the look on Jake's face meant, but he seemed to be pleased that his mother was going to fight his battles.

"Mrs. Malcolm, how much money do you give your son when he comes to the pool?"

Her defenses were up. She eyed me suspiciously. It was her turn to side-step my question.

She's played this game before, I thought.

"I want to know why you've taken my son's season pass."

"And I'm happy to tell you why, after you answer one question for me. Do you ever give Jake five dollars when he comes to the pool?"

"Are you kidding? Who's got five dollars?"

I looked at Jake, and then I looked at her. "Jake does."

"Where would he get five dollars?" she asked, her voice growing louder. She peered at her son who was rubbing his hands on his thighs. "Sometimes I'll give him fifty cents, but that's all I can afford."

"Why don't you ask Jake where he got his money," I said.

"What's Mr. Timins talking about, Jake?"

"Dunno," Jake shrugged.

"What if I told you Jake had sixteen dollars and seventeen cents yesterday?"

Jake suddenly became animated. "He thinks I stole it, Mom."

"I never said that, Jake. Never." I turned to Mrs. Malcolm. "Jake told me you gave it to him. Is that true?"

"Are you saying my son stole that money?"

"Not yet. But if you didn't give it to him, where do you suppose he got it?"

"I don't know. But I'd be damn careful about accusing anyone of stealing," Mrs. Malcolm seethed. She probably knew the truth, but this was her son.

"I haven't spoken to the police, Mrs. Malcolm. I could have, but I didn't. When I asked Jake about the money yesterday, he got really nasty. He yelled 'Fuck you,' at me and then ran out the door and down the street without getting his season pass back. That's why he doesn't have it. No one took it away."

Mrs. Malcolm was staring at the floor when something inside her snapped. Her face reddened, and her eyes filled with tears. She looked at her son. It was as if she saw him for the first time. Without any preamble, she backhanded her son across the face and knocked him completely off his stool. It was a haymaker.

The move flattened Jake, but it also surprised and frightened me.

She stood up and hovered over her son who was sprawled on his back in the office. "Is that true?" she yelled. "Did you actually say 'Fuck you' to this man?" She was shaking visibly and crying. "What is wrong with you?" She had lost all control. "You steal money and then you curse at this man when you get caught stealing?" she screamed.

She sat back down, weeping. I moved toward her but she waved me off.

A quiet rage seethed even as she attempted to calm herself. "I'm sorry," she said. "Call the police if you have to…" She quietly wept as she stood up and grabbed her son by the scruff of the neck. He flinched but didn't balk. Without thinking, she marched her son through the women's locker room and out the front door. She didn't retrieve Jake's season pass.

I don't remember seeing Jake at the pool ever again.

Swimming season lasted from Memorial Day to Labor Day.

Two holidays bracketed the opening and closing of the pool. While the summer calendar and the swimming calendar didn't align absolutely, they were pretty close. And, of course, swimming season revolved around the closing and opening of the schools. There was order in the universe.

I had worked at the pool now for three full summer seasons—and I had been coming to Heil Pool as a patron from the first day it opened. Labor Day always had a wistful feeling to it. Filled with good-byes, it also held the prospect of something new. What Tom had said was "the next chapter."

Despite my own bittersweet response to summer's end, the patrons at Heil Pool never failed to grouse that *it's not the end of summer, you know. That's still more than two weeks away.*

Still, tomorrow all the lifeguards would be returning to school. No one would be left to man the lifeguard chairs. Except for Tom, all of the lifeguards were high school students. Our manager, Tank had actually left a few weeks ago for football camp at the University of Delaware making me the *de facto* manager. Tom and I were both beginning our freshman year at Kutztown State College.

I understood how the adult patrons felt—the ones who were not returning to school or going off to college. It wasn't as if the sultry summer weather—the *raison d'etre* for all outdoor municipal pools—was going to change.

It appears to be a rule that when the pool closes for the summer, and kids return to the misery of non-air-conditioned schools, the temperature and humidity rise. It's a rule. A perverse rule, perhaps, but a rule, nevertheless. The forecast this year was for eighty-degree temperatures and increasing humidity. And no pool for cool.

Today, though, on Labor Day, the late summer humidity was low, which made the 82°F temperature rather enjoyable—especially if there was a sparkling-clear, chlorinated body of water nearby. And there was. There were also about 2,200 people enjoying it, making the pool an SRO affair.

But that was today. Tomorrow would be something else entirely.

I was standing in the office doorway when my neighbor, Mrs. Ortelli, walked past on her way to the concession stand. She took the cigarette out of her mouth and exhaled a smoky cloud.

"I think it would be great to have the pool open tomorrow," she said. Her voice was tinged with hope and authority, as if she could bluff me into saying yes.

I thought staying open would be a great idea, too. The previous pool manager used to joke that running the pool would be a breeze if it weren't for the daily mob of kids.

But some things are just not possible.

"All the kids are back in school," Mrs. Ortelli said conspiratorially. "We adults would have the pool all to ourselves." She gave me the stare that said, *I know you can do this.*

I shot Mrs. Ortelli a resigned smile that said, *I really can't, Mrs. O.*

"Come on, Jacky, you're in college. You can figure it out. You can work around the rules. Staying open would be better than great. It'd be heaven. The adults could finally get some peace and quiet."

Mrs. O—that's what everyone called her—was the mother of three boisterous boys. She lived across the street from me, and she was my mother's best friend.

I could hear my mother saying, "No one craves peace and quiet more than Mrs. O. Especially with that wild bunch she has to deal with."

My smile faded into a more dubious look.

"And don't worry about us drowning, Jacky. Without those little shits jumping on top of us all the time, we'll make out just fine."

You're probably right, I thought as I smiled to myself. *You would make out just fine. And you said the magic words: Nobody drowns.*

Chapter 6
THERE ARE RULES...
AND THERE ARE RULES

Summary 1965

Where stately trees are bending,
Where nature's glories shine,
And loveliness unending
In beauty rare combine
There rise the Kutztown Towers,
And there the college stands,
The wellspring of our powers,
The shrine our love commands.

Kutztown Alma Mater

Summer flew as summers do.

As Heil Pool's assistant manager, my daily regimen consisted of screaming kids in chilly water on humid days, interrupted occasionally by late afternoon thunder storms that emptied the pool. I spent my days talking to lifeguards aloft in chairs, tweeting my whistle, and avoiding sunburn. I also spent time checking the pool's pH, inspecting the men's dressing room—I had one of my female lifeguards help with the ladies' dressing room—and listening to patrons who had grievances large and small. Mostly small.

I loved being the assistant manager, mostly because it kept me out of the sun. Years ago, I learned that blue-eyed redheads—an Irish heritage, for sure—sunburned way too easily in the summer sun. Long sleeves, and a nose slathered with zinc-oxide, ruled my days, as I walked the pool area under brilliant Pennsylvania skies.

Despite my best efforts, Katie jokingly told me that my nose still glowed in the dark, like Rudolph's. I told her she should know because I spent all my in-the-dark time with her. While Katie and I first met at Heil Pool two years earlier, this summer she had gotten her first "real job"—working for Mack Printing on Northampton Street. While I'd be heading off to college after my summer stint at Heil Pool, she'd already joined the workforce.

We spent almost every evening together. Her parents, Dick and Dot, loved me, and I loved them...and their daughter. A couple of times each week, I'd dine with Katie and her family. They were as proud of me as my own family. It was a summer of starlight, moonlight, physical affection...and the New York World's Fair.

Anyone who loved anyone in the summer of '64 took their girlfriend to the New York World's Fair. How could they not? It opened in April 1964 and closed in October 1965, happily allowing two summers to take it all in.

Everyone within shouting distance of New York City—and shouting distance back then had a two-hundred-mile radius—boarded a tour bus to Flushing Meadows out in Queens, New York. So, in July 1964, we caught the bus in downtown Easton to Flushing Meadows for our first excursion. A few hours later, we were walking through the turnstiles at the New York World's Fair in the shadow of the iconic Unisphere. I wore khaki slacks and a blue long-sleeved shirt, and Katie looked lovely in a bright sunflower-yellow dress.

As we rode the bus, Katie and I devoured the "official" brochure. It offered patrons a map of the Fair—a Fair covering almost 650 acres—with the theme of "Peace through Understanding."

"Jesus, Red. Six hundred acres? Maybe the theme should be 'Exhaustion through Walking Around,'" Katie said.

"That means we've gotta pick what we want to see before we ever get there," I said.

"I've always loved a man with a plan," she said, kissing my cheek.

Sticking to our plan, however, proved particularly difficult when we found ourselves standing amidst the fairground's amazing architectural array—a genuine feast for the eyes. As other fairgoers streamed past us, we stood still and gawked. Sometimes, standing and gawking is the only real option.

When we stopped standing and gawking, we commenced gawking while walking. Like so many others who had done any reading about the Fair before arriving, we decided Pepsi-Cola's pavilion, featuring Disney's delightful, *It's a Small World*, would be our first stop. The long waiting line did not dissuade us, because on this beautiful sunshiny July day, everyone seemed happy to visit with their neighboring fairgoers. There were folks waiting in line from just about everywhere in the world—from places way, way beyond shouting distance.

Soon, we were ushered into a small boat that took us on an around-the-world voyage, populated by dancing dolls, all dressed in their national costumes. I have no idea how many countries were represented, but during the entire ride, the taped voices of children sang the song that gave the exhibit its name, *It's a Small World (After All)*. By the end of the ride, Katie and I were both singing.

After the Pepsi pavilion, we decided to snack on a "Bel-Gem" waffle. The brochure assured us that "No trip to the New York World's Fair would be complete without eating a Bel-Gem waffle." They were right. Constructed of a fat, fluffy waffle, piled high with strawberries, and topped with whipped cream, it was a culinary must. They were available all over the Fair.

After waffles, we hiked to General Motors *Futurama*—an exhibit that underlined the Fair's dedication to "Man's Achievement on a Shrinking Globe in an Expanding Universe." True, another long line, but not unexpected. Eventually, Katie and I boarded a moving chair and glided above elaborately-detailed, miniature, 3D-model scenery—sleek futuristic cars, sprinting along smooth highways, sweeping past pristine buildings—all with the implied promise that this might be what life looks like in the "near future."

After experiencing the future, we hurried to the Illinois State pavilion for a date with the past. It was fascinating to watch an animatronic figure of Abraham Lincoln stand up and deliver the Gettysburg Address. Incredible. GM's *Futurama* and Illinois' Abraham Lincoln. The future and the past all neatly available in Queens, New York.

When it was time to return to the bus, we realized we'd only visited a tiny portion of this gigantic exposition. We decided, before we even left the grounds, that we would return next summer.

And return, we did, convinced that we'd explore as many of the previously unexplored pavilions as we could. Strangely, that's precisely what did *not* happen.

Almost as soon as we entered the Fair, we both agreed we wanted to see *It's a Small World* again, and the *Futurama* exhibit, and...well, I don't think I have to explain. As we stood there, amazed that we both were happy just to revisit the exhibits we'd already seen, I had my epiphany—my moment of complete clarity. The New York World's Fair, as wonderful as it was, was not really my destination. Katie was my destination. Where we went and where we were was inconsequential, as long as we were there...together.

We were together...in the present. So much of the Fair seemed intent on showing us the future. That's understandable. Frequently during our previous seventeen years, everyone reminded us that we needed to be ready for the future. *It will be here before you realize it*, they'd say.

I found it amusing when someone would earnestly say, "You've got to be ready when the future arrives." I wanted to smile and say, "That could never happen. The future will always be tomorrow—or ten minutes from now." But I didn't, because a line from scripture quietly counseled me that I'd be a "voice crying in the wilderness."

The future is always looming, isn't it? I asked myself. *Always on the horizon, but never quite here?*

For someone who had just graduated from high school, I knew that I was really lying to myself.

Who could blame me? I was a young man in love with a young woman named Katie; a young man who only wanted to be Heil Pool's assistant manager until he went off to college; a young man who wanted to consider only the immediate present.

There was the present—Katie beside me on the bus coming home from the New York World's Fair—and there was the imagined future. Graduating from college. Marrying Katie. Teaching. Raising a family. It all felt predetermined somehow. Much like the well-understood Catholic life-in-the-hereafter future—which was simplicity itself. Only two options, really: Heaven or Hell. Purgatory was just a detour.

Nevertheless, the earthly, secular future for everyone—Catholic, Protestant, or otherwise—was something we were expected to anticipate, prepare for, and, if possible, shape.

Katie and I watched as the calendar pushed ahead, past July 4th, through a sultry August, to Labor Day. The time for leaving arrived. I was college bound, I was in love, and I had four years to get my degree so Katie and I could exchange vows for our happily-ever-afters. Katie promised to write every day.

For me, as well as for my mom and dad, college was a big deal because I was the first member of my family to attend college. From the moment I received my acceptance letter, I felt an elevated level of anxiety because I feared disappointing my parents. They were both so proud of me. "Our son is going to college" became their conversation opener.

I must not disappoint them.

They'd shown their pride in a hundred different ways, from the moment I'd gotten my acceptance letter, until the moment they drove slowly away from my dormitory. I remembered the look on my parents' faces as they closed their car doors to drive away. Was it pride? Hope? Sadness? Perhaps I witnessed that moment when parents realized that their child was standing at the threshold of adulthood—at the doorway to independence. Unexplored territory. Beyond here, there be monsters.

As I waved good-bye, I felt elation and fear.

I'm actually here. At college. Now, all I have to do is study and succeed. That thought really knotted my stomach, although I couldn't say why. After all, I'd studied and succeeded before, but somehow this felt more important.

Earlier that day, my parents, Katie, and I had explored Kutztown's campus. My dad wanted me to know where the bookstore was. My mother's instincts bent in a different direction.

"Let's find the dining hall. We don't want you starving," she said. We all laughed.

Finally, we arrived at my dorm—my new home. Lots of other students were moving in, too, and the stairwells were filled with voices and banging luggage. My parents and Katie helped me move in—lugging suitcases crammed with clothes and toiletries, carrying my new clock radio, and finally positioning my new Royal manual typewriter on my small wooden desk. All the stuff needed for dorm living circa 1965.

Small talk peppered our conversation throughout the day.

"It's a lovely campus. I love the fountain."

"That clock tower actually looks like an angry chicken, doesn't it?"

"When do classes begin?"

Small talk. It always precedes separation.

It was the same as we moved into the dorm.

"Where do you want this?"

"Should I hang this up?"

"Do you have enough hangers?"

It was my dad who finally said, "Well, that's it. I think we've got everything in."

There was a moment of silence where no words seemed to fit. We all looked at one another, faces full of hope and sadness, tears welling.

After a moment, my mom spoke up. "We know you'll do well, Jack. You always do." She patted my arm and hugged me, kissing me on the cheek. Then she smiled at me, her eyes beaming.

A simple expectation? Doing well? Perhaps. I'd learned that children carry the hopes and dreams of their parents.

We all carry the burden of other people's expectations.

Whether that is fair or not, I don't know. It is simply an obligation imposed when one belongs to a loving family. It is also the honor bestowed by their faith in me.

I remember the last things my parents said that day.

"If you need anything, Son," my dad said, "let us know."

Kisses and hugs all around, and then we all lapsed into silence again, staring at one another, getting lumps in our throats while imagining the future. Dad moved to the door.

"As your grandmother always says, 'When you say good-bye, leave.' Let's go."

I walked them to their car, said good-bye with a brave smile, and kissed Katie a bit more amorously than I normally would.

"I'm going to miss you, Red," she said to me. "Miss you terribly."

"I'm only 40 miles away."

"I know…but you might as well as be a thousand miles away. You might as well be on the moon." She began to cry.

I laughed gently. "But I'm not. I'm right here, and I'll be coming home weekends to see you. Not to do my laundry. Not just to see my parents. I'm coming home to see you. I love you."

"I know. And I love you so very much. Promise me you'll write."

"Cross my heart."

We kissed again. I'd been kissing her since we met, but this felt different. Somehow.

I waved as they drove away.

I was alone, away from home. For the first time in my life. True, I was only 40 miles away from home, but I was on foot and not likely to hoof it home.

I walked back to my room, and said aloud to the room, "What's next?"

My eyes landed on "the books," and I pulled two lonely volumes off an otherwise empty bookshelf.

The summer reading books are next, I supposed.

Soon after being accepted at Kutztown, all freshmen were sent a box with two books for their summer reading list: John P. Marquand's novel, *Point of No Return*, and John Kenneth Galbraith's *The Affluent Society*. I dove in immediately. I read the Marquand novel and enjoyed it, but Galbraith's award-winning economic nonfiction failed to push any attention-getting buttons for me. As it turned out, Kutztown's Admissions Committee felt that reading these two books would give all freshman common ground—books as intellectual icebreakers, suitable to a collegian. I imagined the Admissions Committee dedicating a full evening to the scholarly discussion of choosing a couple of worthy introductory intellectual endeavors for their incoming freshmen. Of course, they would scorn any of the typical "What Did You Do on Summer Vacation?" stuff.

These two books are going to be our touchstones—the things we hold in common—during freshman orientation.

I daydreamed that someone would approach me and ask, "What did you read this summer?," whereupon I would enthusiastically pull out these two books, and a fruitful, intellectual conversation would be launched. That was the theory, anyway. I sat and browsed both books in the late afternoon.

Other than reading the books over the summer, I can't remember ever discussing them with anyone.

I've never forgotten the Kutztown State College alma mater. Is that perverse? The Kutztown Customs Committee—which today would undoubtedly be the subject of a federal investigation for an abusive practice with the benign label, "hazing"—required all freshmen students to be able to sing it, on command, during the first week of school. The Kutztown State fight song was also on the required repertoire, but I can never remember that one. The Customs Committee's responsibilities were to familiarize every freshman with all things Kutztown. And to make sure—after the first few days—that all frosh were indeed familiar with all things Kutztown. Any freshman could be stopped by a Customs member and asked to sing the alma mater—all verses if the Customs person felt so inclined—or asked to state the names of Kutztown luminaries like the football coach, the student body president, or even the president of the college. Freshmen must also know the location of all buildings on campus. Being unable to respond successfully sometimes meant a public berating—ranging from good-natured ribbing to public humiliation—or the worst-case scenario, getting a ticket, assuring a trip to Customs Court.

I never knew what happened at Customs Court. I'm the one who learned the Alma Mater, knew the location of every building, and could recite the names of all the important people.

Memorization was one of the gifts of a Catholic education.

The Customs Committee may have accelerated the campus-familiarity learning curve for many freshmen, but they intimidated many others. Some freshmen avoided the dining hall—breakfast, lunch, and dinner—because it was a Customs hangout. I'm sure the local downtown merchants appreciated the increased grocery business that first week when some freshmen preferred to "dine in" rather than run the Customs gauntlet outside the dining hall.

Customs folk had no difficulty spotting freshman. Imagine 1,500 bobbing heads scurrying across the Kutztown campus wearing dinks—a short-brimmed hat that looked like the bastard offspring of a beanie and a baseball cap. We were expected to wear it during Customs Week. When we registered in Old Main—the oldest building on campus—we received our dink along with the Freshman Handbook that contained all the information frosh needed in order to become *bona fide* Kutztown Golden Bears.

Now, about the dinks. Wearing it was not an option—at least, not for me. My freshman roommate, John Markowski, felt differently, but he hadn't gone to twelve years of Catholic School. Our dinks were the Kutztown school colors, maroon and gold, and emblazoned on the front of each dink was the number 69—our class graduation year.

I should take a moment here and confess something. Yes, I was seventeen years old. Yes, I'd had a girlfriend for almost two years. Still, I'd made it to college thinking that 69 was primarily the number before 70 and after 68. Can you believe that? Upperclassmen crossing campus would intercept me, pat me on the head, and with a perverse smile say, "Hey Frosh, sixty-nine. Sixty-nine."

What's the big deal?

I didn't get it. I finally asked my roommate—who, by the way, *never* wore his dink—about the upperclassmen's behavior, and he looked at me as if I were an alien from outer space.

"Jesus, Timins, sixty-nine. Sixty-nine. Don't you get it?"

No, I don't get it, I said to myself. *What's to get?*

I shot my roommate a bewildered look—what John later called my *Huh?* face.

"Where the hell have you been, Timins?" Markowski asked. When John realized that I clearly did not understand, he decided to broaden my education. "Damn, Timins. Let me make this easy for you."

He went to his desk and dug out a skin magazine and threw it on my bed. John expected me to connect the dots, but twelve years of a sheltered Catholic education had obscured the dots. And it was clear that I had never connected THOSE dots. I was still in the dark.

John grabbed his magazine off my bed, searched its pages for the best full-color illustration he could find, and carefully placed the open magazine on my pillow.

"There. That should help," he said.

I walked slowly to my bed and found myself staring down at a glossy picture of a naked man with a naked woman.

"What's this?" I asked.

Markowski laughed. "That," he said picking up the magazine and holding the open pages right in front of my nose, "is sixty-nine." I looked at the two people intertwined, when suddenly the light went on. I was fascinated...and appalled.

I pushed the magazine away from my face.

"Jesus, Markowski, you're going to Hell for this," I said.

John laughed even harder. "Uh-huh," he said. "I may be going to Hell, but I'll be in charge of your crew." He threw the magazine back on my bed. "Anyway, Timins, now you know what all the upperclassmen are saying when they point at your dink...which is why I never wear mine." He walked out of our dorm room—without his dink as usual—and slammed the door.

Customs officials. Sound innocuous, doesn't it? Just like Gestapo once did. During the first two weeks of school, Customs officials could waylay any freshmen while they were on their way to class.

> *Hey Frosh, give us the first verse of the alma mater. Make it loud.*
> *Hey Frosh, point out the Angry Chicken to us.*
> *Hey Frosh, who is the college president?*
> *Hey Frosh, where's Rothermel Hall?*

I was stopped a dozen times—maybe more. Markowski said it was because I looked like an easy target. "You're a suck-up, Timins. You've got a crew-cut and a goofy smile. You're just the kind of guy that Customs wants to nail. 'Clean-cut frosh snagged by Customs.' They don't know you memorized the damn handbook in record time. Only you would do that. Nobody else gives a shit. I sure don't."

For some reason, I did. Just like in Catholic school, I was willing to play the game. "You don't even wear your dink," I said accusingly.

"Damn right, I don't. So far, they don't know who the hell I am, and I like it that way. I sure as hell don't look like a freshman, and I'll be goddamned if I'm gonna wear a billboard on my head that says, 'Come abuse me.' The first time any of those Customs assholes rags on me for not wearing my dink will be their last. I didn't come here for this bullshit. College is the seat of wisdom—the *sedes sapientiae*. I came here to learn, not to sing songs or kowtow to upperclassmen."

John Markowski was the most brazenly outspoken person I'd ever met. Loud and learned. It was like encountering a new species. He was amused that I hadn't known the meaning of "sixty-nine," and even more amused that I avoided cursing as much as possible.

John said cursing cleared the air. "You should try it some time. Just say what you want to say and tell those Customs jerks to go to Hell. Christ, Timins, try calling a spade a spade." Then he rethought what he'd just said, "On second thought, Timins, better you should call it a goddamn shovel."

I gave him a look that said *I can't*.

"You should try going dinkless," he said. "See if the goddamn sky falls."

I never went out without my dink. In my own way, I kept the sky in place. Looking back, I was certain the hazing didn't bother me because I'd just graduated from twelve years of Catholic School. The Customs Committee reminded me of the nuns I'd met throughout my educational career. Stopping people, for reasons known only to God, and asking them to do something stupid was nothing new. Unfortunately, many of my fellow freshmen were unaccustomed to random harassment—a longstanding Catholic school custom.

As for memorizing facts, that was a piece of cake. That's what Catholic School was all about. I excelled at memorization. To this day, I can still recite various stanzas from *The Rime of the Ancient Mariner*—or portions of a dozen other poems stretching from Shakespeare to Wordsworth to Joyce Kilmer to e. e. cummings. I can still recite poems and lines of Shakespeare at the drop of a hat.

If I recollect correctly, I graduated 15th in my class of 215 at Notre Dame. I really don't remember for certain, but that number sounds about right. If I'd told people I'd graduated first in my class, they'd think I was bullshitting them. Somehow, fifteenth doesn't sound like bullshit. Modest bragging, maybe, but not bullshit.

During my first semester in high school, I had the highest grade point average in Notre Dame's freshman class. No one was more surprised than me. I had some ridiculously high academic average, something like 94.3, and my classmate, Tom Houseman, came in second with 94.2. Notre Dame didn't use letter grades. Nope, they preferred the imaginary precision conferred by numbers. How I eked out a one-tenth point win is anybody's guess, and I preferred not to guess.

No question. College was going to be an entirely new experience. After spending twelve years in the rabid embrace of Catholic priests and nuns, Kutztown was going to be my first secular educational experience.

Orientation week ended and I woke up excited for my first day of class. My clock radio alarm sounded off at 6:30 a.m., and the Rolling Stones were explaining *I Can't Get No Satisfaction* at the same time that Markowski snarled, "You better turn off that goddamn radio, Timins."

Markowski was not an early riser. His classes never began before 9:00 if he could help it, and usually much later than that. The later, the better.

I preferred early morning classes. Markowski would have preferred that I prefer later classes, like he did. But I didn't. Hell, if they'd scheduled classes at 5:30 a.m., I would probably have taken them.

A host of reasons explain why I preferred rising early. For three years, I delivered a morning newspaper, the *Allentown Morning Call.* My newspaper route demanded I rise around 3:30 a.m. three hundred and sixty-one days a year. Additionally, I frequently served as an altar boy at early Mass—usually 5:30 or 6:00 a.m.—something I had done since the third grade. Getting up early was habit.

Markowski groused every day, certain it was unnatural to get up so early, and he told me so whenever I disturbed his slumber. "Nobody gets up as early as you do, Timins," he'd grumble. "Nobody with any sense, anyway."

"Who are you kidding? I'm not the only person in my 8:00 a.m. class," I countered.

"Screw them, too," Markowski would say.

"Perhaps you're unfamiliar with Dibble's First Law of Sociology, John," I said teasingly. "Some do; some don't."

Markowski would pull his pillow over his head, "Tell Dibble he's an asshole."

I clicked off my alarm, showered, dressed, and grabbed my brand-new three-ring binder. Fresh as a daisy, I headed off to the Dining Hall, located just behind Old Main. I am almost ashamed to admit that I never missed breakfast once during my freshman year at Kutztown. Almost ashamed. I never missed breakfast, and I never cut a class. I liked breakfast, and I enjoyed going to class. Markowski thought that was unnatural, too.

My very first college class was Dr. Kneedler's *Introduction to Mathematics*. In addition to being my Math professor, Dr. Kneedler was the oldest professor on campus—the professor given the privilege of carrying the ceremonial mace during the convocation procession. I knew this useless tidbit of knowledge because, sometime during freshman orientation, I'd read the thumbnail biographies of each of my professors.

After breakfast, I made my way to my math class in Old Main. Apparently, I was early. When I opened the door to a dark classroom, I turned on the lights and looked around. The room's twelve-foot-high ceilings and austere hanging light fixtures betrayed its 1866 vintage. A bank of tall sash windows looked out on Main Street. Thirty or so nondescript wooden desks, set in neat rows, filled the room—many of their wooden surfaces etched with years of boredom. I decided to sit in the front row, in the seat nearest the windows.

I was early, and I was ready. I had my binder and pen; I'd purchased the required textbook. I was wearing my brown Harris-tweed sports coat and a pair of pressed brown slacks. As always, I wore a white shirt with a button-down collar, and a print necktie. All very similar to the wardrobe I'd worn throughout high school.

My mother's voice reminded me, *You can never go wrong if you dress up.*

Oh yes, my shoes were shined. Mom always said, "You can tell a lot about a man by his shoes."

Sister Joachim—the harshest disciplinarian at Notre Dame—would have been proud of me, too. While she never said clothes make the man—or the woman—her actions said it for her. *Neatness counts*, she'd always say. *Proper clothes and proper posture guarantee success,* she told us.

I knew I was wearing the proper clothes.

Or so I thought until other students began drifting in. I'd had the classroom to myself for twenty minutes or so before a pair of girls came walking through the door. They wore blue jeans and short-sleeved sweatshirts, and they were laughing about something. One of them asked me if this was Kneedler's math class.

"I hope so," I said. They didn't say another word, as they made their way to the last row and slouched into their desks. Gradually the room filled, and the hum of conversation grew louder as the hands of the wall clock moved toward 8:00 a.m. Then the classroom door opened, and an old gentleman, white-haired, slightly stooped, and wearing a woolen suit jacket, entered carrying a battered, leather book bag. The room fell quiet as he shuffled toward the large wooden desk in the front of the room. The only sound was the scuff of his leather soles on the well-worn wooden floor.

I stood up.

Way back in first grade, I learned that you always stood up when any teacher—or the principal or the pastor from your church—enters the room. It's a rule. It's a sign of respect. If you could believe my first-grade teacher, Sister Mary Adelhearta, people are probably burning in Hell for failing to show this sign of respect. For twelve years, I rose from my desk whenever any teacher walked into the room—just as I always said "Thank you" whenever something was handed to me, or "Excuse me" whenever I'd farted. That's just what you do. It's a rule.

So, when Dr. Kneedler entered the room, I stood up. I had to. It was a rule.

Mine was a solo act.

No one else stood up. Not one other student budged out of a desk. Not one. As I looked around, I realized no other student was wearing a jacket or a tie either. Or a dress. Other than my attire—and Professor Kneedler's—there wasn't a single piece of clothing which would have earned Sister Joachim's approval. If she had been there, she would have seethed and stormed, making them all regret their indiscrete raiment. But Sr. Joachim wasn't there.

I was now a citizen of the secular universe, and the days were past when nuns would berate and belittle me for my clothing and posture. That, however, was quite beside the point. I still had the nuns in my head.

I stood beside my desk. Horribly, self-consciously, alone. I could feel the eyes of my classmates. I was positive they were wondering, *What the hell is he doing?* After all, this was a classroom of strangers. I felt the heat rise in my cheeks—blushing has always been my forte—and I stood there, quietly broadcasting my embarrassment to everyone in the class.

My mind raced. *What should I do? Should I sit down? Should I remain standing?*

I was frozen by indecision, even as Dr. Kneedler placed his book bag on the teacher's desk. He rested his hands on the back of his chair, silently surveying the faces of his class, like a grandfather appraising his progeny. His gaze finally came to rest on me, now bathed in an uncomfortable ruddy glow. A smile crossed Dr. Kneedler's face, and he nodded. "Thank you, young man," he said directly to me. "You may be seated."

I sat. Immediately. I needed no second invitation.

As grateful as I was for Dr. Kneedler's gracious acknowledgement of my gesture, I never, ever, stood up in any college class ever again. If I'd ever wondered if it were possible to extinguish twelve years of behavioral conditioning in a few brief moments, the answer was yes. On that day, I began reassessing so many things that heretofore had been labeled as "a rule."

Sometimes you learn things you don't expect to learn.

The day's lessons were not yet over.

Chapter 7
IT AIN'T ALL BOOK LEARNIN'

September 1965

Perhaps I should reiterate. I did *not* stand up in my *Introduction to Music* class or my *Intermediate German* class later that morning. All my classes were done by noon, so after lunch, I went to the Rohrbach Library.

Good students always go to the library. It's a rule.

Sometime around two o'clock, I returned to my dorm room. Rothermel Hall was a men's dormitory in 1965—during the dark ages of gender-segregated dormitories. Women were not permitted any further than the lobby. If a woman came to Rothermel to see a resident, the resident manning the front desk would page that resident over the PA to come to the lobby. "Jack Timins, Jack Timins, you have a guest in the lobby." Clearly, *guest* meant *female person*—because a guy would have simply walked up to the room. Men arriving at a women's dormitory received the same treatment.

Markowski must have heard me as I began unlocking the door; suddenly, the door was pulled open from the inside—all doors opened inward—and there stood a fuming and furious John Markowski. His face was red and beaded with sweat. My mom would have described him as "spittin' mad."

"Did you see this bullshit?" he seethed, spittle flying everywhere. "Can you believe it?"

I had no idea what he was upset about. I walked past him and put my books on my desk. "What? What's got you so upset?"

"Fuckin' dictator," John fumed. "He gave us demerits! Demerits! Two each."

John had really worked himself into a lather.

"Who gave us demerits?" I asked. "Demerits for what?"

"Goddamn Kervin."

Kervin was our wing's dorm counselor, occupying the room next door, at the intersection of the west and north hallways. If there were any disturbances, all he had to do was step out of his room and look straight ahead or to his right to see the door of every room.

As a dorm counselor, Kervin was responsible for all the residents on Rothermel's second floor, front wing. Dorm counselors established study times—quiet times—and were responsible for enforcing regulations—no drinking, no girls in the rooms, no loud radios, no riots, no shaving cream battles. Any sort of infraction earned demerits. Demerits paved your way out of the dormitory—and maybe out of college. In some ways, Kervin was the cop on the beat.

He was also responsible for our dorm wing's participation in competitive events, like Homecoming or Spring Weekend. Most important, dorm counselors posted the grade point average for their wing every semester. Kutztown was, after all, an educational institution, and dorm counselors' evaluations depended on our academic success. It was the residents' job to make their counselors look good.

"How do you know we got demerits?"

"These were taped to our door when I got back from class."

Markowski showed me two crumpled slips of paper bearing Kervin's signature. One piece of paper had my name, the other, John's name, and two typewritten words on each: "Two Demerits." There was nothing else, except Kervin's barely legible signature.

I smoothed out my wrinkled slip of paper and stared at it. There was no explanation. Just Kervin's signature under those two words.

"He's probably just screwing around, John," I concluded. "That's gotta be it. We didn't do anything wrong, did we? We both went to class, right? We didn't do anything to get demerits." I thought for a moment, then asked, "You can't get demerits for not wearing your dink, can you?"

"I don't know, Timins, but I'm gonna find out."

John moved quickly into the hallway and knocked on Kervin's door. No answer. Then he pounded even harder with his fist, shouting, "Open the door, Kerv. I know you're in there." He kept pounding as he shouted, "Open the door. Open the goddamn door." Other residents on the wing poked their heads into the hallway.

Kervin's door opened.

My mother always advised me to count to ten if I was about to say something when I was mad. It's a rule. Under current circumstances, I should have advised Markowski to count to a thousand. But he ignored rules, and he was bristling.

"Kerv, what's this demerit bullshit tacked to our door?"

I stood right behind Markowski. I wanted to know the answer to that question, too.

"Stop shouting," Kervin said. "I was taking a nap." He did look a bit disheveled.

"I'm real fuckin' sorry I woke you. Just answer my question," John said, his decibel level lowered just a touch. "Demerits for what?"

Kervin stepped out of his room into the hallway, face to face with Markowski. They were about the same height—six feet tall, maybe—but John probably outweighed Kervin by fifty pounds, at least. John waited for the answer, ready to pounce. Kervin was doing his best to look and sound authoritative. "You guys didn't make your beds before you left for class today."

I said earlier, there are questions that are truly bizarre. Today, I found out that sometimes there are answers that are equally bizarre, and totally unexpected as well. This was one of those answers. John turned away from Kervin and looked at me with a *What the hell!* expression on his face. Just as quickly, he turned back to Kervin.

"Whatya mean we didn't make our beds?"

"Just what I said," Kervin said, with a nervous calmness. "You didn't make your beds. That's two demerits each."

"How would you know we didn't make our beds unless you went into our room, Kervin?" John's decibel level had returned to fever pitch.

"I'm the dorm counselor. That gives me the right to enter rooms on this wing."

"Like hell it does, Kerv," John screamed. "You're not my goddamn mother, you're a goddamn dorm counselor. You trespass in my room again, and I'll kick your ass from here to sundown."

Kervin stood in complete silence, his hands on his hips. Fear crept into his eyes. He was unaccustomed to being threatened. A small group of guys gathered in the hallway. Arguments like this might be good theatre, but every-one drew close because this issue affected everyone.

Still seething, Markowski looked over his shoulder and pointed at the guys gathering around. "Any of these guys get two demerits, Kerv? You did check every room, didn't you? Not just ours?"

Without warning, John shouldered past Kervin and entered his room. "Well, I'll be goddamned." John shouted from inside Kervin's room, "Look whose bed isn't made. That's two demerits! Isn't that right, Kerv? You did give yourself demerits, too, didn't you?"

From the moment John barged into Kervin's room, chaos reigned, with Kervin insisting that John leave his room.

To no effect.

"You have no right to be in here," Kervin complained, clearly intimidated. "No right at all. Get out Markowski. Get out of my room. Do you hear me? Get out of my room!"

Kervin's shouted commands competed with John's shouted accusations about Kervin's unmade bed. It was no contest. Markowski's voice drowned out Kervin's.

John exited the room and addressed the hallway crowd. "Hey, everyone, take a look. Kervin's bed isn't made. That's two demerits." He held up the two innocuous slips of paper that Kervin had taped to our door. "It cost Timins and me two demerits each today, because Mr. Gestapo here came into our room without permission. He'll be checking up on you, too. You can be goddamn sure of that. And if your bed isn't made, it'll be two demerits."

John turned back to Kervin and tore up the demerit slips, throwing the torn pieces in Kervin's face.

"Here's two demerits for you, Kerv. Make your goddamn bed." He stepped toward Kervin. They were practically nose-to-nose. "I get any more of those demerit slips, I'll stick 'em up your ass."

He strode back to our room and slammed the door harder than I had ever heard a door slammed. An audible *Whang!* reverberated down the hallway. Nobody could cap a verbal tirade with a door-slamming exclamation point better than Markowski.

Kervin and I stood opposite one another, as the other residents drifted back to their rooms.

"Markowski's going to get two more demerits for throwing those pieces of paper at me."

"Really, Kerv?"

I began walking back to my room and stopped in the doorway. "I don't want you in my room either. If you enter my room ever again, without permission, I won't be shouting like John. I'll be calling the Kutztown police. They'll be happy to read the Pennsylvania State trespassing statute to you."

Of course, I didn't know what I was talking about, but I said it calmly, just as if I knew something that Kervin didn't.

No sooner had I re-entered my room, than Markowski said quietly, "Kervin wants to be a prick? Okay. I'll show him what it means to be a prick." Markowski looked at me. "You in, Timins?"

"He gave me demerits, too," I said.

"Okay, you're in."

Either Markowski had just cast me in the middle of a personal revenge play, or I had just enrolled in Markowski's college course, *Wreaking Havoc on Your Dorm Counselor 101.*

That's how my first class day in college ended. I had been overdressed for every class. Stood up like a fool in Math class. Gotten two demerits for not making my bed. And now I suspected that my roommate and I were officially on our dorm counselor's shit list.

When John and I went to dinner that evening, everyone was trading stories about "My First Day in College." John's contretemps with Kervin led the list, but John barely said a word. The guys who witnessed the brouhaha were more than happy to provide all the details.

"I thought Kervin was gonna shit his pants when John charged past him into his room," said Ken Cressall. "Kervin kept shouting 'Get out, get out,' and John kept telling him to make his goddamn bed."

Everyone was laughing, except John, who seemed preoccupied. I was sure John was enjoying his notoriety, though. I was less sure where this *Havoc 101* course would take me.

"Hey, John. Is it true you're already winning the Demerit Derby?" Ed Schiffer asked. Ed lived on our wing. Digging into his mashed potatoes—the carbohydrate of choice at every dinner—Ed asked, "Did he really give you guys demerits for not making your beds?"

John and I both nodded.

It sounds unbelievable, doesn't it? Everyone's heard of *in loco parentis*, but even my parents didn't expect me to make my bed. My mother had made my bed every day of my pre-college life, and I was sincerely grateful.

"Two each," I said, patting Markowski on the back. "John and I are tied. We both have two."

That tally changed when we returned to our room and John zoomed into the Demerit Derby lead. Another piece of paper taped to the door informed John that he now had two more demerits. Markowski pulled the demerit slip off and looked at it for a moment before unlocking our door. I waited for another explosion, but it never came. Clearly, John's plan for retribution had begun to take shape. He was more nefarious than I could have imagined.

"You have any homework?" John asked. His look told me that he wanted my full attention.

"Nothing that can't wait," I said.

"Good. Come with me."

We went down to the first floor, back wing, and met one of John's friends from Governor Mifflin High School—a guy named Steve. They seemed genuinely happy to see each other.

"How the hell are you, Ski?"

"I'm fuckin' swell except for the four demerits I managed to pile up on day one," John explained.

"So nothin' new?" said Steve, a huge smile spreading across his face.

"Yeah, well, I didn't want to scare off Timins, here, too soon." He motioned in my direction and I introduced myself. "He's my roommate and something of a wuss, but he got screwed today, too, same as me."

I was waiting for John to tell Steve that I hadn't known what "sixty-nine" was, and embarrass the hell out of me, but he never did.

Markowski came right to the point. "I'm going to need your help pennying a guy in his room tonight. Probably around 3:00 a.m."

"Sounds like fun," Steve said. "Who is it?"

"Our dorm counselor," John replied. "A guy named Kervin. Gave us demerits for not making our beds."

"No shit?" Steve sounded truly surprised.

"No shit. I don't know what's going on in his head, and I don't know why he's picked on us, but he's gonna realize that picking on me was a bad first move."

"Yeah, John, he could at least wait until you do something that really pisses him off," Steve said jokingly.

"Damn right," said John. "Getting demerits for not making my bed is an insult. Tonight, I want to give Kerv a really good reason to break out those demerit slips." John and Steve were both laughing.

"So, what's the plan, John?"

"Well, Steve, I want to experiment on your dorm room door to see if it works the same as it did on old man Keller."

I didn't ask who old man Keller was. Clearly, they had done this before. But what was it they had done? I was in the dark.

"How do you penny someone in their room?" I asked. Like so many other things I discovered that day, it ain't all book learnin'.

Here is what I learned as they experimented with "pennying someone in." Call it, *Understanding Your Dorm Room Doors, 101:*

1. To open a door, you turn a door knob. When you turn the knob, the *latch piece* comes out of the hole in the strike plate and that allows the door to open. When the latch is in the strike plate, the door remains closed.

2. When you close a door, the door will close until it hits the *door jamb*, the vertical piece of wood or metal that meets up with the vertical edge of the door. The door jamb prevents the door from swinging through the opening like the proverbial bar room doors always do. Doors with jambs will only swing one way.

Typically, there is a small space between the closed door and the door jamb—maybe as much as a quarter-inch. While this would appear to give the door some wiggle room, it also prevents the latch from being too tight as it rests inside the strike plate. However, if you cram some object—in this case pennies—between the door jamb and the closed door, just above and below the doorknob, the door latch pushes so hard against the edge of the strike plate that you need superhuman strength to turn the doorknob. Kervin did not possess superhuman strength.

They decided to experiment on Steve's door, putting me inside Steve's room while John and Steve jammed pennies between the door and door jamb. When they were satisfied, they asked me to open the door. I tried, but I couldn't. The doorknob, with its latch jammed hard against the strike plate, just wouldn't turn.

Tonight, we would be "pennying" Kervin in his room, and come morning, he wouldn't be able to get out of his room. Fortunately for us—and unfortunately for him—Kervin didn't have a roommate.

Next stop, Kervin's room. 3:00 a.m.

Sometime around 2:30 a.m., Steve knocked quietly on our door. It sounded more like a scratching noise than a knock, but it was 2:30 a.m. in the morning. John, who was already awake—I don't think John had ever gone to sleep—turned out his desk lamp and opened the door to Steve. He gestured for quiet, putting his fingers to his lips. As I sat on the edge of my bed waiting for my orders, John turned his light back on, and he and Steve began whispering to one another. Steve pulled a small oblong block of wood from his pocket, and I heard John whisper, "Good, good, good. That'll do it."

John turned to me and whispered, "You ready for this, Timins?"

I nodded sleepily. "I guess so."

"Steve and I have the pennies," Markowski whispered, "so we're ready." He turned to me. "Okay, Jack, since you're the new guy, you only have to remember one thing. No noise. When we leave the room, no noise. I want you to watch both hallways. Anybody shows up, anybody at all, don't say a word. Just tap me on the shoulder and we'll get the hell back to our room."

"Who's up at this time of the morning?" I whispered back.

"Just us bad guys," Steve said. "Right, Ski?" He and John began to laugh and ended up shushing each other.

"We gotta be quiet," John whispered.

I put on my bathrobe and slippers. Markowski wore only his boxers, a dark t-shirt, and socks.

"We're gonna leave our door open. If we have to get outta Dodge fast, I don't want us looking for a key in the dark." Markowski put his hand on Steve's shoulder. "Thanks for doin' this, Steve." He took a deep breath. "Okay, everybody ready?"

John flicked off the lights in our room. Kervin's room was right next door, and I stationed myself a few feet from Kervin's door, watching both hallways. John and Steve tiptoed to his door, and silently inserted four sets of stacked pennies—two stacks above the door knob and two below. All I could detect was some heavy breathing and a few low grunts like something was being pushed with effort. We weren't in the hallway more than two or three minutes when John tapped me on the shoulder. We returned to our room and John gently shut our door.

"Glad you brought that block of wood, Steve. That was good thinking. Those last pennies are in so tight that Abe Lincoln's gonna suffocate."

"Don't worry, John. Kervin's in his room until some Good Samaritan lets him out. Someone's gonna need a screwdriver to get those pennies out." They both started laughing and shushing each other again. "Hey big guy, I gotta go. Don't forget to make your bed in the morning. You don't want any more demerits."

Steve patted John on the shoulder, peeked out our door, and disappeared quietly down the dark hallway.

"I hope we don't get in trouble for this," I said.

"Relax, Timins, the fun is about to start."

Morning—the part of the morning with sunlight—arrived rather quickly. My alarm went off at 6:30 a.m., just as it had the day before, and Markowski threatened to throw my clock radio out the window—just as he had the day before. His grumblings and threats became part of our daily ritual. I quietly got myself organized—showered and dressed—and went to breakfast. On the way, however, I paused momentarily in the hallway outside Kervin's door to view John and Steve's handiwork. I could barely discern the dark copper penny edges wedged between the door and the door jamb.

While it's true that each person has their own morning routine, almost everyone hears nature's call when they wake up in the morning. Regardless of one's daily routine, getting to the bathroom usually comes first. Kervin was no different.

While I wasn't in the dorm at the time, it was reliably reported that Kervin woke from his slumber and immediately made his way to the bathroom. Or he would have, if he'd been able to get out of his dorm room. His doorknob stubbornly and inexplicably refused to turn. No one knows how hard or how often Kervin tried to turn that doorknob, but it would not yield. Rumor has it the call of nature also refused to yield, forcing poor Kervin to use the coffee cup he kept on his desk.

At this point in our story, it is important to realize that these events occurred in 1965. The old days. No one had a phone in their room. The only phones in the dorm were the pay phones located in niches just outside the shower rooms, one phone for each wing, meaning Rothermel Hall had only six phones—seven if you count the one in the lobby. Kervin was stuck in his room, incommunicado.

When I returned to the dorm later that day, Markowski reported that the incessant pounding from inside Kervin's room, began about 7:45 a.m., probably the same time Kervin had rolled out of bed.

"It was worse than that goddamn alarm of yours," John said, smiling broadly. "He kept yelling, 'I can't get out of my room. Somebody help me.'" John looked satisfied. "Don't ya love waking up to the sound of success? Kervin locked in his room, pounding on his door, sounding pathetic. I stopped outside his door on the way to class and told him he could get demerits for causing such a disturbance."

"Somebody must have let him out," I said. "The pennies are gone."

"Nobody on this wing let him out—not this morning anyway. I hear Dean White had to let him out," John said laughingly. "You'd have loved it, Timins. Kervin shouted at me from his window when I was on my way to class. 'Get me out of here, Markowski.' He yelled some other choice things, too, but I yelled back that I was sorry, but I had to get to class."

"That must have really ticked him off."

"Yeah, it did. What really pissed him off, though, was when I said, 'Don't worry, Kerv, I made my bed. Go take a look.'"

Kervin missed his 9:00 a.m. class that morning. We didn't know that he had a 9:00 a.m. class, and, even if we had, it wouldn't have made any difference. In the spirit of the moment, Markowski commented that Kervin should get demerits for ditching one of his classes.

That evening, the Dean of Men, "Papa Bear" White, called a meeting for second floor, front wing. The meeting was announced over the PA every fifteen minutes from about 3:00 p.m. on.

"Gentlemen on second floor, front wing, there will be a mandatory meeting at 8:00 p.m. in the TV room. Please be there on time."

No mention was made about the reason for the meeting, but no mention was necessary. Everyone knew about Kervin being pennyed in his room. Many had heard firsthand his relentless but futile pounding. No one had let him out.

John and I arrived at the TV room about five minutes before the meeting. The room was noisy, everyone talking about something. We moved to the far wall—the few seats had all been taken—and we were quietly leaning against the wall when Dean White and Kervin walked in. Dean White was a burley, beefy, crew-cut man, fond of khaki slacks and striped, long-sleeved shirts open at the collar. He addressed himself to the thirty-four guys who had shoehorned themselves into the TV room.

Dean White raised his hand, and the room quieted down. The dean took a step forward and stuck his hands in his pockets.

"Gentlemen, I want to keep this brief." He looked thoughtful. "I understand there have been some problems on this wing." A variety of coughs and grunts—and a few unrecognizable words—interrupted the dean and he raised his hand again. "As I said, there have been some problems. But Mr. Smith and I have been discussing those problems, and we believe we have found a solution."

He paused and motioned to Kervin, who stepped forward. Kervin looked directly at John and me. "The demerits I assigned for not making beds will be rescinded." Neither John nor I said a word. "We do ask, however, that all residents pull their bedspreads over their bed, whether your bed is made or not, before leaving the room."

Markowski broke his silence. "Does that mean Kervin has the right to enter our rooms whenever he wants?"

Dean White looked at John. "No, Mr. Markowski, it doesn't. But if your door is open and the room is a mess, you can get a demerit."

"Thanks, Dean White." John continued. "You hear that everybody? Keep your doors closed."

Dean White gave John a baleful look and asked if there were any other questions. Satisfied that there were none, the dean cleared his throat. "There is also the matter of Mr. Smith being locked in his room."

That comment was met with subdued laughter. Kervin was not amused. The dean raised his hand again. "Whoever used those pennies to seal his door shut should be a man and step forward and admit it."

I didn't move. Nor did John. We didn't feel much like being men at that moment. Of course, no one else stepped forward either. I sensed that everyone felt Kervin had gotten what he deserved.

The meeting broke up, and we headed back to our room. I was feeling very guilty. "Dean White said a real man would take responsibility."

Markowski stopped me cold with a withering look. "Bullshit. Real men? Let me tell you about real men. Real men don't get demerits for not making their beds. And real men don't give out demerits when people don't make their beds. Okay? Real men don't give a shit about someone else's opinion about making beds." He shook his head. "If you feel so damn bad about it, go to Confession and tell the priest."

No sooner had we returned to our room and closed the door, than we heard a knock. John opened the door to a glaring Kervin.

"What do you want, Kerv?" John asked coolly.

Kerv was angry. "I'm putting you two on notice. I told the dean I know you guys are the ones who pennyed me in my room last night. You guys just don't have the guts to admit it."

I wouldn't have been surprised if John had inserted a fist into Kerv's smug face. Instead, he invited Kerv to come in, gesturing like a *maître d'*. "Big news,

Kerv. Our beds are made," Markowski said with a saccharine smile.

Kervin walked in.

"You're an asshole, Mr. Smith," John said with mock gentility. "You've decided to make people's lives miserable—for no good reason, except you can. Then, you're surprised when someone returns the favor. I don't know who pennyed you in, but when I find out, I'll give them a medal."

"That's crap. I know you guys did it." He stood there as if he expected a confession.

"No, Kerv," John said. "You *think* we did it. Thinking we did it and knowing we did it are not the same thing at all."

Kervin walked out into the hallway. "Alright. Alright. Mr. Lawyer. Maybe I can't prove it…"

"You can't," John interrupted.

"Maybe I can't." His eyes locked on John. "But this isn't over, not by a long shot. I've decided to give you guys my special attention. You'll screw up again. Especially you, Markowski. And I'll be there with my demerits. I'll bet you're out of here by Halloween." He smiled and walked down the hall.

John slowly closed our door, turned, and flashed me a wicked smile. "Kervin's got that right. It's not over."

"I don't like the sound of that, John." I worried that my academic career was taking an extracurricular detour.

"Kervin wants to make us his special project," John said with a bemused smile. "Okay."

I could see the wheels turning.

"Okay. We'll make him our special project."

Apparently, John had gone to war with people like Kervin long before he ever arrived here at Kutztown.

"We gonna penny him in again?"

"No. But he'll wish that's all we knew how to do. I never like to use the same tactic twice. In a tit-for-tat war, the secret is unpredictability. This calls for a bit of creativity—malicious creativity. I'll figure out something that gets his attention…"

Day 2 of my college career, and here I was on the front lines of General Markowski's tit-for-tat war. Luckily, General Markowski proved to be an unpredictable, creative, and delightfully malicious tactician.

John woke me about 4:00 a.m. "Ssshhhh."

"What's up?" I asked, as quietly as possible.

The dim light from John's desk lamp allowed me to see him standing next to my bed with something tall beside him. I reached out, and my hand recognized the ribbed metal sides of one of the trash cans that stood at the end of each hall.

"What's this trash can for?"

"For our special project. Day number two. Either Kervin goes or we go." Even in the dark I could hear the mischief in John's voice. "I brought this up from the first floor. It's empty. I'm gonna need your help getting it to Kervin's door after we fill it with water. It'll be damn heavy."

John wasn't kidding. We quietly carried the trash can to the shower room, and stood under the shower, holding the can up to the shower head until it was too heavy to hold. John stopped filling it when it was about two-thirds full. He rolled the sloshing waste can to the door of the bathroom and onto two large bath towels he'd placed on the floor. The towels muffled the sound as we dragged the can another ten feet or so until we arrived at Kervin's door.

Now came the tricky part. John rolled the can off the towels, then carefully—and oh, so quietly—leaned it against Kerv's door. I was afraid the sloshing noise might give us away before we tiptoed back to our room.

"When the sun comes up, Kervin's gonna discover why Noah needed an ark," John said, as we both climbed into our beds.

When I headed for the shower room at 6:30, the water-filled trash can was still undisturbed, leaning in place. Several other guys were already in the bathroom, and some of them must have seen the large green trash can leaning against Kervin's door, but nobody was saying or doing anything. Clearly, we had the sympathies of those on the front wing.

From what I could gather, I was in the Dining Hall in the middle of my bacon and eggs when the Rothermel tsunami hit. This morning, Kervin wasn't confronted with a doorknob that wouldn't turn. *Au contraire.* Kervin found that the moment he turned the doorknob, the weight from the many gallons of water—Markowski figured it was at least a hundred fifty pounds, probably more—shoved his door wide open. A deluge ensued. Markowski was still asleep—or so he told me—when the event took place.

You'd think that cleaning up the water would be Kervin's first order of business, but Kervin made no attempt to sop up the gallons of water filling his entire room. Furious, he sloshed out into the hallway and pounded on our door, screaming John's name.

Markowski opened the door, and Kervin stormed in. "You son-of-a-bitch! You did this! I know you did this! I've got an inch—maybe two inches!—of dirty water covering my whole floor. And you're responsible…"

John said Kervin was apoplectic.

Without a word, John walked out into the hallway with Kervin hot on his heels. He stopped at Kervin's doorway, staring in fascination at Kervin's flooded room.

"You better clean that up, Kerv," John said, pointing at the water that was now flowing freely back into the hallway. "Dean White says a messy room'll get you demerits." Then he made his way back to our room. "Don't knock on my door, and stay the hell out of my room. I'm trying to sleep." He repeated his patented door slam.

So this is what revenge feels like. Really feels like, I thought when John described Kervin's tirade.

As a sophomore at Notre Dame High School, I had read Shakespeare's *The Merchant of Venice*. I'd become thoroughly familiar with the idea of revenge because I was the student that Sister Clare Isabelle—known affectionately as Clarabelle, a TV clown on the *Howdy Doody* show—picked to read the role of Shylock, a vengeful Jewish moneylender. My classmates thought this especially funny because seldom had any of them seen a blue-eyed, red-headed Jew. I was the first.

You may remember this part of Shylock's most famous soliloquy:

If you prick us, do we not bleed? If you tickle us, do we not laugh?
If you poison us, do we not die? And if you wrong us, shall we not revenge?

The Merchant of Venice should have been recommended reading for Kervin.

When I returned from class that afternoon, all the water next door seemed to have vanished. Of course, I didn't have access to Kervin's room, so I really didn't know. It probably took quite a bit of mopping.

I unlocked my door, and noticed two envelopes had been slipped under our door in my absence. They were two invitations for a command appearance. Dean White expected both John and me to come in for a chat. His place. Eight o'clock. Sharp. I was sure Kervin would be there, too.

Kutztown's Dean of Men, Dean "Papa Bear" White, lived with his family in an apartment in the rear of Rothermel Hall. Their entrance was on the first floor behind the lobby. John and I agreed that Kervin would likely accuse us of both attacks—"attack" felt like the right word. We would maintain our innocence. What we didn't agree on was the dress code for "the chat." John wore jeans and a Kutztown t-shirt; I wore my sports jacket, brown slacks, and shined shoes.

"You look like my lawyer," John said.

"I think you should dress up, too," I said defending my choice.

"Timins, there's no reason we should both look guilty."

"You think dressing like this makes me look guilty?"

"You look like the scrubbed-up defendant heading for the courtroom. But suit yourself." He stood right in front of me. "Just remember, let me do the talking. Smile a lot and be courteous. I know a good Catholic boy knows how to do that."

"Thanks, Markowski."

"One last thing. Kervin's expecting we'll confess. Don't."

John waited for me to respond. Finally, I said, "I won't."

"Good. Dean White's a nice guy and he won't screw us over without proof—and they don't have any." John seemed quite calm. My stomach was in turmoil. "So, are you ready, Timins?"

Five minutes later, the four of us were sitting in Dean White's living room. John and I shared the sofa, and Papa Bear and Kervin each sat in overstuffed chairs across the room. The dean broke the uneasy silence.

"Mr. Smith has something he wants to say to you," the dean said.

Quick and to the point. My stomach tightened.

Kervin leaned forward in his chair. "I told Dean White that I believe you two are the ones responsible for locking me in my room two nights ago." He paused. "And that you two were the ones who put that trash can full of water against my door this morning."

I looked at John and he returned my look.

Then John turned his stare on Kervin, sitting up straight and placing his hands on his knees. He suddenly leaned forward. "You ever wonder why nobody on the hall likes you, Kervin? You ever wonder about that?"

Kervin said nothing.

He shifted his gaze to Papa Bear. "What do you want us to say, Dean?" John asked. "This guy's been hounding us for three days now. We're still trying to figure out why. First, he illegally enters our room, something he can't do, then he decides to give us demerits…for what?…for what?…for not making our beds? For God's sake."

Kervin tried to interrupt. "That's been taken care of…"

John kept looking at Dean White and would not be interrupted. "…And then last night, after our meeting in the TV room, Kervin comes to our door and accuses us of doing something we didn't do. He tells us, we don't have the guts to confess. Tells us, he knows we're guilty. Mr. Judge and Jury. Says he's sure we're the ones who pennyed him in. Says we're gonna be his pet project. Says that this isn't over by a long shot."

John immediately turned his attention back to Kervin. "Isn't that what you said, Kervin? You did tell Dean White that you stopped by our room after last night's meeting to threaten us, right?"

John turned back to the Dean. "Kervin told you that he came by to threaten us, didn't he, Dean?"

There was an agonizing silence. Dean White looked at John, then at me, and then at his hands gripping the arms of his chair. He did not look at Kervin.

Papa Bear pulled himself out of the chair and hiked his belt. "Gentlemen, thanks for coming so promptly. I appreciate it. You can go. Have a good evening."

"Thanks, Dean White," John said. "You have a good evening, too."

I echoed John's thank you, and we walked out the door.

"You did good, Timins," John said as we climbed the stairs to our wing.
"I didn't do anything."
"That's what I mean."

We never knew what Papa Bear and Kervin discussed after our departure. As I said, this was 1965, the old days. These were the sweep-it-under-the-rug days, and the Dean kept his own counsel. Did he think we might be guilty? Maybe. I was certain, however, that the Dean knew Kervin had trespassed some pretty clear boundaries, and that he'd lost the trust of everyone on second floor, front wing. As Dean, it was his job to fix that, if it could be fixed.

Nothing happened for a few days. Perhaps the war was over. I noticed that Kervin opened his door slowly and carefully, never knowing when the next flood might arrive.

I kept getting up at 6:30 a.m., and John kept complaining about my alarm. For the most part, Kervin kept to himself, not even responding to a hello when one was offered. Then he called for a meeting in the TV room, where he announced that, in the future, he would conduct surprise inspections. He would knock on the door, and we would have to let him in. Inspections would begin the following week.

Here's the interesting thing. John and I spoke to guys who lived on the other wings, and they couldn't believe what they were hearing. As one of them said, "Looks like you guys drew the short straw." When we told Kervin that none of the other dorm counselors were implementing his draconian policies, he said he didn't care.

Back in our room, I tried to reassure John. "We don't have anything to worry about."

"You're kidding, right?" John replied. "When there's an asshole like Kervin on the loose, we all have something to worry about."

The next day, John said we had some shopping to do.

"For what?" I asked.

"You'll see. You can't fight a war without the proper weapons." John was concocting another scheme. "Come on, Timins, this'll be fun."

As we walked down Main Street, I had no idea what we were after…or why. We bought two cans of Barbasol shaving cream at one store, and a blue bottle of Aqua Velva after-shave lotion in another. John found the bottle below a poster of a bubbly Mamie Van Doren confiding to the world that she "just loves an Aqua Velva Man."

"I never took you for an Aqua Velva Man, John," I said. "You wanna tell me what we're doing?"

All he would say was, "You'll see."

On the way back to the dorm, we stopped at the bookstore, and bought two large manila envelopes.

"Timins, we are armed and ready for tomorrow."

All I could do was shake my head. "If you say so."

If you have a perverse imagination, a devious mind, or both, you can go to war with people who have decided to make your life difficult. John considered it a kind of *quid pro quo*. In this case, John had decided we were going to *quo* before Kervin had a chance to *quid*.

Until the moment arrived, John let me wonder how shaving cream, Aqua Velva, and manila envelopes might be used as weapons.

When Kervin left for his 2:00 p.m. class the next day, Markowski watched him until he walked out of sight.

"Kervin's gone to class, so get ready," John said to me.

"Ready for what?"

"War."

His monosyllabic answer sounded so simple—and so calculated.

"Grab yourself one of those manila envelopes…and grab a can of shaving cream, too."

I did as I was instructed. It was amazingly simple. I filled my manila envelope with Barbasol shaving cream and slipped the open end of the envelope under the Kervin's closed door. Then I stomped on my shaving cream-filled envelope as hard as possible. I repeated that process until all my ammunition—shaving cream—was exhausted. For his part, Markowski filled his manila envelope and then sealed it shut. Then he cut a two-inch-wide hole at one end.

"Why did you do that?" I asked.

"Distance," he said gleefully. "Make the hole smaller, increase the pressure, and the shaving cream flies lots further. I'm hoping I can hit his windows." He began laughing. "Isn't science great?"

A locked door stood between us and the results, and we could only imagine the foaming mess we'd caused, because we were never able to get in the room.

Nevertheless, as we finished, John declared, "Voila! Kervin now has a freshly decorated dorm room with the fresh scent of Barbasol. I hope he can appreciate it. Only one thing more to do," John said. "Get rid of the evidence."

After he returned from class, Kervin didn't come pounding on our door, raining accusations down upon us as he had previously. Nope. He kept his door locked and went in and out of his room as if he had the Hope Diamond in there.

But John and I knew his secret. Little did Kervin realize that the day's foaming attack was only the first half of our campaign. Part two would come later—actually early the next morning. That's when I learned how Aqua Velva figured into our campaign.

Aqua Velva was an after shave that was wildly popular in the 1950s and 1960s. From what I can tell, it still is. It probably battled with Old Spice for dominance in the smelling-clean-and-fresh department. For our purposes, it was useful to know that Aqua Velva's alcohol content exceeded 40%...which meant that the liquid would burn at a relatively low temperature on a hard surface...without burning the surface. In the dark of night, when poured over a linoleum floor—and all Rothermel Hall dorm rooms had linoleum floors—burning Aqua Velva produced a clear blue hypnotic flame, swirling across the top of the shallow pool of aftershave.

That night, at about 2:00 a.m., John and I poured the whole bottle of Aqua Velva—7 fluid ounces—under Kervin's door, using straws to blow it across his linoleum. John lit the match, and the rest, as they say, is history.

John pounded once on Kervin's door, and then retreated to our room without a word. Kervin woke up to see a blue flame snaking across his floor. I could only imagine what it was like, waking from a sound sleep to flames waltzing across his bedroom floor. Panicked, Kervin burst out of his room and pulled the fire alarm across the hall. Pandemonium reigned.

More than 200 guys, in all stages of undress, evacuated Rothermel Hall, stumbling down dark stairwells into the cool September night. Dean White and his family, like all the residents of Rothermel, joined everyone on the lawn that bordered Main Street. Sirens, sounding in the distance, shattered the early morning stillness, and indicated rapidly approaching fire and police. One would have to be blind to miss the scowl on Papa Bear's face.

The whole scene, with its crush of emergency equipment, possessed an eerie aura, with its profusion of flashing red lights and bright spotlights playing across the brick face of Rothermel Hall, as if it were a prison cellblock. Everyone convened in small groups, yawning and stretching, some even lying down on the grass, as the firemen attempted to determine if there really was a fire.

There had been.

Sorta.

We saw Kervin, in animated conversation with the fire chief and Papa Bear. I suppose he admitted pulling the fire alarm, but I couldn't say if Kervin explained to the firemen, or Dean White, that he had panicked when he saw the flickering blue Aqua Velva flames dancing across his floor.

If John or I had been real men, we would have confessed to our role in the evening's drama, but we didn't feel much like being real men that night either.

The next day, Kervin moved out of Rothermel Hall. We never knew where he went, and we didn't care. His departure meant there would be peace in our time. No one ever asked John, or me, who had done the deed. I don't know if the powers-that-be even thought there was a deed worth asking about. We were not inclined to reveal our secret.

As for me, I realized that there was a lot to learn that wasn't sandwiched between the covers of a book. Markowski taught me that sometimes you can color outside the lines, when the lines are oppressive or onerous. That idea alone overruled twelve years of my Catholic school conditioning.

I discovered that sometimes life demands an *ad hoc* response if you expect to survive, and John Markowski was a veritable encyclopedia of *ad hoc* survival skills. As I said, Markowski was a new species. Whenever I asked John where he learned all this stuff, he'd shrug and say, "Don't really know. Here and there." Well, clearly, I had never been "here" or "there," but John had, and I was the beneficiary of his acquired knowledge and experience.

On the bright side, our new dorm counselor turned out to be a really reasonable guy. Always a good thing.

When I walked to class the next day, wondering if I should go to Confession for any of my shenanigans, I didn't wear my dink.

Chapter 8
THE PLAY'S THE THING

Fall 1965

School had begun in earnest. Kervin, our first dorm counselor, had been vanquished. And the Freshman Hazing Period with mandatory dinks receded into the past. I was glad Kervin was gone, but I felt bad about having lied—mostly through omission—to the Dean of Men about my role in the events that eventually made Kervin disappear.

My roommate did not share my misgivings. Not one bit.

"You do know that telling the truth might have gotten us kicked out?" John asked.

I said nothing.

"Look, Timins, if you feel so damn guilty," he sighed and shook his head, "go to Confession. That seems to be your solution to almost everything. Tell the priest what you did and tell him you're sorry—because it certainly sounds as if you're sorry."

"Don't you feel bad at all?" I asked.

"Hell no. Kervin was mean. He didn't have to be mean, but he was. I'm glad he's gone." Then he smiled that wicked ear-to-ear smile at me. "I want you to know how much I appreciated your help."

I went to Confession.

Kutztown's only Catholic parish was Saint Mary's, one mile east on Main Street. Most Catholic churches had Saturday night Confession, and St. Mary's was like most Catholic churches. The church door was wide open—held open with a small metal hook attached to a metal banister. I walked inside and noticed that I was the only one going to Confession—at least for now.

I began as every penitent begins. "Bless me, Father, for I have sinned."

Typically, the priest blesses the penitent and says something that resembles a prayer. But not this time. A familiar voice asked, "Is that you, Jack?"

I recognized the voice immediately—an unmistakable baritone.

"Father Gaffney?" I hadn't realized that Father Gerry Gaffney had been assigned to St. Mary's, so you can imagine my surprise when I found myself getting reacquainted with him in the confessional. Father Gaffney and I had history. He'd been the assistant pastor at St. Joseph's, my home parish, when I was a third-grader becoming an altar boy. He was the first priest I ever served with on the altar.

"That's me," he said.

I could hear him laughing. He was always easy to talk to.

"Hey, Father, I have some things I want to get off my chest. How much time do I have?"

In the dim light of the confessional, I could see him consult his watch, and then he opened the door to his own small confessional closet. A moment later, he pulled aside the heavy drape on my side of the confessional. He extended his hand as I rose from the kneeler. It was good to see him. He always reminded me of Friar Tuck, short, round, and jovial.

"I think all the sinners have come and gone tonight, Jack. Slow night. Not a lot of sinners, and the sins have been universally dull." He offered me a welcoming smile. "Let's say we get a cup of coffee in the rectory kitchen, and you can tell me what's on your mind."

He placed his hand on my shoulder as we walked to the rectory's back door. "Boy, was I ever surprised when I heard your voice. Didn't expect to see you here…"

"You mean in the confessional?" I asked, half-jokingly.

"No. Here in Kutztown. I never knew you wanted to be a teacher."

"I'm hoping to be an English teacher, Father."

"That's great. It really is. By the way, call me, Gerry. Okay? I think we've known one another long enough, don't you?"

He held the door open, and I found myself in a small kitchen, the early-evening light casting shadows across the floor from the potted begonias on the windowsill.

"Probably ten years. I was in third grade."

He gave me a look full of reminiscence. "Ten years ago. Wow. And look how far you've come."

"I've got even further to go, Father. Sorry…Gerry. But I'll get there."

He pulled a kettle from the back burner and filled it with water. "Mrs. Hathaway has the weekend off, so let me boil some water for coffee. I didn't ask, but I'm assuming you drink coffee."

I laughed. "As a matter of fact, I started drinking coffee just last week."

He shook his head. "Probably the beginning of a beautiful, lifelong beverage relationship. I never drank coffee until I went into the seminary. Still going strong."

He put the kettle on the stove, and turned on the burner. He pulled a quart of milk from the refrigerator and joined me at the table. He was still wearing his stole—the long thin garment that a priest drapes around his neck as the symbol of his priestly authority to forgive sins.

"Well, Jack, you're a male college student, a young man in the bloom of youth, on a college campus with twice as many girls as guys, who gave up a perfectly good Saturday night to come to Confession. What's up?"

It took two cups of coffee—with milk and sugar—before the tale of Kervin, the Dormitory Counselor, was finished. I would have told my story more quickly, but Father Gerry's laughter interrupted me in mid-sentence more than a few times.

"You really did that?" Laughter. "That's incredible!" More laughter.

When I was finished, I had to wait for Father Gerry to catch his breath. I was especially glad we weren't inside the confessional. I can't imagine what anyone in the church might think.

"So, that's why I'm here. My problem has nothing to do with girls."

"I can assume that every word you're telling me is the truth?"

I could see the amusement in his eyes.

"Ah, Gerry, we just wanted Kervin to lay off, to give us some space. We never expected he'd get fired."

"Well, did he get fired?"

"We really don't know, but what we do know for certain is that he's gone. We don't even know if he's still on campus. I told my roommate we could ask the dean, but he said, 'Timins, get it through your head. It's over. O-V-E-R. Kervin's gone. G-O-N-E.'"

"So, Jack, what do you want from me?"

"You know, I'm not really sure. I deliberately lied to the dean—and to Kervin."

He put both his palms on the table as if he was about to make a pronouncement. "Let's look at this in a slightly different way. Let me assume that Kervin was abusing his authority—or perhaps more accurately, let me say that *you* thought Kervin was abusing his authority."

"I did think that."

"You and John went to war with Kervin. Kervin had demerits in his arsenal, and you and John had pennies, water-filled waste cans, and Aqua Velva after shave." He began laughing again. "I would have loved being there. Your roommate is a rascal."

I waited for Father Gerry to stop laughing. "Rascal? That's one possible word—but yeah, he sure knew how to deal with Kervin. I would never have thought to do any of those things. But here I am, a little amazed and a little ashamed that I did all of those things…and then lied about it."

"Are you more upset with the doing or the lying?"

"Probably the lying. I kind of agree with John that Kervin got what he deserved."

Father Gerry nodded. "Yeah, I understand. This whole lying business is where the whole concept of sin gets sticky."

"I thought a lie was a lie."

"Come on, Jack, we both know that's not true." He stood up and took his coffee cup to the sink. "Let's say you had told the dean the truth. 'Sure, Dean, we pennyed him in, and then we leaned that great big barrel of water against his door.' The dean would have had to do something, right? You were only leveling the playing field. It wasn't as if you could give demerits to Kervin. You had no demerits to give, so you fought back with the weapons available."

"If it makes a difference, Gerry, Kervin fired first."

Gerry laughed. "Yes, he did, and I'm betting he wishes he hadn't. So, let's take the war off the table."

He rescued the milk from the table and put it in the refrigerator.

"As for the lies, I can only imagine far worse and unjust consequences if the truth had been told. The only truth worth recognizing is that Kervin was probably unsuited for his position of authority. People in authority need to temper their decisions with mercy. Imagine how different things would have been if Kervin had knocked on your door that first day and said, 'Hey guys, I'd like you to make your beds before you go off to class.'"

"You mean, give us a warning…a heads-up?"

"That would have been the kindest thing he could have done, don't you think?"

"Yeah, you're right. Thanks, Gerry." I took my cup over to the sink. "Are you saying I don't need absolution from my sins tonight?

"You probably don't. You probably need a good night's sleep more than absolution. So, go back to your dorm. Right now, the only person who needs to forgive you, is you."

As we walked to the rectory's front door, he patted me on the back. "The year's still young, Jack—and you are a young male college freshman." His smile was clearly evident. "Let me know if I can ever help."

As he opened the door, he counseled me, "Don't ever be like Kervin, Jack. As you walk home, keep one thing in mind. Only the weak are cruel or unkind. Gentleness—kindness—can only be expected from the strong. Be gentle with others, and be gentle with yourself."

"Dr. Monroe thinks I should try-out for *Much Ado About Nothing*. I just finished *Barabbas*. That play swallowed up all my time. Took my weekends, too. I don't know if I should try out or not."

"You really are a Catholic tight-ass, Timins," Markowski replied. "Your Dr. Monroe invites you to try out for her show—and you do, and you get the lead, and you do great. Great! Now she tells you that you should audition for a famous Shakespearean play. What's your problem? What the hell more do you need? You'll be a shoo-in. Are you just playing hard-to-get?"

"If I am a tight-ass, just blame it on a lifetime of being Catholic. Change comes slowly for me, you know."

"Slowly? Now who's kidding who? Don't forget, you ditched that Harris Tweed jacket after your first day of school. You haven't worn it to class since.

And you helped get Kervin off our backs and out of this dorm. So, I know you can change. Don't say otherwise. I'll make an atheist out of you yet."

"Not gonna happen, John," I said, suddenly realizing that certain life-long behaviors had truly already been reversed.

"Well, I think you should try out for the show. Christ, Timins, first your professor suggests you should try out for *Barabbas*, and then she says you should try out for *Much Ado*. Who the hell gets *two* invitations from a professor?"

He was right. I expected certain changes when I came to college, but, so far, the changes that had happened during the first few weeks seemed to be altering the entire trajectory of my life.

I'd enrolled in Dr. Annette Monroe's course called *Oral Interpretation* because it sounded interesting. It sounded a bit like theatre—and I'd long been interested in plays and musicals. We'd scarcely begun the third full week of class when Dr. Monroe, chairman of the Speech and Theatre Department, told me I should try out for her Reader's Theatre production of *Barabbas*.

"They're open try-outs. Anyone can audition," she said. "I'm directing. I think you'd do well at try-outs. They're Wednesday afternoon."

"I've never really done theatre," I said. "Other than when I played an angel in second grade."

"That's alright," Dr. Monroe assured me. "No experience is required."

"But I don't know anything about...what's it called?"

"*Barabbas.*"

"He's mentioned in the Bible, right? During the Passion. Isn't he the man—the criminal—who was released instead of Jesus?"

"He's the one. Pär Lagerkvist wrote a novel about him in 1950. I always thought I'd like to make it into a staged presentation. I adapted the novel this past summer."

I felt a bit cornered, but I also found myself intrigued. Invitations from superiors—particularly from the director—are always seductive.

"I've never read the book," I said.

"That's alright, too. I begin all try-outs with an explanation of the story. I'll be surprised if anyone else has already read the book."

Even as I felt the tug of my own interest, I also felt fear welling inside.

"What if I'm no good?" I asked. My face betrayed me. It always has.

Dr. Monroe smiled reassuringly. "These are just try-outs," she said. "I really think you have untapped talent. You ought to come to try-outs."

I stood silent.

"Good. Wednesday. The Little Theatre. 4:00 p.m. It's downstairs in Schaeffer Auditorium. You'll see the signs," she said, as she picked up her briefcase and walked out the door. I didn't think I'd said yes, but I was wrong. My face had "yes" written all over it.

When I walked into Dr. Monroe's class on Wednesday morning, she handed me a copy of *Barabbas*. "Here, Jack. Here's the novel. If you get a chance, you can read through this. It's my copy. Just bring it to try-outs, okay?"

I managed to say something like "Thanks" or "Sure thing." Then later that afternoon, I found myself waiting, seated on one of the folding chairs scattered around the Little Theatre. About twenty-five other students had come to try-outs, too. I had Dr. Monroe's novel but no one had scripts.

"Did you read through it?" asked a swarthy man nodding at the book in my hands. He slid into the chair next to me. I wondered if this man with long black hair, heavy features, and a two-day growth of beard could be a student. He certainly wasn't a teenager.

"Uh, not much. Just the first few chapters."

"Sorry. I should introduce myself. I'm Dale Rome. This is a great story, don't you think?"

"I'm Jack." I hesitated, looked at the book on my lap and then at Dale. We shook hands. A brief silence descended.

"I've never been to an audition before," I admitted.

"You've got nothing to worry about," he said. "Dr. Monroe is a great director. She's a quiet, introspective director. She wants you to discover what you already have inside and just let it emerge. She knows what she wants and she knows how to help you find it inside yourself."

Everything went just as Dr. Monroe said it would. She handed out scripts to those without them—including me—then she explained the plot and described the characters.

"Okay, let's get started," she said.

That was it.

Two and a half hours later, after reading a half-dozen times for a half-dozen different roles, try-outs concluded. Dr. Monroe thanked everyone for their energy and enthusiasm, and said we all should check the callback list she would be posting outside her Old Main office the following morning. I had no idea how things had gone.

Gravity may be an irresistible force, but curiosity can give it a run for its money. The following morning, I went to breakfast just as I always did, trying to keep my curiosity in check. The last time I'd focused so intently on "making the list" was as a high school senior when Coach Molnar announced the starters for the first varsity football game of the season.

At breakfast, my distraction grew by the moment. I pushed my scrambled eggs around my plate. *Were they too watery?* Nibbled on my over-done bacon. *Too crisp, maybe?* And wondered if my name appeared on Dr. Monroe's list. I realized I hadn't heard anything anyone had said at the breakfast table. My friend, Ed, asked me if I was alright. I wanted to shout, *I don't know. I haven't seen the list.* But all I did was shrug my shoulders.

I surrendered. I abandoned my unfinished breakfast and ran from the Dining Hall into Old Main, up the stairs to Dr. Monroe's office. Scotch-taped to the wall next to her office door was the typed list—<u>CALLBACKS</u> was scribbled in black magic marker across the top.

My name was second on the list. I was still deciding if that was good news or bad when I heard a voice behind me.

"If you get called back, that means she's definitely interested in you being in the show," Dale remarked. "It doesn't mean you've got a part, but she thinks you're a good candidate for one. See you this afternoon." Dale's name was on the list, too.

Perhaps some background might help. I fell in love with theatre the way kids fall in love with ice cream.

It wasn't until years later, after I'd left fifteen years of classroom teaching to join Harper & Row publishing, that I realized how much I viewed life through the lens of theatre. After I left the classroom, someone asked me what I missed most about teaching. Without hesitation, I blurted out, "Five shows a day."

My mother frequently used a phrase to describe my love of theatre that seemed particularly apt: "From inauspicious beginnings." Those were the words she used after she attended my opening night performance in the production of *Barabbas* at Kutztown State College.

"Jack began his thespian career as an angel in St. Joseph's Christmas play," my mother happily informed all who had gathered around. She was beaming. "I think you were in the second grade."

The memory of my alleged angelic participation remains fuzzy. I remembered my father rigging up foil-covered, cardboard wings—wings that were actually taller than me. They were fastened across my shoulders, back, and chest with brown twine. I remember this because photographic evidence of my angelic role exists. The upper arch of my wings loomed above my head and they stretched all the way to the floor. That's all I really recollect from my first performance—and I don't know if I actually recollect it, but I've seen the pictures.

For the rest, I rely upon my mother's memory. "Sister Rita Ann was so impressed with the wings your father had created, that she designated you as the lead angel. That meant you starred in the central tableaux—the one with the Christ child in the stable at Bethlehem."

That's probably the only time any one would ever call me the "lead angel."

Mom explained how I'd stood on a rickety ladder behind the jury-rigged stable, while first-graders, dressed as sheep, cows, and camels, occasionally destroyed the tableaux effect by wandering around or waving at their parents. According to my mother, I maintained my reverent stillness atop the ladder because I was frozen with the fear I might fall. Finally, I uttered my one and only line: "Alleluia."

After my drama debut, my mother told me I looked wonderful—before offering a bit of stage advice. "You could have been a bit louder delivering your line."

Line? It was only one word.

"You must learn to project," my mother advised. But like moms everywhere, she sugar-coated her criticism. "That's okay, we knew what you were saying."

After my initial Christmas pageant appearance, my Catholic school stage career ended. True, I joined the Notre Dame HS Glee Club, and when Notre Dame staged *Camelot* during my freshman year, the Glee Club acted as the chorus. The fact that the chorus never actually walked on stage meant it was a quasi-theatrical experience. Neither costume nor choreography were required.

But *Barabbas* redefined theatre for me. After my rookie collegiate performance, my mother beamed. "From inauspicious beginnings," she said. "You're the lead—and you're only a freshman. I'm sure there will be many more roles. You were wonderful. Look how much you've learned. Look how far you've come." And then, as if recalling my initial angelic performance, "And I could hear every word."

Perhaps I was fated to love theatre—my mother loved it and spoke often of her thespian years at Alexander Hamilton High School in Elmsford, NY. Even in elementary school, I'd arrive home and find my mother listening to Rodgers and Hammerstein's *South Pacific* or Mario Lanza's *The Student Prince* while she smoked and knitted. My parent's fairly extensive collection of LPs included numerous musical theatre albums like *The King and I*, *Showboat*, and *Finian's Rainbow*. I loved them and often found myself humming the infectious show tunes as I delivered the *Allentown Morning Call* newspaper in the pre-dawn hours. Once I sang *"How Are Things in Glocca Morra"* so loudly, I worried that I'd disturbed the sleep of an entire block.

When I told my mom what I'd done, she said, "You come by it honestly. I love theatre, too."

Of course, New York City's proximity enhanced my love for theatre. My hometown, Easton, is only sixty or so miles from The Great White Way. The truth is both my parents saw themselves as New Yorkers. My father was a native of Hoboken, NJ—just across the Hudson from NYC—and my mother hailed from Elmsford, NY, in Westchester County, just a short train ride north.

Shortly after beginning my freshman year, I took advantage of the inexpensive buses covering those sixty miles to the NYC Port Authority. My girlfriend, Katie, and I went to see a new musical, *Man of La Mancha* just after Thanksgiving. I hadn't gotten home on weekends as I'd promised I would, but I had the notion that inviting one's girlfriend to a Broadway show would be a clear indicator to her that our relationship was serious.

My roommate—as annoying as he was savvy—wanted to know if I'd gotten the tickets to *Man of La Mancha* to convince Katie or to convince myself. I had a love-hate relationship with John's astute comments.

Still, few things are more delightful than going to New York and seeing a show. I was seventeen when I saw my first show, and more than five decades later, my love for Broadway shines as brightly as The Great White Way—even as other loves have fallen by the wayside.

I went to callbacks. Excited and nervous. By the end of the day, I knew I'd be playing the role of Barabbas. I'd gotten the lead. The lead, for God's sake. I was gratified…and terrified. That evening, I called Katie to tell her I'd gotten the part. We were both giddy with my success, both of us blithely unaware that I'd just fallen in love with a mistress that would occupy my time and my thoughts continually. Theatre does that.

My first genuine stage experience changed my life. Changed it entirely. *Carpe proscaenium*—seize the stage. And the stage seized my days. I quickly learned that girlfriends and theatre both make great demands on your time. Rehearsals swallowed the weekends I'd promised Katie. Running lines and impromptu gatherings with fellow actors occupied time previously given over to letter-writing. My letters home to both my girlfriend and my mother—that had initially been copious and garrulous—now became so infrequent that my own mother wrote a quick, one-sentence letter to me that fairly boiled over with maternal frustration:

> *Dear John,*
> *Are you still alive?*
> *Love, Mom*

Katie's almost-daily letters became increasingly concerned, asking questions like, "Do you still love me?" These were questions that deserved honest answers, but I was too cowardly to give her an honest reply. I wanted her, and I wanted my life in the theatre—at least as long as I was in college.

As we rode home from our *Man of La Mancha* excursion, I mentioned to Katie that I was thinking of trying out for *Much Ado About Nothing*.

"Will you be rehearsing on the weekends?" she asked. "Like with *Barabbas*?"

After an extended silence, I offered up a weak, "Probably."

Her face told me that my answer was unappreciated.

"What about us?" she said. "I write you almost every day. I write because I love you." Tears welled up, and I can offer no good defense where tears are involved.

The remainder of our homeward-bound bus ride conversation was anything but warm. I can't remember whether she sulked and I pouted or if it was *vice versa*. But I knew that I'd soon have to make a choice.

Looking back, I suppose I made my choice when I went to the *Much Ado* auditions.

I know what Shakespeare would have said, "Ay, there's the rub ."

Chapter 9
LOVE AND DRAMA

Late Fall 1965

My parents were amazed to find themselves part of *The Greatest Generation*—
the manufactured name bestowed upon those born between 1901 and
about 1927. It amused my mother that someone, somewhere, decided it was
necessary to name her generation or any other.

"Greatest?" Mom would ask, a bit befuddled. "We just did what we had to
do." My dad agreed.

What Mom and Dad did, along with my grandmother and my Uncle
Ted, was roller-coaster through three decades—barreling through the Roaring
Twenties, suffering through the Great Depression, and sacrificing during the
Second World War.

"We just did what we had to do," she'd reiterate whenever I became curious
about the years that pre-dated my birth.

Remarkably, despite a lifetime of upheaval, *The Greatest Generation* managed to evolve into *The Profusely Polite Generation*—*please*, *thank you*, and *may
I?* were coins of the realm.

Much of their politeness was anchored by the conversational ballast we call
euphemisms. As I grew up, I absorbed this euphemistic penchant long before
I knew that such a linguistic phenomenon even existed. As the *Baby-Boomer*
child of two members of *The Greatest Generation*, euphemisms quite naturally
insinuated themselves into my conversations.

For example, when the eight-year-old son of my Little League baseball
coach tragically tumbled over a cliff and died, I remember saying *Jeffrey passed
away*. When our Little League shortstop died of cancer, I sadly acknowledged

that *God had called Joey home.* From what I recollect, no one ever simply died when I was a child. They may have *passed away* or been *called home by the Lord*—but they didn't die.

Polite euphemisms flooded every aspect of life. Women experienced *that time of the month.* People were never cheap, they were *frugal.* If Mom wanted us out of the house, she'd say, *I could use a little peace and quiet.* That was code for *get out*, but saying *get out* was simply not in her nature.

After going toe-to-toe with enough uncomfortable realities to fill two lifetimes, my parents employed euphemisms to dull the sharp edges of a difficult world.

One delightfully ironic euphemism that I particularly recall is, *Things got out of hand.* That expression could apply to incredibly diverse situations—from spinning uncontrollably on an icy highway to behaving uncustomarily *in flagrante delicto.*

In either case, my parents were likely to respond with a simple *things got out of hand.*

During my first week as a college freshman, I'd quickly come to realize that the euphemistic expression, *things got out of hand,* aptly described my relationship with my dormitory counselor.

Before that week, I had seldom allowed anything to get out of hand. I wasn't a control freak, but I was a follower of rules. If I rebelled at all, I'd rebel quietly. Well, mostly.

Once the drama bug had bitten, I found nothing short of involvement in a show could scratch that itch. It was an addiction. Things had gotten out of hand. The jury was still out on whether that was good or bad.

I'd auditioned for *Much Ado*, hoping for a lead role, but our director, Miss Bartlett, had other ideas.

"Timins, as you know, I've given you the part of Balthasar. It's a small part. But you'll have a song to sing. I hope you can sing. By the way, you don't play the lute by any chance, do you?"

I should have used the very words of my character, in my best Shakespearean English, to explain to Miss Bartlett why that wasn't a good idea.

"Tax not so bad a voice to slander music any more than once."

But I didn't. And before I could explain that I was no musician of any sort, she said, "Never mind. We'll get a lute player for you. Small parts are always fun. You'll have to be okay with that."

What Kutztown's take-no-prisoners director, Professor Betty Bartlett, meant was, "Take it or leave it."

I took it. I didn't complain. Small part, big part? I was where I wanted to be. *Much Ado* was only my second show, but already I knew I liked being with theatre people—probably because theatre folks exuded a fascinating combination of high seriousness and delirious comedy. I've often wondered if those qualities were opposite sides of the same coin.

While I had only a small part, everyone was expected to attend every rehearsal. At our first cast meeting, Dr. Bartlett made that rule abundantly clear. "I never know what scene I'll want to see. Or what order I'll want to see them in. I can't be worried about whether you're here or not—so you'll be here. If that doesn't work for you, tell me now so I can replace you with someone who will be here."

Her ubiquitous cigarette, firmly planted between her lips, bounced as she spoke. Her hands were busy shuffling through sheets of paper on her lap.

"By the way, that includes Friday evening rehearsals. For those of you intent on going home for the weekends, you've got to choose…choose this play, or going home."

She found the sheet she was looking for, and pulled the cigarette out of her mouth. She bent her head back, exhaled a long stream of smoke, and held up the paper with her left hand.

"Here's the rehearsal schedule. Samantha will give everyone a copy before you leave tonight. We go on six weeks after the second semester begins. You've got all the dates there. Tonight and for the rest of this week, we'll get started on the read-through and character interpretation."

Her student director whispered in Miss Bartlett's ear.

"Right. Everyone gets measured for costumes before you leave on Christmas break. We're doing this full–Elizabethan—none of that modern crap—so don't get fat over the holidays. Dr. Thomas will be here tomorrow night to give you some Shakespearean background. On Thursday, our stage designer, Dr. Barnet, will be here to talk about…well…the stage design."

The bright, burning tip of Bartlett's cigarette punctuated everything she said. "One last item. I want everyone off book after Christmas break. Get your girlfriends and boyfriends to runs lines with you over a cup of grog or beneath the mistletoe. Everyone off book! Any questions?"

There were seldom questions. Gray, short-haired, fiftyish, stocky, chain-smoking Betty Bartlett was a legend among Kutztown's theatre community.

"You'll want to be in her shows," several theatre majors told me. "She may be gruff—sometimes she's a real bear—but she's never had a bad show. That's because she doesn't mince words. She wants what she wants when she wants it. And she always knows what she wants. If you give her what she wants, she'll be happy—and that means you'll be happy."

They were right. Everybody scrambled to give her whatever it was she wanted. Including me.

After several weeks of rehearsals for *Barabbas*, it occurred to me that acting was a kind of schizophrenia. Being two people at the same time. When I played Barabbas, I deliberately and consciously immersed myself in the part. As I dove deeper into the role, I wondered: Why was it ultimately so freeing, so satisfying, to not be me? To be someone else? In the day-to-day world—the one I occupied every minute I wasn't on stage—I was me. The strong me. The weak me. The brave me. The cowardly me. The Catholic me.

But that me was never that person I played on stage. When I performed on stage, I was someone else. And rehearsals were simply an opportunity for me to practice being that someone else. I'm saying this because I know acting changed me. Imperceptibly. One small change at a time. And I never really recognized those changes until later. Acting helped me move into emotional realms I would never have explored if I'd been just plain, old me. Suddenly, I was feeling things I'd never felt before—or never allowed myself to feel before. Suddenly I'd begun wondering, what is my character thinking?

Life changes you. So does theatre. And I had a foot in each.

As I sat in the Little Theatre of Schaeffer Auditorium waiting for *Much Ado* auditions to begin, I had no warning that things were about to get out of hand—little by little and bit by bit—until my proverbial footsteps had me spinning uncontrollably and behaving uncustomarily.

Familiarizing myself with the audition pieces, I looked up, a bit surprised, as someone plonked down right beside me. The theatre seats eight hundred, and there were only about fifty people waiting to audition.

"You don't mind if I sit here, do you?" asked a lovely stranger.

I wondered, *How could I say no?*

"You're Jack, right? Jack Timins? You played Barabbas?"

"Yes," I said, both flattered and a bit confused.

"I'm Diana Schiavano. I came to see your show opening night. I thought you did a terrific job. That was a tough role."

"Thanks," I said. No one had ever called *Barabbas* "my show"—until now. I could feel my cheeks color up. Blonde-haired, blue-eyed Diana was smiling at me, complimenting me, and I was blushing like a kid with his first crush. I was sure she couldn't possibly miss my embarrassment, so I blurted out the first thing that occurred to me. "Did I meet you after the show, Diana? If I did, I don't remember. It's all kind of a blur."

"No, I would have liked to congratulate you that night, but I have a two-year-old son who needed me back at home. He's the little guy who interrupted my education. I just returned to school in September—to finish my degree."

"Good for you," I said. "What year are you in?"

"I'm a senior. I plan to student teach next semester."

"Are you a theatre major?"

She laughed when I said that. "No. I thought I'd better get a degree in a subject area where I'd always be in demand. I'm an English major."

"Me, too."

"English teachers unite," she said as she shook my hand. "Lots of the folks auditioning tonight aren't theatre majors. But I think we all love theatre. If I get a part in *Much Ado*, I'll have been in seven plays during my college career."

I could tell she was proud of that.

Professor Bartlett, was sitting a few rows back from the stage, talking to her student director, and rummaging through a stack of papers. Miss Bartlett stood up and turned toward us.

"Okay," she said loudly. "Okay. We're going to get started. If I don't have your audition sheet in my hands, you better get it to me in the next minute or so." She held up the stack of sheets to emphasize her point, and then she handed the sheets to her student director.

A few students moved quickly, handing their audition sheets to the student director. Betty Bartlett took that moment to take a long drag on her ever-present cigarette.

"Okay. Auditions are going to happen in the order I received your audition sheets. First come, first served. When you're finished with your audition, you may stay or leave. Whether you stay or leave, do it quietly. Quiet doesn't mean you whisper. It means quiet." She stopped for a moment for emphasis and exhaled a long plume of smoke as she surveyed all those waiting in the auditorium. "Quiet means quiet. Everyone gets a fair shot. No interruptions unless the building is on fire."

A few people laughed, quietly.

"The results will be posted outside my office by tomorrow morning," she said. "So, let's get going." Her student director handed her one of the audition sheets. "Okay. Bill James, take stage."

"Let's talk after the auditions, okay?" Diana said. "Bartlett hates anyone talking when auditions are going on. Let's meet out in the lobby after, okay?"

I think I managed a "Yeah, sure," and then Diana moved across the row about ten seats.

What just happened? I asked myself.

Perhaps I should have asked, *What is happening?*

We both stayed in the auditorium after we'd finished. We knew auditions were over when Miss Bartlett stood up and spoke to an almost empty auditorium. "That's everybody, right?" She looked around just to be sure. She stubbed out her cigarette, handed a ream of paperwork to her student director, and collected her purse.

Diana was sitting about ten seats away from me, and as I made my way over to her, Betty Bartlett shouted in our direction. "Good to see you, again, Diana."

"Thanks, Miss B," Diana shouted back. "Nice to be back."

Diana turned toward me and said, "Walk me to my car." She looped her arm through my arm, and we walked out the side door into a chilly, clear December evening.

"So, how do you think it went?" I asked as I zipped my jacket against the cold.

"Can't say for sure. We'll know in the morning," she said as she pulled me closer and steered me toward the parking lot. "Brrrrr. I'll bet it's ten degrees colder than when we went inside," she said.

The voice in my head repeated the question. *What's happening?*

"What part are you hoping to get?" she asked me.

"I really don't know. Benedick? Don Pedro?"

I could feel the gentle pull on my arm tighten. "Hate to break it to you, Jack, but you're probably too short—and you've got this delightful baby face. If this were radio, maybe you'd make a great Benedick, but this is live theatre. Not radio."

"How about you?" I asked.

"I really don't care. This may very well be the last time I'm on stage, so I honestly don't care. I'm just trying out because I want to perform—even if it's just one last time."

"Well, I hope you get a part," I said. "That would be great."

"And I hope you get a part, too," she said. "I'd enjoy spending some time with you—that is, if you don't mind. You showed me you have some theatre chops when I saw *Barabbas*. I think it would be fun spending time with you."

I started to blush again. The cold air was no barrier.

"Can I ask a favor?"

"Yeah, sure," I said.

As she fished through her purse for a pen and piece of paper, we arrived at her car—a blue and white 1958 Chevy Impala.

"Nice car," I said.

"It was my dad's. When I had Michael—that's my son—Dad said I needed a car." She leaned against the roof of her car and scribbled something on the piece of paper. "Here's my phone number. My first class tomorrow isn't until noon. And I tend to run late. But I'll be dying of curiosity. Could you see if I made the cast? Call me either way, okay?"

"What time do you leave for class?

"I take Michael to my mom's apartment about 11:30. Mom lives in the apartment next to mine. It only takes about fifteen minutes to drive here from my place. If you call before 11:15, I'll be there, okay?"

"Alright," I said. "I expect I'll be looking at the cast list by 9:00 tomorrow morning. My first class is at 8:00. I'll call you as soon as I know."

"That's sweet, Jack. I really appreciate that." She kissed me on the cheek and asked, "Could we have lunch together tomorrow?"

What was it I was suddenly feeling? Panic? Fear? Arousal? All of those?

I took a deep breath. "What if one of us doesn't get a part?"

"Does it make a difference? When we have lunch, you can play the part of Jack Timins, freshman thespian, and I can play the part of Diana Schiavano, senior and future English teacher."

I smiled and shook my head. "Okay, lunch. What time?"

"How about one o'clock at the Old Main dining hall?"

I watched her Chevy pull out of the parking lot. As I walked back to my dormitory, I didn't know if I should congratulate or scold myself. I never mentioned Katie to her—the girl I expected to spend my future with. And I wasn't certain I'd mention Katie at lunch the next day, either.

Oh, Jack, I asked myself, *what's happening?*

We exchanged biographies at lunch the next day. Once upon a time, Diana Schiavano had gone off to college, hoping to become a high school English teacher—a goal we both shared. Things were going well for her during her first three years—her GPA nestled between a B+ and an A-. Twice she'd made dean's list. Better still, she enjoyed performing in one show after another. Then, in April of her junior year, she discovered she was pregnant.

She never married—and I never asked her why not. In my world—the Catholic world—a pregnant girlfriend meant a quick, sometimes quiet, wedding. No shotgun was required. A guilty conscience and the unrelenting pressure from Catholic peers "to do right by the girl" was all that was required. The unwritten Catholic code said that fathers and mothers were obligated to marry to legitimize the child. Later in my life, I would wonder if the Catholic Church felt that nuptials were a kind of punishment. I still don't know.

Theatre allowed her to combine her academic interests with a meaningful activity that advanced those same interests. She admitted to being stage struck the day she first played a small part in *The Pajama Game* when she was a high school sophomore.

"After that, I couldn't wait until the next year and the next musical," she explained. "I was hooked, Jack."

"I know what you mean," I said. "Until I was in *Barabbas*, I'd never been on the stage—unless St. Joseph's Christmas pageant counts. I was in second grade."

"In theatre, everything counts, Jack. I recommend you put your second-grade role on your résumé. What did you play?"

"I played an angel."

She laughed. "Hmmmm. An angel. Are you an angel?" she asked coyly.

"Mostly," I said.

"Mostly angel? Sometimes devil?" she asked, raising her eyebrows.

I began to blush—the response I've never been able to outgrow or suppress.

"I'm sorry," she said, as she saw my face redden. "I'm just teasing. Take a deep breath."

I took a deep breath. And we sat in silence for a moment.

"When I was a junior, I got the lead in *Show Boat*." Diana instantly shifted into a delightful southern drawl. "I want you to know, suh, that ah played Miss Magnolia Hawkes. People called me, Noli, the Suthin' belle on mah Daddy's boat, the Cotton Blossom."

"Nice accent," I said.

"Thanks," she said smiling at me. "I love parts that require accents. They're tons of fun—and if you end up teaching high school English, they'll come in handy. Your students will love 'em."

"Were you in a show your senior year?"

"When I was senior," she said, "I had the lead in *Once Upon a Mattress*. I played a princess—Princess Winnifred. If I hadn't gotten the part, I think I would have died of despair."

"Now that sounds a bit melodramatic. Try that 'died of despair' line with a southern drawl while you collapse with the back of your hand to your forehead." I placed my right hand on my forehead in a *Gone with the Wind* gesture.

"So, now you're a director?" she asked me in a coquettish tone. She leaned over and kissed me lightly on the lips.

I blushed; she laughed—something that became a familiar interaction.

Let me point out that I don't really know whether she was being coquettish or not. Memory sometimes plays tricks on us, cleverly deceiving us so we are always the "good guy," the "innocent party." Was she trying to seduce me? Maybe. Did I want to be seduced? Probably. All I want anyone to know is this: I was enthralled by her. She was a lovely "older" woman who sought out my company, sat next to me at auditions, encouraged me to walk her to her car, and invited me to lunch. She exuded sexuality. She wore it like a perfume. It was all very seductive—and, looking back, I'm sure I wanted to be seduced.

Now, with a two-year-old son to care for, and a mother who would happily babysit, Diana had returned to Kutztown to complete her senior year. We both had small roles in *Much Ado*—I played Balthasar and she played Margaret.

"No big role for me, Jack. Can't do it now. Next semester, after Christmas break, I'll be student teaching. I don't have time for a major role," she explained. "I'll need the time for lesson planning and grading papers. I can just as easily do most of that during rehearsals. And when I'm done, we'll either be rehearsing on stage, or just spending time together."

"I know we don't have a lot of lines, Diana, but most of my lines happen with you on stage with me," I told her. "Should we practice together?"

"I'd like that. See you tonight at rehearsal."

I should have known better.

I can hear my mother saying, "Famous last words."

Still, I should have known better. The first night of rehearsal, we did a complete read through of *Much Ado*. Before we ploughed through the text, Dr. Thomas, our resident Shakespeare scholar, crammed our craniums with all the English Renaissance trivia we could digest.

The second night, Dr. Barnet walked us through his imagined, not-yet-erected, multi-level set design, and our imaginations got a visual workout.

Rehearsals began in earnest that second night, and Diana and I retreated to the Little Theatre to run our lines, to begin memorizing our parts. The Little Theatre was perfect. We could speak in normal tones and not interrupt the rehearsal upstairs on the main stage.

But our lines were few. After the third run through, she leaned over and whispered in my ear. "Have you ever been on the catwalk above the stage?" she asked.

The question seemed innocent enough.

"The catwalk?" I asked. "No."

"It's the best seat in the house to watch rehearsals," she said. "I've spent hours up there watching everyone on stage. During rehearsals and during shows."

"Do you think we should we go up?" I know I sounded unsure.

Her voice betrayed no timidity at all. "Absolutely. As a senior, it's my duty to show you—a freshman player—the stage upon which we shall tread—or is that trod? I shall show you the wings of the stage—where we shall make our entrances and our exits. We shall visit the lighting board. And finally, yes finally, we'll climb to the heights—to the catwalk, where we can watch everything below from up above." She said it all with a comically haughty oratorical tone.

"You're sure it's okay?"

"Come thou, with me, Balthasar," she said, playfully calling me by my character's name. "Come with Margaret, and thou shalt see things that doth dazzle thy mind and imagination."

I began to laugh. Diana had transformed into an Elizabethan P.T. Barnum. So much silliness and fun. I followed Diana to the ladder in the wings of the main stage, and we climbed into the dim heights above the Klieg and Fresnel lights. We sat on the catwalk, enveloped in almost complete darkness, watching the rehearsal unfold forty feet below our dangling legs.

"Makes me feel like God," she whispered in my ear.

"It's incredible," I whispered back.

Then she kissed me. Not a peck on the cheek. Not a modest, I-like-you kiss. No. Nothing at all like that. This was a kiss that expelled the darkness.

What is it about darkness and unexpected kisses...unexpected passionate kisses? Something like the Zombies' song, *Tell Her No*, began playing in my head. Feelings I'd never felt before set my mind suddenly awhirl with fireworks and red flags. Delight mingled with doubt. Doubt dissolved into fear—and imagined legions of nuns with their "thou shalt nots" attempted to countermand my lustful impulses. *Tell Her No.*

I sought clarity and found none. *Can I do this?* morphed into *Am I permitted to do this? Isn't this wrong? Shouldn't I Tell Her No?*

Without a word, I jumped up, and in the darkness, my hands traced along the cold metal railings that led me to the cold metal ladder. I needed to go somewhere else—anywhere else. I needed to be alone. I needed to clarify my muddled mind, understand the overwhelming contradiction between my mind's admonitions and my body's desires. I raced down the ladder from the catwalk and never stopped until I'd reached the stage floor in the wings.

During my descent, as my hand traced along the metal, it apparently caught a jagged edge. I don't remember that happening; I don't remember the pain, but, as I stood in the darkness in the wings, I could feel something liquid on my hand. I brought my hand up to my face and pressed it against my cheek. What was it? Water? I walked outside the stage door to the lighted stairwell, and I saw the palm of my right hand covered in blood.

Like my father, I don't do blood very well, especially when it's my own. On several occasions, I have fainted at its sight, and that's what happened.

I fainted.

One of the stage managers found me unconscious on the stairwell landing, and ran out onto the stage to the footlights, shouting, "Miss Bartlett, something's happened to Timins. He's unconscious and he's got blood all over his face." At least, that is what Diana told me. She was watching everything from the catwalk.

Rehearsal ground to a complete halt. Apparently, everyone came to see Jack Timins, unconscious in the stairwell just beyond the stage door. Bartlett barked a stream of orders, dispatching her stage manager to call the emergency squad, directing others to place something soft beneath my head, and commanding, "Somebody find a damn blanket. That floor must be cold."

I never woke until the emergency squad arrived. They used smelling salts to rouse me, but told me to lay still because of my head injury.

"Don't move," a man ordered. "I'm one of the medics, and it looks like you've got a head injury. We're going clean the wound first, and then we'll make an assessment about transporting you to the hospital."

I'm sure I was a bit woozy, but I didn't remember hitting my head. I began to say what I was thinking…*Oh my God! The hospital?*

"No. Don't talk. Let us do what we have to do. I'm sure you're going to be fine."

He asked for gauze and some kind of sterile solution, and then he began gently swabbing my bloody right cheek. He was quite amazed when he couldn't find any kind of head injury. With the blood on my face removed, he extended his search—my scalp, my neck, my shoulders, my arms, my hands. Finally, he spotted the ugly, bloody gash across the palm of my right hand. Mystery solved.

"I'm going to clean this wound and close it with some butterfly adhesives," he said. "Could you sit up for me?"

While the medical folks tended to the wound, Betty Bartlett—whose rehearsal had come to an abrupt stop—hovered over the wound-dressing operation. Her gruff tone betrayed that she was in no mood. "How'd you cut your hand, Timins?"

When one of the medics working on bandaging my hand began to respond, he was immediately hushed with a wave of Bartlett's hand. "When I have a question for you," she said to the well-meaning but now-silent medic, "I'll ask you."

She turned back to me. "I need an answer, Timins. How'd you cut your hand?"

I was fearful and hesitant—Miss B was a force of nature—but then I accepted that this stairwell had become another confessional. A bit more public, perhaps, but a confessional.

"I was up on the catwalk, Miss B," I confessed. "I was watching the rehearsal from up there." I made no mention of my amorous companion. "I'm pretty sure I cut my hand on the ladder somehow, probably when I was coming down. I'm really sorry, Miss B. I really am."

Every Catholic Confession ends with an act of contrition—a *Sorry I did it and I won't do it again* moment. Saying I was truly sorry felt like the right thing to do.

After my hand was properly bandaged, Miss Bartlett straightened up. "Get yourself into the theatre, Timins." She turned to everyone gathered around the stairwell. "Everybody, into the theatre. We're going to nip this nonsense in the bud right now."

When Bartlett wants something to happen, it happens, and it happens quickly. In just a few moments, the whole cast was assembled and seated in the two front rows. I was front and center, and Diana sat immediately behind me. Miss B's assistant director stood next her as Miss B lit another cigarette. She looked directly at me, then she looked away, smoke billowing over her assistant's head.

"Okay," she said. "First, the catwalk is off-limits, every day, all the time—except for the tech people. No spectators allowed. Is that understood?"

Everyone nodded, even me.

"I can't hear your heads," she said impatiently, "only your words. Does everybody understand?"

A cascade of yeses flew her way.

"Good, we're unanimous. Second, Mr. Timins, here, is our object lesson in bad decisions—decisions I don't want anyone else to make. Every time you look at his bandaged right hand, I want you to say to yourself, 'I'll never do something like that.'"

She moved toward me. She pulled my right arm and bandaged hand into the air as if I were an unstrung marionette.

"So, what are you all going to say?"

A somewhat mumbled jumble of words spilled out, with everyone responding half-heartedly with a sentence that sounded vaguely like, "I'll never do something like that."

"That was awful," she said, her cigarette jiggling crazily on her lips. "I can see that line is going to need some rehearsal. You've got to say it with conviction. Okay? Okay?"

Everyone said okay.

"Good. Let me show you what I want." Miss Bartlett offered the cast a rhythmic, almost sing-song, "I'll never do something like that." She did that twice. Then, in a bright, energetic voice, she said, "Okay, everyone," and she conducted her cast like a concertmaster, using her cigarette like a baton.

After the cast had successfully taken Miss B's direction, and when she was finally certain that no one would ever do something like that, she turned to me.

"Stand up and apologize, Timins. You've wasted everyone's time here tonight. C'mon, stand up. I expect you to apologize, and it damn well better be convincing."

I stood up and apologized. I have no idea what I said, but later that night, in the dark confines of the Little Theatre, Diana told me my apology was very convincing. And then she kissed me like she had on the catwalk.

All calm disintegrated. Desire and Lust wrestled with Fear and Love—an emotional tag-team match with no referee—spinning uncontrollably and behaving uncustomarily.

Tomorrow's calendar was crashing down on me. I would be going home to spend the Christmas holidays with my family, and with the woman I love.

I could hear a disapproving voice in my head contradicting me.

You mean you'll be spending the holidays with the woman you say you love. You still haven't mentioned her to Diana. Not once. Why is that?

I had no answer for myself. Things had gotten out of hand.

Tell you what, Timins, you're gonna need a Christmas miracle.

Chapter 10
THE HOMECOMING
Late December 1965 / Early January 1966

Homecomings should be joyous moments. Particularly at Christmas. I was about to celebrate my 18th birthday—it felt like eighteen was the magic number that truly opened the door to adulthood—and my first semester in college had gone better than even I had ever expected. Academically and intellectually, anyway. Psychologically, things were, as my mother would say, "discombobulated."

That was me, "Mr. Discombobulated."

I involved myself in various tasks and activities to divert myself from me. At the moment, I wasn't really talking with myself because I wasn't particularly pleased with myself.

One of the things I disliked most about myself was that I was quite capable of reminding myself that I'd failed on several fronts.

You promised to write every day, didn't you?

I'd written a paltry number of letters—especially when I could bundle all of Katie's letters into a stack that was ten inches high. She'd kept her promise, writing to me three time a week. Sometimes more. After the first few weeks—when I did write almost every day—my numbers had dwindled. Somehow, I was only writing once a week, maybe once every two weeks.

Don't worry, Katie, I'll be home on weekends. It's only forty miles away.

My promise to be home on weekends went largely unfulfilled. I could plead my case, saying, "I'm busy with theatre rehearsals," but I'm sure all Katie heard was, "I'd rather be busy with theatre rehearsals than with you."

And then Diana happened.

Even as I write those words, it makes Diana sound like a car accident—or getting caught in a blizzard or a hurricane. As if it was awful, and I had no control over what happened.

But Diana was no accident, no blizzard, no hurricane. In truth, I wanted it all to happen again when I returned to school the next semester. I wanted to rehearse *Much Ado* in the Little Theatre with Diana. I wanted the kind of kiss that expelled the darkness.

OK, Jack, what do you plan to say to Katie?

Saturday morning, my father knocked on my dormitory door at 9:00 a.m. Dad was the most punctual man I've ever met. If he had said he'd be there at 8:45, I would have heard the knock fifteen minutes earlier.

I opened the door.

"Hi, Dad, come on in. I'm just about ready to go."

Across the room, John called out, "Hi, Mr. Timins, Merry Christmas." He reached under his desk and pulled out a box wrapped in shiny white paper, bound with a big red ribbon. "Mr. Timins, this is for you and your wife. My mom makes really great Christmas cookies, and she insisted I give these to you. She figured I owed you and Mrs. Timins for sending Jack my way. He's been pretty great. So, it's my way of saying thank you."

A gift for my parents…and me with nothing for John's folks. "Thanks for letting me know, John," I said. I was, indeed, surprised.

My dad was gracious, as always. "Thank you, John." He walked over to John and took the box and shook John's hand. "Merry Christmas to you, too. And to your mom and dad."

"Well, I'm outta here," I said. "When are you heading home, John?"

"When my dad gets here—or my mom. I'm guessing they'll be here after lunch. We really didn't talk about a time."

"Well, Merry Christmas to all the Markowskis," Dad said. Then he turned to me. "You ready to head home, Son?"

I picked up my suitcase, and my gym bag and we headed out the door.

"What did you do to your hand?" my dad asked.

"Oh, this?" I said, putting down my suitcase. "It's nothing. I cut it during rehearsal for *Much Ado*. It's fine."

"I told Jack he shouldn't get involved in a sword-fighting scene. But he never listens to me," John said.

My dad laughed at John's quip.

"It's really nothing, Mr. Timins. Jack will be fine in no time."

I'd told John about my encounter with Diana and with the medics when I came back from rehearsal.

That's when he told me, "You better use your Christmas break to figure out who the hell you are, Timins." I could hear some disapproval in his voice. "There's theatre, and there's real life. You know what I mean?"

And today, as I was leaving for Christmas break—and real life—I turned to John and said, "Thanks for everything, John. I'm glad you're my roommate. Merry Christmas."

"See you next year, Timins," John called, as Dad closed our dorm door.

As we walked to the stairwell, Dad explained all the things that would be occupying my time. "Your mom wants to decorate the archways and the mantelpiece the way she always has. She needs greens. She's sending you and your brothers up Morgan Hill to collect some fir branches and pine boughs."

"You mean Will and Denny haven't made the annual pilgrimage, yet?"

"Not yet. They say they're waiting for you. They said it's an annual ritual."

That was true—or my brothers and I saw it that way. We'd been traipsing up the side of Morgan Hill since we were in grade school. Every December, a bunch of guys with saws and twine and canvas bags—sometimes in sunshine, sometimes in rain, and sometimes in snow—collected greens for all the moms on Line Street to decorate their homes. None of us knew who owned the trees on the land where we collected our greens. There were no houses anywhere near the pine and fir trees we preferred. It felt like the middle of nowhere—except we played in the middle of nowhere every summer.

Besides, nobody ever told us we couldn't, so we always did.

As we drove home, my dad did most of the talking. He talked about what he'd gotten for Mom—"Don't say anything. It's a surprise." He mentioned that Uncle Ted and Aunt Marian were coming for a visit the Tuesday and Wednesday before Christmas—Christmas was on a Saturday. They lived about seventy miles away in northeastern New Jersey and we tried to get together about twice each year. Uncle Ted is Dad's only brother—just a few years older—and, as much as I loved my Uncle Ted and Aunt Marian, I loved their visits because I'd get to spend some time with my cousin, Moira. I happily admit that I had a huge crush on my cousin. She was gorgeous and sophisticated... and gorgeous.

I'm pretty sure my brother, Will, had a crush on her, too, but his experience with the opposite sex was much wider and more varied than mine. Will's life was replete with crushes—and conquests. Even our neighbor, Mr. Vargo, insisted that Will "had left a string of broken hearts in his wake." I can't say if that's true, but the girls always flocked to my older brother, way more than to me.

Was I jealous? Damn right, I was.

Decades later, when anyone asked who gave me my first real kiss—a kiss I genuinely enjoyed—I'd say "My cousin, Moira." I can say with great satisfaction that my cousin's twice-yearly visits were always sandwiched between two kisses—the first when she arrived and the second when she departed. Of all the kisses of my youth, I loved her cousinly, modest kisses most of all...until I met Katie.

And then Diana happened.

I wanted to tell myself to shut up.

Right after early Mass on Sunday, Will and I hiked up Morgan Hill, on our way for the annual cutting of the greens. Our brother, Dennis, who normally would have come along, was busy Christmas shopping. I was happy that it was just me and my older brother. That's when I told Will I really needed to talk with him.

When I said that, Will stopped on the path that led up to the ridge. The day was cold. The air, crisp and clear. The sky, a brilliant blue, as only winter skies can be. We both turned around to soak in the view. We could see damn near forever. To the north, south side Easton spread out below us, and the twin steeples of St. Joseph's Catholic Church thrust high into the air. Beyond that—across the Lehigh River that was invisible from our observation point—we could see the thin spire of the courthouse, and beyond that to the east, some of Lafayette College's rustic, brick, colonial-style buildings on College Hill. If we looked north to the far horizon, you could see the rolling hills around the town of Nazareth, and to the northeast, we could see sunlight glinting off the Delaware River as it flowed lazily south past Easton.

"Don't you just love that view, Red?" Will asked. "We come here every year, but I never get tired of it."

"Yeah," I said. "I love it, too. There's one of the things I love most," I said, as I pointed to a distant house. "We can see our house from up here. It looks so small, doesn't it?"

"Everything looks small from up here," Will said. "So, what's up, Red? You sound like you've got something serious going on. You're not in trouble, are you?"

Will looked at me waiting for an answer, but added, "Does it have anything to do with that gauze bandage you've got wrapped around your hand?"

"Well, yes and no."

"Okay, Brother Jack, when someone tells me it's yes and no, that usually means yes."

I told Will how I'd injured my hand coming down from the catwalk above the main stage. And how the emergency squad was called, because the stage manager found me unconscious with a bloody face, and she was certain I was severely injured.

I'm pretty sure Will found the whole situation amusing.

"That's the whole story?" Will asked.

I hesitated, and Will gave me that older brother look that says, *Spit it out.*

Only then did I tell Will the whole story, beginning with Diana's passionate catwalk kiss, and then her post-rehearsal reprise of a second, equally passionate kiss.

"Jesus, Will, no one has ever kissed me like that. Not ever. Not even Katie. When Diana kissed me, all I wanted to do was kiss her back. I just wanted to keep kissing her. I didn't want to stop."

Will chuckled at my discomfort.

"It's not funny," I said. "I never mentioned Katie to Diana—not once. Not during the auditions…not when we were up on the catwalk…"

"Seems to me, Red, sooner or later, you're going to have to ask yourself. 'Why haven't I mentioned Katie?' Well, why haven't you?"

"I've been asking myself that question since I left the Little Theatre on Friday night."

"And still no answer?"

I shrugged. "Not yet."

"Here's the hardest part, Red. *You* have to answer that question. You. You're the only one who can. If you're looking for an answer from me, I'm afraid I can't give you that answer. Think about that as we walk."

In silence, we followed the path to Spring Valley—our name for the place where we always played as children during the summer months and where we always collected Mom's Christmas greens.

Once there, cutting and trimming the greens absorbed our attention for the next hour. As we tied the boughs together with twine to comfortably carry them home, Will said, "I think we've got enough. Whatya think, Red?"

My despondent response was "Probably."

Will sat down on the trunk of a fallen fir tree and patted the bark—an invitation for me to sit down.

"I thought we're heading home," I said.

"We are, Red, but sit down for a moment, okay."

I sat.

"I've been thinking about what you told me. About Diana. Before we go back, there are some things I feel I need to explain. I heard what you said, and I hope I can help. I'm not sure if I have any useful advice, but I think I have a different way of looking at things. The truth is, I know how you feel. I've been there, and I still don't know what to tell you. But…"

"But what?" I asked.

"Here's the thing, Red. Katie is your first serious girlfriend. Right? She really is. I know you love her—you told Mom and Dad you love her, and that's gotta count for something. You guys have dated for what?…maybe two years? I know you guys have talked about getting married after college. But that's still years down the road."

"I know, Will. And I haven't written Katie every week, like I promised, or come home on the weekends…like I promised…"

"Hey, Red, don't beat yourself up. Here's what I want to tell you. You've got to realize that the whole direction of your life has changed. Pure and simple. Anyone can see that. You thought you'd be going to class for four years, sending letters to Katie every day, and coming home every weekend. Then you'd get a teaching job, get married, and have kids. Right?"

I nodded. "Yeah, that's what I thought."

"Well, that's not the direction your life has taken, Red. Not anymore, anyway. You're on a whole different path. You're still growing up. You're in college. Who the hell knows what twists and turns are in store for you—or for me or for any of us for that matter."

He seemed to be searching for the right words. "You can't close the book when you're barely past the first chapter, man. That's where you are. You've got to find out what life is about, not punish yourself for things that just happen."

"I feel so guilty."

"Well, you've always been good at that. You're better at feeling guilty than anyone I know. So, go ahead and feel guilty if you want to, Red, but it's nobody's fault. Not yours. Not Katie's. Not even Diana's. But it's clear you like theatre. And from what you've said, I think you'd like to find out a bit more about Diana, too. Am I right?"

I nodded, again.

"Then, my advice—older brother to younger brother—is this. You've got to tell Katie."

A third nod. "What should I say?"

"Don't ask me, Red, 'cause I don't know. I know she won't be happy—it is Christmas after all. But I'd tell her *before* Christmas. I'm just saying."

We began our trek home, bouncing along with boughs of Christmas greens across our shoulders. As we began moving down the side of Morgan Hill, we could see the gathering dusk, and Will paused right where we'd stopped on the way up and put down the greens he was carrying. We could see Easton's Christmas candle, erected annually around the war monument in Easton's Centre Square. It was always fun seeing Easton's Christmas light, shining brightly in the distance.

"It's gonna be dark in another half hour. Take a good look at Easton, Red. This has been our home just about forever. But there's so much more—good, bad, and otherwise—in every direction. So much to explore. So much to learn.

You're only turning eighteen this week, Red, not fifty. Jesus, your life's just beginning." He began to laugh. "I sound just like Dad, don't I?"

"Yeah, just like Dad."

"Well, that's all I've got to say. That…and enjoy your life. Spend the rest of your years in college living and learning and…oh, yeah…loving." He smiled at me as he said that. "Don't spend those years waiting—or making Katie wait."

He picked up his evergreen boughs and slung them over his shoulder.

"Let's get home before dark."

As we moved down the side of Morgan Hill, along a very familiar path, I said, "Thanks, Will."

"That's what we older brothers are for."

My own personal countdown had begun. It was the Monday before Christmas. Uncle Ted and Aunt Marian would be coming tomorrow, on Tuesday. This evening Katie and I were supposed to go shopping together because Easton's downtown stores extended shopping hours as Christmas approached.

So, tonight would be the night when I'd tell Katie.

I didn't know exactly what I'd be telling her, but I knew exactly what the outcome would be. As the day moved inexorably toward evening, Neil Sedaka's *Breaking Up Is Hard to Do* played incessantly in my head.

> *Don't take your love away from me.*
> *Don't you leave my heart in misery.*
> *If you go, then I'll be blue,*
> *'Cause breaking up is hard to do.*

I realized that I wasn't just breaking off my relationship with Katie, I was breaking up with Dick and Dot, her dad and mom, too. And her brother. And her wonderful grandmother. Neil Sedaka's song said nothing about collateral damage, but whenever I imagined our break-up scenario, I felt increasingly like a villain.

Katie and I planned our shopping excursion weeks earlier. I would pick up Katie at work around 4:30. We'd drive downtown for dinner. After dinner, we would go shopping. Then, I'd take her back to work to pick up her car, and we'd go to her house and wrap presents.

The only thing that went as planned was the picking-up-at-work part. As we drove toward downtown, I was unusually quiet.

"Something's wrong, Red," Katie said. "Tell me what's wrong. I felt it Saturday night when we went to the movies, and we spent less than five minutes talking on the phone last night."

I wanted to tell her the truth, but I didn't know how. Not about Diana. Not about the massive internal confusion I was feeling. For a person whose words too often flowed like water, my words had dried up. My mind was a desert.

Katie turned to face me in the car. "Do you still love me?" she asked.

A simple, straightforward question deserves a simple straightforward answer. I pulled the car into the A&P parking lot and turned off the engine.

I gripped the steering wheel and shook my head. "I don't know, Katie. I don't know."

Her face crumbled and she began to cry. "I think that means no," she said. "Please take me back to my car."

I did what she asked. No argument. No hedging. I felt ashamed.

As I drove her back to her car, I wanted to say, *I'm just trying to be honest* or something that could ease the hurt. But I doubted saying that would ease anything. As she climbed out of my car, she looked at me as if she really didn't know me—a look I easily comprehended because, at that moment, even I didn't know me anymore.

I looked at her and said, "I'm sorry."

"Me, too, Red," she said. "I'm sorry, too. Please don't call me until you can answer my question, one way or the other."

She was right, she deserved a definite yes, or a definite no. So did I.

As I write this, I feel myself immediately transported back to that cold December day. A day that should have been wonderful, even a bit magical. After all, it was the season of Christmas. It should have been a day Katie and I would recall years later in our dotage—happily married, our kids grown, our grandkids growing—as we gathered around our very own Christmas tree in our very own home. It should have been a day filled with love, laughter, and warm embraces. It should have been a day we'd be wrapping gifts together at Katie's home, Christmas carols playing on the phonograph, while we comically did our best to sneak peeks at what we'd gotten one another for Christmas. Naturally, each of us would lovingly scold the other, "It's a present. Don't ruin the surprise." Then we'd kiss and gently tell the other to "Go away, nosey. No peeking."

Sometimes, that's the day I imagine, and my heart begins to ache at the never-to-be-realized memory. Neil Sedaka was right. Breaking up is hard to do.

From the moment I realized I loved Katie, I'd played it safe, my sails set to a certain shore. I was convinced that's the way it should be, the way it must be. But without me realizing it, attending college shifted the winds. Now I was sailing toward an unknown destination, wondering where I would arrive, wondering when I would arrive. Wondering if arriving somewhere or sometime was even possible or necessary. The new and unexpected sense of mystery intrigued me, excited me—and also scared the hell out of me.

Since falling in love, Katie had been my destination. My only destination. She was my date for movies, for Saturday night dances at Notre Dame Bandstand with Jumpin' Gene Kaye, for Broadway plays, for New York World's Fair excursions, and for the senior prom. She joined me around my family's table—or I joined her around her family's table—for Thanksgiving, Christmas, New Year's, Easter, the 4th of July, and all the birthdays. She was my companion of choice for every other day, too. We read each other's minds; we took care of each other's hearts.

Her love helped me live a life that was safe and worry-free. I never had asked myself—*So what the hell is wrong with safe and worry-free?*—because the answer was self-evident.

However, when my life changed course, a new, very different question presented itself. *Wouldn't you like to explore the wide, wide world and all of its possibilities?* Until I went off to college, that question never occurred to me. But now it did.

A different question demanded a different answer. Part of that answer came in the form of theatre—acting on stage, stepping into a different self. Becoming a person who is *not me*. That was scary, but also irresistibly intriguing and exciting. Theatre demanded taking risks in front of a whole crowd of people—most of them strangers, who have come because *the play's the thing*.

Another part of that answer came in the person of Diana, someone even more irresistibly intriguing and exciting—and scary—than theatre. Diana felt like a kaleidoscope of unexplored possibilities.

I knew that when I answered that newly-framed question, *Wouldn't you like to explore the wide, wide world and all its possibilities?*, the answer was yes. There could be no going back.

When I walked in the back door that night, Will met me in the kitchen, while our dog, Impy, sat patiently waiting for a pat on the head. They could both see I'd been crying. Impy licked my hand as I stooped to pet him.

"I see you told her," he said.

"Yeah. Too many tears tonight, Will," I said, as I scratched Impy's chin. "I feel like a real shit."

"I think you did the right thing, Red. I really do."

"Why does doing the right thing feel so awful?"

"I dunno. I wish I did. Let's go tell Mom and Dad," Will said. "They love you, and they'll understand. That's what parents do."

I'd thrown a monkey wrench into Christmas. Katie wouldn't be coming here, and I wouldn't be going there.

My father and Katie's father both came to the rescue when they met at the 25th Street Shopping Center on the evening of December 23rd, my birthday. My dad handed over the gifts intended for Katie's family, and Katie's dad did the same.

I can just imagine them both, standing outside their cars in the cold parking lot, telling war stories. Katie's dad had driven a truck across France with Patton's Third Army, and my dad had piloted a B-24 bomber for the 8th Air Force out of England.

I don't know what they said to one another, but when Dad came home, he said, "How are you feeling, Son?"

"Like I've hurt someone I promised never to hurt."

"Well, cheer up, Son. All gifts have been exchanged. And Katie's dad is a real gentleman. He told me that he hopes you do well in school, and that you have a Merry Christmas."

"Thanks, Dad."

"Life goes on, Son. It always does. Try to make the best of it."

I think that was my dad's motto. *Try to make the best of it.* Coming from a man who had flown thirty-five missions over German-occupied territory, I truly believed that my father understood one simple principle: No matter how bad things may seem to be, they could be far worse. He'd watched planes, flying with him in formation, tumble earthward with broken wings, while he prayed that the crew members would parachute to safety.

I think when Dad finally returned stateside in August 1944, he married Mom and gave himself permission to be happy, even in tough times—because things could always be worse.

I loved that about my dad, and so did my brothers.

Chapter 11

KISSING, ET CETERA

Late December 1965 / Early January 1966

My Uncle Ted arrived on Tuesday, and it helped me forget how miserable and upset I was—at least for a few days. Mom and Aunt Marian immediately went to the kitchen and began baking, while Dad and Uncle Ted sat together at the piano on the sunporch to play four-handed Christmas carols. Soon, music mingled with the smell of fresh baked cookies, and we all agreed that Santa Claus wasn't coming to town—he'd already arrived.

Whenever our two families got together, Will and I spent most of our time with our cousin, Moira. We always felt that Moira was far more worldly-wise than we were. Perhaps because she lived in the New York City metropolitan area, perhaps because she was a gorgeous young woman who paid attention to things that Will and I never did. She'd regale us with stories about glamorous movie stars, like Debbie Reynold's broken heart when Eddie Fisher left her for Liz Taylor, or Liz Taylor's torrid affair with Richard Burton when she left Eddie Fisher. Broken hearts and easy virtue were always riveting topics. We'd spend hours listening to her, because we loved the music of her voice and her beautiful face. That's the simple truth.

At some point mid-story, however, she interrupted herself and looked directly at me. "Why so sad, cuz?" she asked.

I didn't respond with my usual effervescence—probably because I didn't feel effervescent. In fact, I just sat in silence. She turned to Will and asked, "What's going on with Jack? He looks like he's lost his best friend."

"Pretty close," Will replied. "Pretty close."

Will pointed at me, as if it were my turn to talk.

"Katie and I broke up."

"Oh my God, Jack, that's awful. Are you okay?" She paused for a moment and then waved her hand. "Well, that was a silly question, wasn't it? Of course, you're not okay."

Moira walked over to me and gave me a warm hug, and, as she released me, she turned to Will and said, "It will be our job, Will, to cheer Jack up. We cannot have him out of sorts—not with his birthday tomorrow and Christmas on Saturday."

"My birthday is the day *after* tomorrow," I pointed out.

"Well then, we have an extra day to cheer you up, don't we?"

"Be careful, Moira," Will said, "Jack isn't sure that there is life after Katie."

When I heard what Will said, I feared that somehow he would begin teasing me about Diana—and somehow give me away. But he didn't.

"Of course, there is life after Katie," Moira said gently. "Broken hearts are a part of life, Jack. Nobody wants one, but sooner or later, everybody gets one. If you want to talk about it, I'm happy to listen. If not, let's talk about something fun…like what you got me for Christmas."

Her teasing tone and playful smile had a way of making us smile.

I don't recollect if we actually discussed gifts at all, but Will mentioned that he was giving serious thought to enlisting in the Marine Corps. That got us talking about our dads' military service.

And I began worrying about Will.

As the conversation wound down, Moira looked at me and said, "We won't allow any long faces, Jack. Not while the house is filled with the sound of music and the smell of cookies. It's Christmas. What can I do to make you happy?"

"Would you like to help me memorize my lines for my part in *Much Ado About Nothing*? I've got a part—just a small part—and we have to be off book when we start rehearsals the first week of January. I think I've committed my part to memory, but it would help if someone read the part of Margaret."

"I can do that," Moira said.

I ran upstairs and got my script and opened to my first scene, and off we went. I even sang a terrible rendition of *Sigh No More, Ladies, Sigh No More*. As I said, I sang badly.

Moira rocked back, clapped her hands, and laughed. "You're really going to sing that song on stage, Jack? In front of a crowd? You may know the words, but you better practice the tune." Will and Moira agreed that I'd memorized all my lines pretty well, and Moira told me how wonderful I was—except for my singing—and wanted to know when I'd make my movie debut.

"Maybe you'll get to share the screen with Liz Taylor. Who knows?"

The laughter grew even more raucous. Moira always had the gift for turning frowns into smiles.

And that's how things went.

We talked, listened to Dad and Uncle Ted play four-hand piano, stole fresh cookies from the kitchen, and played an intermittent game of Monopoly over two days—a game we never really finished. Nobody won. Nobody lost.

We celebrated my birthday a day early.

Uncle Ted, Aunt Marian, and Moira went home for Christmas.

On Christmas Eve, my family visited several neighbors to deliver Mom's delicious anise cookies before we attended midnight Mass.

We opened our Christmas presents on Christmas morning while Dad played Christmas carols on the piano.

We sang *Auld Lang Syne* on New Year's Eve.

We watched the televised bowl games on New Year's Day.

In so many ways, my life was scripted. Each year, I'd spent Christmas the very same way, always feeling content, sometimes joyous—even exuberant. Three years ago, Katie became part of my Christmas joy—and I truly expected that she would be incorporated into my life's script forever.

Unfortunately, forever doesn't always last as long as one hopes, and this year, one of my forevers proved to be short-lived, and a very definite sadness crowded out some of the joy. I did my best to hide it, but as my mom always said, "Jack, you've always worn your heart on your sleeve."

The holidays were over. I was packed and ready to return to school. Will sat at the edge of my bed as I zipped up my gym bag.

"You gonna be alright, Red?"

"Yeah. Classes start tomorrow, and we start rehearsals for *Much Ado* tomorrow night."

"Okay," Will replied. "I expect that Diana will be at that same rehearsal, right?"

"I guess so."

"Come on, Red. You're hoping she's going to be at rehearsal, aren't you?"

I nodded.

"Well, just be careful. Watch out for yourself. And for God's sake, don't climb up to the catwalk or faint again. Mom and Dad don't know anything about that first episode, so let's not repeat it."

Just then, Dad poked his head into our bedroom.

"Ready to go, Son?"

"Yeah, Dad. I'm ready. Will, you take care of yourself, and let me know what decision you make about the military. Gotta go."

"Study hard, Jack. Love ya."

The Tuesday following New Year's Day, Dad drove me back to my dorm.

I had an inkling that my return represented far more than just the start of my second semester. Still, I found comfort in certain constants. John and I would again be roommates. I felt good about that. At least one thing hadn't changed. Or so I thought.

As John and I sat drinking some hot cider at *Chez Nous*, the campus snack bar, we agreed that our Christmases had been epiphanies for us both.

I told him that Katie and I had broken up.

"Sounds like you did all the breaking up, Timins," he said, blowing on his cider.

"Yeah. Okay. You're right."

"Of course, I am," he said. "But it's not the end of the world, Jack. Once you get back into the swing of things here…what with classes and rehearsals, you won't have time to feel sorry for yourself." He took a careful sip of his cider.

"So, tell me about your Christmas," I said.

He sipped his cider, then wrapped both hands around the warm cup. He seemed to be summoning the courage to say something.

"What's going on, John?" I asked.

"I'm pretty sure I'm gonna quit after this semester," John said.

"Quit what?" I asked nonchalantly.

"What the hell do you think I'm gonna quit?"

I should have seen it coming. Once again, change had crept up behind me and banged its damned drum.

"What? School?" I'm sure I sounded a bit confused. "Why would you quit?"

"Because it's not what I want, Timins. Seems there's a lot of that going around."

My face betrayed the sting of his words.

"Look, Jack, I'm sorry. Damn it, I shouldn't have said that. You can have any girlfriend you want. I'm sorry." He was clearly frustrated. "Hell, I don't know what I want. You can see that, can't you? I didn't know what I wanted when I graduated from high school, and I still don't know. I just know that I don't want this. I know you love it here—you've found your niche—but it's not for me."

I listened, but I wasn't quite sure what to say. All I could offer was, "Are you going to get a job?"

"Already have. And a good one, too. Over the holidays, I told the Army I'd enlist in June. I went to see the recruiter in downtown Reading, and he told me that if I did a deferred enlistment now, I'd get choices I wouldn't get any other way. You know, Jack, when you get drafted, they can do anything they want with you."

I hadn't been sure what breadth of changes might be afoot after first semester, but this one had come straight out of left field.

"You enlisted? Already?"

"Already signed the papers."

"You sure about this, John?"

"I better be. It's too late now. I know two things for sure. I don't want to be here—I don't know what ever made me think I'd like to be an elementary school teacher—and I don't want to get drafted. I also know that when I leave here in June, I'll be draft bait for sure. So, I figured I'd enlist, get the kind of military assignment I'd like, and see if I can figure out what I actually want to do for the rest of my life while I'm in the service."

"For how long?"

"Three years," he said.

He could see the concern in my face.

"Don't worry about me, Jack. I'll get time off for good behavior."

"Very funny," I said.

So, there it was. The ever-constant sea of change lapping up on my shore. Is it possible to get used to change—especially unexpected change? Suddenly turning left when you'd always turned right? Talking about change in the abstract is one thing—but when change creeps up behind you and bangs its drum, how does anyone know what to do?

Until I arrived at college, there was a discernible, identifiable rhythm to my daily life—my weekly life. Wake up, go to class, go home and study, eat dinner, say my prayers, and go to sleep. Repeat. Go to Mass on Sundays. I'd grown comfortable with my life's rhythms.

Then college happened. College gave me the freedom to make decisions about where to go, when to go, and who to spend time with. I had ample opportunity to overthrow my lifelong rhythms. I could decide to skip breakfast, ditch class, or skip doing my homework. I could, but I didn't. A lifetime of Catholic school had conditioned me to be "the good student"—whether my parents were looking over my shoulder or not. I was now the boss of me, and my boss wanted me to continue being "the good student."

Then Diana happened, and I felt out of control—doubting if I really was the boss of me anymore. That was my fear, as I walked down the aisle of Schaeffer Auditorium to the first January *Much Ado* rehearsal.

Betty Bartlett pulled me aside. "Timins, how's your hand?"

"It's fine, Miss B," I said.

"You practice your song?"

I reflected on what Will told me after another awful rendition of the song I was expected to sing. "Practice doesn't make perfect, Red. Perfect practice makes perfect. And you're a lot of miles from perfect."

"Learned my lines, practiced my song, Miss B," I said. It wasn't a lie—and it wasn't the whole truth.

"Good. No more shenanigans."

Then she turned to the assembled cast and said, "Hope you all got plenty of sleep over the holidays. We've got a show that goes on seven weeks from now. This is Shakespeare, boys and girls. Let's make the bard proud. Dress rehearsals will be the 21st, 22nd, 23rd, and 24th of February. You can each invite two friends. First show is February 25th. Let's get started. Act 1, scene 1. On stage please. You can carry your scripts and write in your blocking, but I want everyone off book."

As Miss B lit her next cigarette, I took the stage. I didn't have any lines, but I had to know my entrances and exits.

After my opening scene, I sat in the auditorium, and Diana slid into the seat next to me. Without a word, she took my arm, squeezed it, and kissed me on the cheek. She whispered in my ear, "We'll talk after rehearsal." Then she reseated herself about three rows behind me. She was student teaching this semester, and I think she was working on her lesson plans.

Rehearsal lasted a little more than two hours. It's always slow going when actors are scribbling blocking instructions—so they know where to move, when to move, and how to move. Of course, all stage movement was up to Miss B, who had the habit of saying, "No. I don't like that. Let's try it this way."

Immediately after rehearsal, Diana rejoined me at my seat. "We've gotta get out of here. They're locking up Schaeffer in a few moments. Walk me to my car, okay?"

It was a cold, clear January night.

"Hop in," she said. "I'll get the heater going."

As the car warmed up, she slid across the bench seat and kissed me. I would have recognized that kiss anywhere.

"Did you have a good Christmas?" she asked.

"Yep," I lied. "How about you?"

I didn't spend a lot of time with Diana on Wednesday evening. She'd asked me about my worst Christmas ever, and I tried to make it sound like the complete opposite. I couldn't bring myself to tell her that I'd broken up with my girlfriend, my first love, the erstwhile love of my life—the girlfriend I'd never once mentioned to Diana because I wanted her to kiss me again like she had just before Christmas break.

The morning I left for Christmas break, my roommate Markowski told me that Katie would probably kiss me that way, too. "She must love you a whole hell of a lot. You get a letter damn near every day. Sometimes two. You know how many letters I've gotten from home? Zippity-doo-dah! Zero! You're bottom desk drawer is nothing but Katie's letters. I'll give you odds she'd be happy to kiss you just like Diana does, if you only just let her."

I didn't say anything. John took one look at my face.

"Yeah, I know. You feel guilty just thinking about it, don't you? Well, you shouldn't. You just shouldn't. Be an adult. For Christ's sake, Timins, if you plan to sin—those are your words, not mine—why not sin with someone you've told me you love. What's the attraction of sinning with a stranger?"

Naturally, Diana's Christmas had revolved around her son.

"My mom got Michael a little red wagon. She just put a big bow on it and placed it under the tree in her apartment. It was fun. After we gave him his first ride, he kept climbing back into the wagon and waving his arms, asking for a ride. You'll know what I'm talking about when you have kids. My advice: Don't buy a little red wagon."

That made me laugh.

We both seemed preoccupied on Thursday night—I had a writing assignment in my Advanced Writing class the next day, and Diana was heads-down working on lesson plans. Other than saying hello, and blocking one of our scenes on stage, we were like...well, like strangers. It felt awkward—at least for me. I decided that when I went to Friday's rehearsal, I'd plunk myself down right next to her.

Diana was already seated in the auditorium when I arrived for Friday night's rehearsal. We had about a quarter hour before Miss B would crack the whip, and I could see Diana was already working on something. Nevertheless, I did what I'd decided the night before.

"Well, hello, stranger," she said.

"How's my favorite student teacher?"

She closed her binder and took my arm, just as she had on Wednesday night. She gave me a squeeze and kissed me on the cheek.

"Have you started actually doing any teaching yet?" I asked.

"I'll be starting on Monday. American Lit, 11th grade English. Right now,

Mr. Barrett—he's my supervising teacher—has me sitting off to the side in the front of the room. He teaches and I watch and listen. But we did something really unexpected today."

"Like...?"

"Before Christmas, Mr. Barrett told his two American Lit classes that they would be having a student teacher at the beginning of the second semester. At the time, all he knew was my name. And he told everyone to write down one question they'd like to ask me on the day that I arrived. He mailed all those questions to me over Christmas."

She handed me the note he had enclosed.

Welcome to the world of teaching, Miss Schiavano. I look forward to your arrival at Reading High School and working with you during the next quarter. The questions in this envelope come from my American Literature students—young men and women who will soon be <u>your</u> American Literature students. You'll see that all the questions are signed. I think you'll find that useful. You'll also notice I have not censored any of the questions. (There are two questions that I was tempted to toss, but then, I thought it would be best to leave them there, just as they'd been written. Feel free to address those questions when you arrive. Or not.) I'm fairly certain that the students' inquiries will help you become acquainted with them—sight unseen—and help you know what they might be curious to know about their new teacher, Miss Schiavano. That's you, of course. In the meantime, Merry Christmas.

Sincerely,

William F. Barrett

William F. Barrett
Chairman, Department of English
Reading High School

"Today, I answered their questions."

"What were the two questions that Mr. Barrett was tempted to toss?"

"One of my third period students wanted to know if I'd be interested in dating a young man who was 'mature beyond his years.'"

"Oh, my. What did you say?"

"Well, first of all, I asked Skip Burkhardt to stand up."

"Did he?"

"Oh, yeah. If Mr. Barrett asked you to stand on your head, you only ask if you should do it at your desk or along the wall. Yeah, Burkhardt stood up."

I could tell she was enjoying the retelling of this story.

"What did you say?"

"I said, 'No.' Then he began to sit down, and I told him that I wasn't finished with my answer. That's when Mr. Barrett told him to 'Stand up straight, Mr. Burkhardt. No slouching.' Everyone laughed. Then I said, 'Look around, Mr. Burkhardt. You have all these lovely women, right here in this class. Women your age. Women who understand a sixteen-year-old boy like you, Mr. Burkhardt. By the way, do you have a real first name? Skip isn't your given name, is it?' He shook his head. 'My real name is Franklin.'"

"I pointed out that Franklin was a mouthful for a sixteen-year-old. He said that's why he liked Skip better. So, I told him that when he decided to put Skip away and become Franklin—the name of a man who might well be mature beyond his years—he should give me a call. Then I told him to resume his seat."

"What did Mr. Barrett say?"

"He congratulated me. He said he knew there was a reason I was named after the Roman goddess of the hunt. Said I'd hit my target dead center."

Sometime in the midst of talking about Diana's student teaching experience, Miss B decided it was time to begin rehearsal.

Diana leaned close and whispered, "We have to be quiet now. But stay after rehearsal, Jack. I have a question for you. Okay?"

Rehearsal unexpectedly ran for almost three hours. It was ten o'clock and I was tired. Apparently, so was everyone else, because I found myself sitting in a huge, completely vacant auditorium. I looked around. It was empty. It felt a bit like church on a Sunday afternoon, when everyone has gone home. I knew

Diana wanted me to stay after rehearsal, but I was the only solitary soul in the room. I stood up and stretched and began walking up the aisle.

Suddenly, the door to the lobby opened, and there stood Diana, with two three-ring binders cradled in her arms. She walked towards me, and I walked towards her.

"I was afraid you'd gone home," she said. She placed the binders on one of the theatre seats, put her arms around my neck, and kissed me…and kissed me…and kissed me.

I felt something melting inside, something I'd never felt before. I heard a small voice in my head—a voice that I'd always heard and usually obeyed. Tonight, I decided to disobey. I kissed her back. Passionately. Enthusiastically. Tenderly.

When I finally stopped kissing her, I looked at her warm, well-kissed, smiling face and felt a bit embarrassed.

"Oh, Diana. I'm sorry. Forgive me. I got carried away."

She smiled, rubbed the back of my neck with her fingers, and laughed ever so quietly.

"You don't need forgiveness from me, Jack. It's been quite a while since anyone's kissed me like that."

I know I began to blush. "You said you wanted to ask me a question after rehearsal, didn't you?"

"Yes, I did," she said. She drew my face close to hers, and I could feel the warmth of her breath. "But I think you just gave me the answer I was hoping for."

"I did?" I asked.

"Uh-huh. You certainly did."

She kissed me again. And I surrendered to the moment.

Isn't this exactly what you wanted, Jack? Didn't you say you wanted to explore all the possibilities? Isn't Diana one of those possibilities?

This surrendering, this allowing myself to actually feel what I was feeling, and giving myself permission to feel it—this was new. During all the years I dated Katie, I'd spent untold hours scolding myself whenever the desire to pursue my desires welled up inside me—just as it was welling up now. I'd tell myself that I shouldn't be feeling what I was feeling—warning myself that what I was feeling was somehow unnatural or debased. A lifetime spent in class and in church with nuns and priests cautioned me—with infallible certainty—that pursuing my desires was lustful and sinful—and a straight road to Hell as well.

Despite my older brother, Will, telling me I should sin a bit more often, or my good friend, Sterling, saying that dirty deeds are way more fun than dirty thoughts, I could never convince myself to accept their advice.

Until now.

I have no idea what changed, but something had definitely changed. After another session of insatiable kissing, I asked Diana, "What was it you wanted to ask me?"

She whispered in my ear, as quietly as if the eight hundred empty theatre seats were each occupied. "Would you spend the night with me?"

I don't remember if I said yes, but I know I didn't say no. I'm sure my kisses answered for me.

She gathered up her binders, looped her arm through mine, and as we walked through the lobby, she said, "Michael is spending the night at my mom's. We have all night."

We stepped into the chilly January night air, and Diana huddled close to me.

"I love how warm you are, Jack."

I don't know if it was the cold air or the gentle tone in the things she said, *We have all night* or *I love how warm you are,* but I felt my breath quicken.

When we reached her car, she unlocked the door, handed me the key, and said, "You drive."

She slid ahead of me into the car, and snuggled up against me as we drove to her apartment.

I want to say that my mind was a blank, but it wasn't. For some reason—which I cannot explain—it was filled with poetry. Shakespeare's sonnets invaded my thoughts:

> *Let me not to the marriage of true minds*
> *Admit impediments.*

and

When my love swears that she is made of truth,
I do believe her, though I know she lies.

I wanted this moment—this night—to continue forever. I wanted it to unfold just as her kisses in the aisle promised it would. I knew I would never be able to stop time altogether, but I was sure I could make it linger.

As I parked in front of her apartment, the words of the 17ᵗʰ century English poet, Andrew Marvell, rattled around my brain.

Thus, though we cannot make our Sun
Stand still, yet we will make him run.

All I could do was smile. *Why in the world did Marvell's words pop into my head?*

I had the answer by morning.

Saturday morning, Diana drove me back to Rothermel Hall. I was exhausted. We'd spent the night at her apartment—my sleep was constantly interrupted.

"Get some sleep," she said as she leaned over and kissed me. I could hear the quiet smile in her voice.

"When will I see you again?"

"Definitely Monday. At rehearsal." She smiled an enigmatic smile.

"That's not what I was talking about," I said.

"We can talk about that on Monday, okay? And Jack, you were wonderful last night."

I never realized how much energy was required for lovemaking. Until last night, I had never realized the emotional connection that making love can create. I was certain I was in love. I had made love—I don't know how many times—and I was holding on to the love that I'd made.

I opened the door to my room, exhausted, but in love.

Despite my best efforts to be quiet, my roommate woke up.

"Where the hell have you been, Jack?" He swung his legs over the edge of his bed. "Christ, I've been worried about you all night."

"You knew I was at rehearsal," I said. I know I sounded defensive.

"Until eight o'clock this morning?"

"No."

"So, let me repeat myself. Where the hell have you been?"

Even if I wanted to lie, I couldn't. My mom was right. I wear my heart on my sleeve. I have no idea what John saw on my face, but he looked at me intently and shook his head.

His words came slowly. "Jesus Christ, Timins, you got laid."

Why did "got laid" sound so tawdry—so ugly? So sinful?

"It wasn't like that, John. I went home with Diana last night—she invited me—and she was…I don't know…wonderful. Wonderful to the tenth power. I never knew I could ever feel like I felt last night."

I know John heard me, but he was clearly peeved.

"You could have called to let me know, Jack. I was damn worried about you. Did it ever occur to you that I'd get worried when you didn't come home last night?"

"Sorry."

"I was so worried I went over to Louie's room, figuring that the two of you were catching up after Christmas. But Louie said he hadn't seen you since breakfast, yesterday. So, I came back and tried phoning you at home. I thought maybe you'd gone home to patch things up with Katie. Your dad said you hadn't come home, and as we talked, he sounded just as worried as me. I told him you'd call home as soon as you showed up here."

"Thanks, John. Sorry to make you worry. I'll call my folks."

Perhaps some eighteen-year-old boys can discuss their first sexual experience with their parents—a night of supreme embarrassment and delirious pleasure—but I wasn't one of them.

Sure, Dad. She's a senior—six years older than me. She's got her own apartment off campus, lives next to her mother who takes care of her two-year-old son while she does her student teaching, and she's wonderful in bed. You'd like her a lot.

So, I lied.

I struggled with my feelings until Sunday afternoon. I phoned Father Gerry.
"Father Gaffney," he said.

I blurted out, "Father Gerry, it's Jack Timins. I need to see you."

"Hi Jack," Father Gerry said. He sounded calm. "Are you okay? You sound upset."

"I am upset—and I need to see you as soon as possible. I couldn't think of anyone else to call."

"Alright. I'll be here at the rectory for the rest of the day," he said. "I've got no plans to do anything. Nothing you can tell me will be worse than the Philadelphia Eagles lame 5-9 season. If you want, come on down. I'll put on a pot of coffee and we'll sit in the kitchen and talk."

This is why I always loved Father Gerry. He had a gift for defusing my persistent childhood fear that I'd end up in Hell's fiery furnace.

"I'll be right down," I said. I grabbed my overcoat, my maroon and gold Kutztown knit cap to keep my ears warm, and my warmest gloves. Then I walked straight down Main Street to the east side of town.

When I rang the doorbell, the rectory door opened immediately.

"Must be something important going on, Jack," Father Gerry said. "You got here in record time. Come on in. Take off your coat, and join me in the kitchen. I've got fresh coffee and doughnuts."

As I took a seat at the kitchen table, I noticed that my coffee cup was already full. In the middle of the table, a plate of doughnuts kept the quart of milk and the sugar bowl company. Father Gerry handed me a teaspoon even as he put on his stole—his official and required confessional garb.

"What's up?" he asked. He sounded kind, concerned.

It took me a moment to find my voice. I practically whispered, "I had sex, Father."

For a moment he said nothing. I had no idea what he might say. I certainly wasn't the first confessant to say those three words to him, and I wouldn't be the last either.

He sat down. "Of course, you did," he said calmly. "Sooner or later, almost everybody does. It's what human beings do. It's the biological imperative, Jack. Cole Porter even wrote a song about it. 'Birds do it, Bees do it, even educated fleas do it…'"

"Priests and nuns don't," I said.

"Sure, they do," he said, "and then they go to Confession. Just like everyone else."

I wasn't sure if he was kidding, or being serious.

"Sex is a very special category, Jack. Look, some people have the urge to rob banks. Some are tempted to kill another fellow human being. Some. But almost all of us are tempted to have sex."

"And some of us give into that temptation, Father Gerry."

"Okay, Jack. Just so you know, you're in good company. Talk to me. I'll listen. You came here because you have something you feel you have to say, right? Just talk to me about what happened, Jack."

It took me a moment to begin. I was nervous—and a little scared. The last time I confessed anything remotely like this, I was told I had to break up with my girlfriend. But Father Gerry had always proved himself to be a kind, gentle human being first—and a priest second. I'm pretty sure the Catholic Church would take a dim view of that, but I needed someone who understood me as an 18-year-old who was battling temptation—an 18-year-old who finally decided that losing that battle was worth it.

So, I told him. I began by telling him about the kiss—actually kisses, plural. I told him how outrageously good Diana's passionate kisses made me feel. Then I told him about accepting her invitation to spend the night.

"We did a lot of kissing, Father. And a lot of touching. And a lot of…uh… *et cetera.*"

He gave me a knowing smile. Like I said, a human being first, a priest second.

"Did all that *et cetera* meet your expectations?"

"Would it be a sin if I said yes?"

He shook his head with a quiet laugh. "Oh, Jack, you'd never made love before?"

"No, Father. Never. I wanted to—at least I think I wanted to, but my inner voice always ambushed me. Always. Until Friday night, all I ever heard was

Thou shalt not."

"Let me ask, did you hear any *Thou shalt nots* this time?"

I put both hands atop my head and nodded.

"Yep. But I didn't care, Father Gerry. I just did not care. A beautiful woman wanted me to spend the night with her"—I took a sip of my coffee—"and I wanted to spend the night with her. It's not like it was her fault."

"It was a good night then?" Father Gerry asked.

"Good? Oh, my God. It was fantastic. How can something that feels so incredible—so wonderful—so…I don't even have the words for how I felt, Father Gerry. I could run through every superlative I know, and I'd still fall short. Damn it, how could that be wrong?"

I waited for Father Gerry's reply as he sipped his coffee and took a bite of his glazed doughnut. Clearly, he was thinking about his reply.

"Jack, the survival of the human race depends on that incredible, wonderful feeling you're talking about. Sure, people have sex because they want to have children, but most people have sex because there is no pleasure in the world like it. Nothing even close."

The voice in my head wanted to challenge Father Gerry's comment by asking, *How do you know?* But he probably knew the same way I did. Maybe, many years ago, before he decided on the priesthood, a beautiful young woman whispered an invitation in his ear.

"So, what should I do, Father Gerry? I don't feel the least bit sorry. I'm pretty sure I have to be sorry for my sins, and promise to go and sin no more, to receive absolution."

Father Gerry gave me the priestly look that said, "Yep." He paused. "Do you think you love this woman, Jack?"

"Would that make a difference, Father?"

"Love always make a difference, Jack. Love is larger than lust—love is more generous, more open, and far more fulfilling than lust. Lust satisfies the body, but love satisfies the soul."

"I really don't know if I love her, Father. I wish I knew, but I'm just not sure. Besides, how would I know if it's love or it's lust?"

"Experience."

"And how can I get experience if experiencing it is a sin?"

"Well, it appears you've had your first full dose of experience, Jack. And I may be wrong, but it sounds like you plan to get another full dose of experience as soon as possible. Am I right?"

I couldn't meet his eyes. I stared at my empty coffee cup.

"Welcome to the human race, Jack." I could hear the calm, parental tone in his voice. "As an adult, you get to make your own choices—wise or foolish. That's the difference between being an adult and being a child. The church hasn't declared sex outside of marriage a sin because they're mean and want to make the lives of teenage boys unbearable. They declare it a sin because it's dangerous, my friend, for a whole host of reasons. When it comes to love and sex, people often get hurt, even when neither person meant the other any harm. It's like my mother told me when I was your age, 'Gerry, sex is the only sin that causes people.' Your young lady learned that the hard way. Be sure you don't. I hope you're being careful."

"I am," I assured him. "And you're right about people getting hurt, Father Gerry." That's when I told him about ending my relationship with Katie just before Christmas.

He gave me an incredibly sympathetic look. He stood up and walked to the sink. He stared out the window at the dying winter light as he rinsed out his coffee cup.

"I don't think you're ready to go to Confession right now, Jack. And I completely understand why. You're enjoying your sins way too much for me to give you absolution." He turned and gave me an amused look. "It's like you've had ice cream for the very first time, and the only word in your head is 'More.'"

We both laughed. I stood up and took my cup to the sink.

"That's true, Father. Thanks for listening. I'm not sure where this relationship is going, but I need to tell her how I feel."

"You do that, Jack. And let me know how it goes—and how you are, too. I'm usually here on Sunday afternoons, doing the New York Times crossword and eating doughnuts. If you need to talk—or if you get tired of ice cream and want to confess and tell me you're truly sorry for your sins—I'm here."

I've known priests practically from the day I was born. Some were martinets, cold and unforgiving, relentlessly adhering to all the rules and regulations. And then there was Father Gerry, who always made me feel okay about being a flawed human being.

Chapter 12

WATERSHED MOMENTS

Winter and Spring 1966

I'd gone to see Father Gerry without ever once feeling sorry for what I'd done. I knew that spending the night with Diana was forbidden—and I also knew that I had enjoyed what was clearly forbidden—what the Catholic Church designates as a mortal sin. I phoned Father Gerry because I worried that the fate of my immortal soul might be in jeopardy, but therein was my dilemma: Being sincerely sorry for one's sins is essential to making a "good Confession," but I wasn't sorry, ergo, no "good Confession."

My lack of contrition—I didn't even feel a vague ambivalence at that moment—surprised me more than I realized. Before Diana, I'd always felt guilty and contrite.

"That's just who you are, Timins," Markowski would say. "Catholic from the top of your head to the soles of your feet."

Could he be wrong?

I decided it was time to have a stern talk with myself. After sleeping the morning away, I decided it was time to rise and shine—even if I didn't feel much like shining. I walked into the men's bathroom with my shaving kit, and I stared into the mirror, looking hard at the dark circles still under my eyes. I rubbed the stubble on my cheek. I looked really tired.

I spoke to my reflection. "What's going on, Timins? You spent an entire night with a lovely woman, sharing her bed and doing everything that twelve years of Catholic School have explicitly told you are forbidden to anyone outside of marriage."

"Yeah, I did," I said to myself.

"And if you died this very second, you'd spend eternity in Hell."

"Yeah, I would."

"So, what's going on in that head of yours?"

"I have no idea."

I'm pretty sure I'd gone to see Father Gerry because I wanted to find out what was going on in this head of mine. I'm not sure I found any answers.

The same questions that had plagued me last night as I returned to my dorm afflicted me still.

Am I in love with Diana?

Does Diana love me?

When would I see Diana again?

Why is what we did sinful? Diana enjoyed it. Me, too.

What was it we learned in Religion class about love, marriage, and sex?

My mind drifted back to a rather humorous moment in my high school Religion class—I think I was a junior—when Sister Angelica explained that every marital bed is shared by three: the man, the woman, and God. As Sister turned to put the *Man>God<Woman* diagram on the blackboard, someone spoke out just loud enough for the class to hear, "Sounds a bit crowded to me."

The laughter that erupted, quelled quickly as Sister Angelica whirled round and gave us all a withering look. She was not amused.

Still, that memory always provoked amusement.

Perhaps my night with Diana was a watershed moment.

Immediately, it was last September, and I was back in my first day of English 101 with Dr. Gable.

After taking role and making meticulous notations in his roll book, Dr. Gable stepped around his desk, folded his hands, and surveyed a sea of waiting freshman faces.

"My English 101 class will be the most important course you will ever take in your life." His articulation was clipped and precise—to say nothing of his audacious assertion. It might be hyperbole, but no one contradicted him.

Who was this professor? What we saw was a middle-aged man with no sharp edges. His balding head was round, his face was round, his cheeks were round, his eyeglasses had round lenses, and he himself was…well…comfortably round. Not obese, just round.

But he was impeccably dressed in a brown, three-piece, tweed suite. His tie, in Kutztown's school colors, had a neatly knotted Windsor. If any of us thought this was for show on the first day of school, we were mistaken. Dr. Gable proved to be—how did my classmate, Patty, put it?—"a fashion plate."

"Ladies and gentlemen," Dr. Gable said, "Today is Monday. I am asking you to have your first writing assignment completed by Wednesday—two days hence. My goal is to assess each of you as writers. Since I am not a mind reader, I'll have to be an essay reader."

Louie, a freshman with whom I'd struck up a conversation in our earlier Music Appreciation class, leaned over and whispered, "Wow, Jack. Day one and already we've got an essay due."

Louie raised his hand.

"Yes, young man," said Dr. Gable.

"Dr. Gable, do you have a topic in mind, or may we choose whatever topic we wish?"

"What's your name, young man?"

Louie paused for a moment, and then replied, "Louis, sir."

"Well, Louis," Dr. Gable walked down the aisle to Louie's desk, "that's an excellent question, and I particularly appreciated that you said 'may we choose' rather than 'can we choose.' And no, you may not choose your own topic, because I've already chosen one."

Dr. Gable returned to the front of the room.

"Ladies and gentlemen, your topic will be," and here he turned to the blackboard, "*Watershed Moments*." He wrote *Watershed Moments* on the blackboard in exquisite handwriting.

"Your essays may not exceed 1000 words, nor be less than 500 words. They must be typewritten on standard, clean, 8½ x 11 typing paper, or written in ink on standard, clean, 8½ x 11 three-hole notebook paper. Essays written in pencil, or on sheets torn out of spiral notebooks, or with words or sentences crossed out, will be unacceptable. I am a stickler for the proper presentation of content, as well as the content itself. Are there any questions?"

From somewhere in the back of the room, a young lady raised her hand.

Dr. Gable asked, "Please tell me your name, young lady, and then ask your question."

"My name is Grace, Dr. Gable. I'll be happy to write about a watershed moment, but first, I've got to find out what it is. I have no idea."

"Thank you, Grace. I can enlighten you. If you will all take out your notebooks, I'll write the meaning of a watershed moment on the board."

He went to the board, and wrote in his beautiful script.

A watershed moment is a turning point, the exact moment that changes the direction of an activity or situation. A watershed moment is a dividing point, after which things will never be the same. It is considered momentous, though a watershed moment is often recognized only in hindsight.

I struggled to find a watershed moment I wanted to write about. I made a list:

- My First Confession and First Communion.
- Serving my first Mass in third grade.
- Serving for the Bishop when he came for Confirmation.
- Getting my first job as a paperboy and actually buying my parents Christmas gifts with my own money.
- Falling in love with Katie when we were lifeguards at Heil Pool.
- Earning my varsity letter on Notre Dame's undefeated football team.

I finally settled on the day I received my acceptance to Kutztown. I figured, if being accepted by a college isn't a watershed moment, then nothing is.

I asked Louie what he planned to write about.

Louie jokingly said, "I was thinking I'd write about the day I was born, but I just can seem to recall anything about that day."

"Thanks, Louie. Now that I know what you are not writing about…"

"I'm writing about my first home run in Little League. That was really something. My mom, dad, aunt, and uncle were all in the stands—a bunch of neighbors, too. They went crazy. Until that homer, my teammates just saw me as a short, skinny second-baseman. Suddenly, I was the star of the team. I played football and baseball every year since then."

It occurred to me that if I were given that same assignment now, I'd be tempted to write about my night with Diana. It was definitely a life-altering moment. After meeting Diana, after spending the night with Diana, nothing would ever be the same.

But I wouldn't. I couldn't.

Some life-altering moments are too important to be public—too meaningful to be broadcast to anyone else, except perhaps in modest before-and-after references.

The next few weeks were a blur. I attended class every day, and every evening I went to rehearsal. *Much Ado* was taking shape, and my small singing part improved when Miss Bartlett decided to make me a trio.

Much Ado's last regular rehearsal was the Friday that preceded our six scheduled performances. Our final week would be all dress rehearsals—a full show with costumes and lights each night.

After that first night with Diana, I was on an emotional high. I wanted to be with her as much as possible—even though she was off campus all the time except for rehearsals. As a student teacher, she drove to Reading High School in the morning, drove home in the afternoon, and drove to rehearsals in the evening. That was in addition to looking after her son, too. She was exhausted—and I was an 18-year-old boy, too foolish and too horny to understand what had actually happened between us. Making things worse, I was positive that I was in love with this woman who had allowed me to share her bed and her body on one fateful Friday night.

At rehearsals, she had lesson-planning to do, while I did my best to get my reading done and complete whatever homework had been assigned. What I really wanted was another evening of passionate kisses and lovemaking. There were a few stolen moments, but far fewer than I had expected.

Right around the beginning of February, at the beginning of one of our regular rehearsals, Diana asked me to stay behind. I stayed. After everyone had gone home, she put all her work aside and gave me her full and undivided attention.

From the look on her face, I knew what was about to happen.

"I think I owe you an apology, Jack."

I sat in silence. *Apology? For what?*

"The truth is, I've been celibate since long before Michael was born. I'd begun to feel like a nun."

I looked up. "I went to twelve years of Catholic school, Diana. You don't have to talk to me about celibacy…or nuns."

The comment was supposed to be comical, but neither of us felt inclined to laugh. We both fell silent for the moment.

"I needed you that first Friday night after we came back from Christmas break," she said. "I never realized that it would be your first time—until—well, you know what happened."

"Yeah, Diana, I remember it only too well." I felt embarrassed. I'm sure I began to blush. "I sure made a fool of myself in record time that night, didn't I."

"No, Jack. No, you didn't. You were wonderful. I was flattered that anyone would find me as attractive as you found me, and respond…as quickly as you responded."

"I made a hell of a mess."

"No harm done, Jack." Her voice was quiet and soft. "That Friday night was one of the most memorable nights of my life. Those kinds of messes are easily cleaned up. But other messes…" She stopped herself in mid-sentence, clearly frustrated.

"I should have said something, Jack. I should have warned you that whatever happens between us, please do not fall in love with me. I'd planned to say something like that as we drove to my place, but we were both just so… involved? Is that the right word? I wanted you, and you wanted me. And we spent the night giving ourselves to each other."

"And I fell in love with you, Diana."

"I can see that."

"I think about you all the time. And when I'm not thinking about you, I'm daydreaming about you. I have no idea how to make my feelings for you stop."

I was in uncharted territory. Madly in love—physically and emotionally—with a beautiful older woman. A beautiful older woman with a son. What was I thinking? Why was I so willing to sin with her? I was addicted, and I didn't know how to quit.

"I know, Jack. I'm sorry. That was my fault. I allowed myself to get swept off my feet when I was a junior, and I have a son to prove it. It took me more than a year to get my feet firmly under me again, and my son and my work must be my first considerations."

I knew she was right. But knowing something and feeling something—well, those things can be miles apart.

"Neither of us can continue this way. We just can't. I like you, Jack. A lot."

"I understand," I said. I really didn't understand, but I didn't know what else to say. My heart ached.

"We're both in very different places, in different times of our lives. I hope to get a teaching job by June, and who knows where I'll end up? You've got three more years to go. Right here. You can't leave. You shouldn't even think about leaving. You're going to be on stage, performing, being the thespian you were born to be. Who knows where any of that will take you? At some point, you'll find someone—someone who's not me—someone to share your love and your passion with."

I felt suddenly sad, completely drained. Empty. I had no words.

"Like I said, Jack, I owe you an apology. My life is out there. Your life is right here."

She leaned toward me, kissed me gently on the lips, and stood up.

"See you tomorrow night."

I felt as empty as that empty auditorium. I sat until a janitor walked by and asked me why I was still there.

"Gotta lock up," he said.

I pushed myself up and returned to my dorm room. As soon as I walked in, Markowski asked me what was wrong. Apparently, my heart was on my sleeve, as usual.

Exhausted, I sprawled across my bed, my head on my pillow.

"Diana said, 'I'm sorry, but I can't be in love with you, and you can't be in love with me.' She says my life is here and her life is out there." My voice was flat and emotionless.

"Sorry, Timins. I really am," John said. "I know how you feel about her. My sister always told me that it's a bitch when love and logic collide. Looks like you've had a collision tonight."

What's the adage? *'Tis better to have loved and lost, than never to have loved at all.* In December, I was the one telling the woman I loved that I couldn't love her anymore, and, barely a month later, I was the one being told. It didn't matter which side of the equation one was on—they both felt rotten, and Tennyson's perspective offered little consolation.

I wasn't sure I could take any more watershed moments.

It was a bit awkward, continuing to rehearse with Diana, finally realizing that my feelings for her were much like the title of Shakespeare's play, *Much Ado About Nothing*.

Our performances went off without any problems. The school newspaper said wonderful things about the staging and the costumes, and life went on. With no evening rehearsals, no Diana in my life, no dorm counselor to abuse, and no impulse or reasons to write letters to Katie, my life reverted to the banal and predictable.

Get up. Shower, shave, brush my teeth. Get dressed. Go to breakfast. Go to class. Go to lunch. Go to class/library. Go to dinner. Go back to the dorm. Brush my teeth. Get undressed. Go to bed.

Repeat.

I did write a few letters to my parents.

And one more predictable thing. I went to Confession. Once again, Father Gerry and I gathered around his kitchen table.

"I came to see you in *Much Ado*, Jack," he said as he poured me a cup of coffee. "I really enjoyed it. It's none of my business, but did I see your love interest?"

"Yes, Father Gerry. It was the woman who played Margaret."

"The maid? The one who sang with you?"

"Yes, Father, that was her."

He shook his head knowingly. "We are all in the thrall of beauty, Jack. I can see why you succumbed."

No priest had ever said that to me before. He might as well have said, "No wonder you sinned." I'm glad he didn't.

"I'm here to make my confession, Father Gerry, if that's alright."

I can't say that I was sincerely sorry for my sins, but I was sorry. I had begun to understand how sex and love and lust get jumbled up inside people's minds—and my mind in particular—and how people get hurt. I've come to believe that hurting people is the real sin…and that's what I was truly sorry for.

Then it was Holy Week. On Holy Thursday night, my brother Will showed up unexpectedly at my dormitory door.

I opened my door when he knocked because almost nobody knocks. I thought it must be a stranger—and there stood Will.

"Hey, Will, spring break doesn't begin until tomorrow night," I said lightheartedly.

"We have to get home," Will said. It was almost a whisper. His somber face spoke of sadness and pain.

"What's the matter, Will?"

"It's Uncle Ted. He's dead."

I think I said "What?" but I really don't remember.

Another watershed moment.

Chapter 13
WORDS FAIL
Spring 1966

Dad drove me back to college the Sunday after spring break in our '62 Dodge Dart. A bright blue sky and warming weather prompted us to roll the windows down as we went. My youngest brother, Dennis, who had gotten his driver's permit three weeks earlier—every teenager's treasured rite of passage—sat in the front seat next to Dad.

As we drove west along Route 22, Dennis fiddled with the radio from time to time, looking for good songs. After a few twists and turns, he dialed up WABC in New York City and landed mid-song on *California Dreamin'*. Clearly in a good mood, Dennis sang along with the Mamas & the Papas, while I sorta hummed along from the backseat. Dennis's mood had gotten a boost when Dad told him he'd be driving home, once I'd been dropped off and they were out of the bumper-to-bumper campus traffic. I could see that Dennis was anxious to get behind the wheel.

"It'll be my longest drive so far, Jack. I've gotten real tired of driving around Food Lane's parking lot."

"We all got our first driving lessons in big empty parking lots, Denny," I explained to my brother. "Dad always picks big parking lots in the early morning because you can't hit something that isn't there. Isn't that right, Dad?"

Normally, Dad would toss in a comic quip like, "I'm sure Dennis could hit plenty of things that aren't there," but Dad didn't respond at all. During the entire drive back to campus, I don't think Dad said more than a handful of words.

"You got everything, Son?" "Okay, time to go."

I could see that his mind was elsewhere—always on his driving, of course—but I knew he was thinking about his brother whom we'd buried just a few days after Easter. Dad's only brother, who had survived the Depression and fought in World War II against Hitler's army, was gone. Uncle Ted's uproarious laughter and enthusiastic embraces…gone forever.

A kind of impenetrable sadness surrounded Dad, and that was something I'd never seen before. He'd make eye contact in the rearview mirror with me for a moment—I could see the pain in his eyes—and then he'd just look away. I wished I could have taken his pain away, but Mom said that the only thing that could do that was time.

I hoped Mom was right, but I remember what Dad said to me when we left the viewing at the Berwick Funeral Home for little eight-year-old Jeffrey Seitz. Jeffrey was our baseball coach's son—and our team's batboy—and he died tragically and suddenly. Then our coach quit. I asked my dad about our coach's quitting.

"You saw young Jeffrey in his casket, Jack. His dad decided to bury his son in his baseball uniform. Just imagine him seeing all of you out there playing baseball—in that same uniform. Some reminders are just too painful, Son. Some wounds never heal. He buried his coaching career with his son."

Dad was still at Uncle Ted's and Aunt Marian's when Will and I arrived home from Kutztown that Thursday night before spring break. Dad would be making the funeral arrangements.

During our drive home, I asked Will how he was feeling.

"I don't know, Red. I'm just feeling numb. I almost feel that I'll wake up tomorrow, and this will all be nothing but a bad dream."

"How about Dad?" I asked.

"It's probably too soon to tell. His heart has got to be breaking. On the phone, he kept asking Aunt Marian, 'Why would Ted kill himself? Why didn't he call me?'"

As we drove along in silence, listening to the radio, Will made an absent-minded comment.

"At least someone else besides Uncle Ted will win when we play Crazy Eights."

Crazy Eights was the card game that Uncle Ted always won. No one knew how.

Will's comment started me thinking about the vacations we'd all taken at Lake Oneida in upstate New York. Grandma and Grandpa lived in Utica, New York, and they'd always wanted to get both our families to come north for "a summer vacation at the lake."

"Grandma said, we'd love it, Will. And looking back on it now, I'm sure we did."

"Jesus, Red. Remember the bungalow?" he started laughing just thinking about it.

"You mean '*The Refugee Camp*?'"

"Yeah. Grandma said the bungalow would sleep ten."

"It did sleep ten. Kinda."

Will snorted. "Only if everyone was laid out like a mosaic on the floor. If you had to get up at night to pee, you'd manage to step on damn near everyone on the way to the bathroom."

"I got stepped on plenty," I commented.

We both laughed.

"And remember swimming in Lake Oneida?"

"Oh, yeah. Lake Oneida. More like Bug Beach. Boy, I sure remember the huge patches of dead bugs floating on top of the water and washing up on the beach."

"Don't forget the dead fish floating in, too."

I don't know why we found any of this funny—except it was. For three summers, we spent a full week all together at *The Refugee Camp*, eating breakfast each morning before walking to Bug Beach. After returning, we'd eat hotdogs and hamburgers that Grandpa cooked on the grill, play Crazy Eights until past midnight, and sleep in our sleeping bags until Grandma called us for breakfast the next morning.

Right after dinner, we always played Crazy Eights at the dining room table—all six adults and four kids—and it didn't matter who dealt the hand or where Uncle Ted was sitting. He always won. Always. Well, it seemed like always.

One evening, after Uncle Ted had won for the umpteenth time, Moira told her dad that he would have to trade places with her. He did…and he still won.

"Remember that, Will? Moira said it was witchcraft."

"Yeah, Red, I remember."

A brief, sad silence descended once more.

Will turned off the radio. "One thing's for sure, Uncle Ted was a wizard at the piano. I'm going to miss that."

"Whenever Aunt Marian would say that they were going to visit someone, the first thing Uncle Ted would ask was, 'Do they own a piano?'"

"That's right. No piano, no visit."

I pointed out how much I enjoyed Dad and Uncle Ted "tickling the ivories" together—whether at our home or theirs.

"That's why Grandma made sure the bungalow had a piano," Will said. "She used it as bait to get Uncle Ted to come up to Lake Oneida."

Our car ride home, while only an hour, was an Uncle Ted lovefest, filled with remember-whens.

"Remember when Grandma told us that Dad and Uncle Ted went to enlist on the very same day—in January, 1942—without telling her or her mother? Uncle Ted said that everyone had to do his duty, and serve his country."

"Remember when Uncle Ted said he made more money in the Army during WWII by playing the piano in Officers' Clubs than by fighting the Germans?"

"Remember when Uncle Ted told us he actually got to play Hitler's piano at Berchtesgaden—the Eagle's Nest—when the U.S. Army turned Hitler's Bavarian retreat into an Officers' Club?"

"Remember that night at Lake Oneida when there was that fire in a nearby bungalow? We all stood around and watched the firemen do their best to contain the fire, and all Uncle Ted said was 'I hope there wasn't a piano in there.'"

"Remember when Dad and Uncle Ted took us to the Polo Grounds to see Willie Mays play? How old were we? Were we even in Little League?"

"Remember when Dad and Uncle Ted would be watching a Giants game on TV, and something would happen, and they'd both be inches from the television screen screaming at one of the football players as if he could actually hear them?"

"Remember when Uncle Ted said, 'Never root for the Giants. They'll always break your heart.'"

On our drive home, Will and I discovered that there were many moments to remember—many reasons for our heartache.

My trip back to campus took a little more time than the usual hour or so—probably because six-thousand students were returning at the same time. We found ourselves in a very slow, rolling traffic jam on Main Street, about two blocks from my dorm. I told Dad to turn left.

"Your dorm's another two blocks," Dad said.

"I know, Dad, but I can walk the rest of the way. Remember, I'm returning, not moving in. If you turn now, you'll be out of this traffic, and Dennis can drive you home."

I had almost nothing to carry. A gym bag filled with some books and underwear Mom had laundered, but nothing else. The dark, navy-blue suit I'd worn to my uncle's funeral was hanging in my closet at home.

"Okay," Dad said, as he turned left onto College Boulevard.

"Just pull up in front of Kemp—that's the building right there." I pointed at a one-story brick building crowded by maple trees.

Dad pulled up to the curb, and I hopped out on the driver's side.

Dennis started laughing, "Does that street sign say *Normal Avenue*?"

"Yes, it does, Denny."

"Why would anyone name a street Normal?"

"Why not?" I replied. "It's better than Abnormal Avenue, right?"

Dad stepped out of the car, and I could see he was doing his best to smile. I hugged him. "I love you, Dad. We all love you." As I embraced my father, I could feel his sadness, his weariness, his resignation. Dad and I stepped around to the curb even as Dennis scooted across the bench seat to get behind the wheel.

"I'm in the homestretch here, Dad. The end of my first year. I'll be home before the end of May, and then I'm back for another summer at Heil Pool."

Dad looked at me, his usual broad grin smothered beneath his grief. He sighed deeply. "I love you, too, Son." He looked toward campus. "I know you'll do well. You always have. I'll tell your mom that we got you back safe and sound. Give your mom a call tonight, okay?" He opened the car door and slipped into the passenger seat.

I walked around the car to offer the "new driver" some brotherly advice. "Do you know the best way to get back to Main Street?" I asked.

"Not really."

"Okay, let me make it easy." I pointed straight ahead. "You're on Normal. So, it's Normal to Noble to Main. Left on Noble. Right on Main."

"Second star to the right and straight on 'til morning?" Dennis quipped.

"Hey, wise guy, did you hear what I said?"

"Relax, Red, relax. Normal to Noble to Main. I got it."

Perhaps there was something about being in college that made me feel slightly parental. I lowered my voice, and it suddenly struck me that the seriousness in my tone sounded just like Dad. "Dennis, you be real careful. Okay? You've graduated from grocery store parking lots to real roads with real cars and real people. Your objective is to get home without hitting anything—and without anything hitting you, either. You think you can do that?"

Dennis flashed me a determined smile. "Yeah. I can do that."

Then I lowered my head and whispered in his ear. "Denny, take care of Dad, okay."

Dennis nodded.

I walked around to the curb and leaned over to place my hand on Dad's arm as it rested on the window ledge. "Safe trip, Dad. Love you."

I stood back from the car and Dennis pulled away, slowly at first, waving high out the driver's window as he headed down Normal Avenue.

I turned to walk across campus, wondering if John had beaten me back to the dorm.

He had. When I walked into our dorm room, he was sitting at his desk.

As I tossed my gym bag on my bed, John remarked, "I was wondering when you'd get back."

I flopped down on my bed, saying nothing.

"I've been worried about you, Timins. Ever since I got your cryptic note." He pulled a crumpled piece of paper from his pants pocket and began reading. "Sorry John. Family emergency. Gone home. See you when I get back."

"Yeah. Look, John, I know I should have called you at home. To explain.

Except I really didn't want to talk about it until we were together—you know, until we were here, face to face."

John pulled his chair over to my bed. "Well, we're here, face to face. What's going on? Are you okay?"

I sat up. I wasn't sure how to begin. I looked up at John and I could see the concern on his face. "My Uncle Ted committed suicide." I could hear the disbelief in my voice. "He hanged himself sometime on April 7th—Holy Thursday. He's my dad's only brother."

John gently punched the mattress. "Shit," he whispered, and his shoulders slumped. "Suicide?"

"Yeah. He got fired from his printing press job, and when he got home, he saw that his music gig was cancelled for that weekend. Bad news, times two, on the same day." I realized I was listening to myself, as if listening carefully enough to my own words would help me make sense of it all. It didn't.

"His daughter, my cousin Moira, came home from school and found him in the basement. Thursday afternoon. My dad got a phone call from my Aunt Marian—that's Uncle Ted's wife. Jesus, John, she's a complete wreck. My dad jumped into the car, and he got to my Uncle Ted's house about the same time the coroner arrived." I didn't have to say anything more.

"How's your dad?"

"I really don't know. I've never seen my dad so sad. Dad drove me back to school today, and he hardly said a word. He brought my brother, Dennis, along, so Denny could drive home. Denny just got his learner's permit a month ago."

"I don't think I need to ask you how Easter was."

"Thanks. How was your Easter?"

"Well, in keeping with my personal habit of shunning religion, I didn't go to church. But I made sure the house was all vacuumed and everything was dusted and picked up for when my mom's relatives swept in for the annual Easter dinner. I even set the table. The best china, the sterling flatware. Carefully folded spring-green napkins. My mom was impressed."

"We muddled through at home. I went to Easter Mass, but I was thoroughly uninspired. It felt like everything was out of sync. In slow motion."

"Yeah. Jack, I'm so sorry about your uncle. If you ever want to talk about it…"

"I do. But I don't even know where to begin. You know, John, when I was in grade school, and I'd get together with other kids from school—or with the neighborhood kids—we'd sometimes talk about our uncles, aunts, and cousins. Just stuff about relatives. Some relatives walked on water, and some were real nightmares. I'd always tell my friends that if I had my choice of anyone in the world to be my uncle, I'd choose my Uncle Ted."

"Sounds like you really loved him."

"Yeah. He was warm and loving and gentle—a lot like my dad—and funny and bonkers about the New York Giants. And he could play anything on the piano." I could feel my voice crack. "Anything." I started crying.

John sat down beside me, just sitting there, just being there.

I shook my head. "As I walked back to the car at the cemetery, Mom said it's a shame that Uncle Ted is in Hell. She had a real tortured look on her face."

"You don't believe that, do you, Jack?"

"Suicide's a mortal sin, John."

"Yeah, that's what I've heard—but years ago, when I was attending religion class, I just couldn't wrap my head around the whole business of sin and Heaven and Hell."

"Why not?"

"Look, Jack, you said your uncle was a good man. Do you really believe that?"

"Absolutely."

"So, let's say a really good person has one moment of weakness—a moment of despair—and he commits suicide. Why send the guy to Hell? Does one bad act erase a lifetime of good deeds? Or flip the situation around. Let's say Hitler had gone to Confession just before he died? Yeah, I know he committed suicide in his bunker, but let's say the Russian shelling killed him. Does he get to pass through the Pearly Gates? Hitler was responsible for millions of deaths. If he goes to Confession and gets absolution, does he get a free pass? Is St. Peter gonna be standing there saying, 'This way, Adolf'?"

"I'm not a religious scholar, John. I just do my best to follow the rules."

"That may be, but if Hitler could end up in Heaven and your uncle goes to Hell, where's the justice? Where's the fairness?"

He paused for a moment.

"Let's talk about the rules, okay? Let's talk about the rules in the Garden of Eden."

I think I looked a bit confused.

"What did God tell Adam and Eve? He said, 'Don't eat the apples of that tree.' Right?"

"Yeah."

"Did He warn them about the snake?"

"I don't think so."

"The answer is no, if you believe the *Book of Genesis*."

"But they disobeyed God, the Father."

"They were kids, Jack. Fresh from the hand of the Almighty—well, Adam, anyway. Eve was fresh from Adam's rib. Kids. What did they know about anything? They couldn't have been worldly-wise because the world had just been created. They didn't know what the rules were. Just being alive must have been a real trip."

"God told them they couldn't eat the fruit from that specific tree." My voice had lost some of its conviction.

"Yeah, you said that. Did God Almighty say if they ate the apple they'd be kicked out? Do you think Adam and Eve could know anything of consequences? They were newbies, Jack. The first human beings ever. God's greatest creation, right? Let me ask. Have you ever broken any rules at home?"

"Sure. I expect almost everyone has."

"And your dad kicked you out, right?"

"What? No."

"Why not?"

"'Cause I was just a kid. I probably didn't know any better."

"You didn't get the old heave-ho?"

I couldn't help but laugh. "No."

"Let me see if I understand. Your dad let you come home even after you disobeyed him?"

"Sure, why not? He's my dad."

"Really? Then your dad's way more decent than God, the Father—the God every priest and preacher declares to be almighty, all-loving, and all-merciful. They're talking about the God who threw Adam and Eve out on their keisters after their first mistake. Their very first mistake. No do-overs. No second chances."

"Come on, John, the story of the Garden of Eden is just a story. It's not literally true—at least, most people don't think humans landed here fully formed only 6,000 years ago. I certainly don't."

"Good for you. But if there's a moral to the story, it doesn't paint a pretty picture of the Lord God, Almighty, does it?"

"I suppose not."

"No supposing, Jack. God, Almighty, is not a nice person. Can you say Sodom and Gomorrah? How about Noah's Flood? Reading *Genesis* in religion class is what started turning me away from the Catholic Church—and religion, in general. I was in third grade. I was maybe eight or nine. I said to myself, *I wouldn't want him for my dad.* After reading *Genesis*, I could never figure out how Father Vandervelt could conclude that God was all-loving, all-merciful, and all-just. So much of what we were learning in religion class was beyond belief."

"That's what faith is all about, John."

John looked a bit baffled...and disappointed. "Faith? Is that what I need?"

He stood up and snatched something from the top of his desk. John tossed his copy of *Time* magazine across to me.

"Tell that to *Time* magazine," he said. "Looks like their editors are running a bit low in the faith department, too. Look at the latest edition. They published it this past Good Friday. Great timing, I'd say."

I looked at the cover. It consisted of three words, in bold red letters, against a stark black background. There was the question I'd begun asking: Is God Dead?

"Is this a joke? What the hell...?"

"They're thinking the same thing I've been convinced of for years, Jack, probably since the third grade. And my answer to their question is yes. But that's just me. I ran out of faith a long time ago. Believing in the unbelievable...well, that's not my thing."

It was late Sunday night, but I called Father Gerry—because the rectory kitchen seemed like it would be the safest place in the world.

Father Gerry picked up. Before he could even finish saying hello, I blurted out, "I'm not sure I believe in God anymore."

"Jack?" Father Gerry asked.

"Yeah, it's me."

"I must admit, Jack, what you just said is a real conversation starter—for me, anyway, being an ordained priest and all. Do you want to come down and talk?"

I trotted the entire way down Main Street to St. Mary's. The street was still clotted with cars filled with returning students.

I knocked on the rectory door and Father Gerry pulled the door open.

"Come in, Jack. We're out in the kitchen. Pour yourself a cup of coffee if you'd like. I'll be with you in a moment."

The noisy street outside gave way to the quiet, as I walked to the back of the rectory. That's when I realized that much of the noise was in my head. I poured myself a cup of coffee and sat down.

Father Gerry joined me in the kitchen, and sat down across from me. He immediately saw the *Time* magazine that I'd placed on the table.

He picked it up, and stared at the cover for a moment. "I have my own copy, Jack. Thanks," he said with fake nonchalance.

"Father, *Time* published this issue on Good Friday," I hesitated, hoping to find the right words, hoping to hold back my tears. "The day after my Uncle Ted committed suicide. He died on Holy Thursday."

He put down his coffee, staring for a moment at the dark liquid.

"Oh, Jack. Jack, I'm so sorry to hear that." His words were soft, and full of pain. I'm pretty sure Father Gerry was determined to let me lead the conversation.

"My Uncle Ted was a wonderful person, Father. I mean, really wonderful. And now he's dead and burning in Hell."

"And why would you say that, Jack?"

"It's true, isn't it? Suicide is a mortal sin. I know that. Every Catholic in the world knows that. As we were leaving the cemetery, my mom said it's a shame he's burning in Hell."

"Jack, your mom is not in charge of who goes to Heaven and who goes to Hell."

"I know that, but what about the rules? Mortal sin? The sin of despair?"

"I don't have the answers you want, Jack."

"Well, who does?"

"Our Lord, Jack. He's got the answers."

I wasn't sure if the Lord was on speaking terms with me.

"So where was Our Lord"—I said his name rather sarcastically—"when Uncle Ted really needed Him? Tell me. Where was He? My Uncle Ted hanged himself in the basement right next to his piano, Father. This was a man who could make any piano sing so beautifully…where was Our Lord when Uncle Ted…died…?"

"I don't know. All I can say is that it's all in God's hands now."

"I'm sorry, Father. For more than a week now, I've been looking for some sign—something that will assure me that Uncle Ted…" My voice was swallowed in sorrow.

Sitting opposite one another at the kitchen table, I could see that Father Gerry very much wanted to comfort me.

"As I walked down here, Father, one question kept popping into my head. After a lifetime of being a good person, can someone be condemned for eternity for the very last thing they do?"

"That's the $64,000 question, isn't it, Jack?"

"I concluded that there's really only two possible answers."

He gestured as if to say, *Go on.*

"Either we have a cruel and indifferent God, who doesn't have the time or the inclination to help people like my Uncle Ted when he's in real trouble, or there really is no God. I mean, that second option is so much more preferable, isn't it? Why would anyone worship a God so oblivious to the pain my Uncle Ted was feeling?"

I looked at Father Gerry, hoping I could find the answer to my question somewhere in his face, in his eyes.

Father Gerry asked me what was going on in my head.

"I really don't know," I said. "I know I'm supposed to have faith because what I'm asking you is unknowable. It's a mystery, right? It's in God's hands. That's the way all the mysteries of the Church are handled. But any God who would send a man, as loving as my Uncle Ted…to Hell…well, He doesn't deserve my adoration."

"I understand how you feel, Jack. I really do. You are angry with God. You won't be the first person to feel that way, and let me tell you, you won't be the last. One of the biggest mysteries in all our lives is trying to understand what God wants for us. Trying to understand why certain things happen."

"I've been trying to understand what God's been doing for a long, long time, Father. I remember being in the Cub Scouts—maybe I was eight?—and the Boy Scout attached to my den died of polio. He was only sixteen. We went to see him in an iron lung a few days before he died. A couple years later, when I was playing Little League baseball, my coach's son fell over a cliff and died. He was only eight."

"None of us know why these things happen, Jack."

"Yeah? Sixteen years old? Eight years old? I wish God would show up and explain why these two died. This can't be God's will, can it?" I shook my head. "And Uncle Ted. You can't believe that God wanted my uncle to commit suicide?"

"No. I don't. I really don't. I wish I knew why, but I don't."

"Me, too, Father Gerry. Me, too."

Somewhere in the back of my mind I heard the nuns reminding me that I had to have faith; that I shouldn't surrender to doubt. I needed faith to believe the unbelievable, to accept the unacceptable—acknowledging that some things will always be unknowable. Such things will ever be mysteries.

I had that kind of faith, once. Where did it go?

I stood up, and reached out my hand to Father Gerry to shake hands. It felt rather strange to both of us because we'd never really shaken hands before.

"Thanks, Father Gerry. I better get back to the dorm. I haven't been sleeping well, and it's back to class tomorrow."

"I'm truly sorry to hear about your uncle. Let me say one last thing, Jack. Trust that God will do the right thing. If your uncle was the man you knew him to be, I expect he's in the presence of the Almighty right now."

"I hope that's true, Father. But like you said, my mom can't send him to Hell, and you can't send him to Heaven. After what's happened, I really wish God would just show up and talk to me."

Father walked me to the rectory door.

"See you next Sunday, Jack?"

It was more of a question than a statement.

I left without responding, only flashing Father Gerry a resigned, defeated grin. God might be in his Heaven, but all was not right with the world.

I walked back up Main Street recalling a conversation I had with my room-mate soon after we'd become roommates. I forget what we were arguing about, but I'd called John an atheist—as if it were an insult. He didn't disagree. He just stared at me, and then asked me to sit and listen.

"I know you're a Catholic, just like my parents and my sister, Jack. Just like my grandparents. Just like I used to be. As far as I can see, religious folk have every right to believe in their particular God, and every right to expect every-one who subscribes to their particular religion to comply with their rules. The Jews have Yahweh, the Catholics and Protestants have Jesus, and Muslims have Allah. Each is sure they've got the right God and the right set of rules. By the way, I don't subscribe to any of them."

He shook his head as if he needed to clarify something.

"Let's look at religion from your perspective. Let's say, for the sake of argu-ment, there are 50 religions in the world. As a Catholic, you don't believe in 49 of them, right?"

"That's true, but…"

He interrupted me. "Hold on, Jack. You've got your Catholic religion—one out of 50. Your Jewish friends don't believe in 49 of them either. Each religion dismisses the 49 others—the ones that they're not. That's why you're not Jewish, and they're not Catholic, right? As you said, Jack, I am an atheist. That means I don't believe in any of the 50 religions—but the truth is, I reject only one more than you."

I found his logic oddly therapeutic. When John explained atheism that way, the distance between us began to disappear.

Is there a God? Isn't there a God? I didn't know, and I wondered if I could ever really know. Father Gerry wanted me to trust God, to accept things on faith—a faith that grew weaker by the day. As I walked back to the dorm, I felt increasingly empty. All I had was a hollow ache that I didn't know how to fill.

I hauled that empty feeling into my dorm room and flopped down on my bed. John was on his bed reading a Kurt Vonnegut novel—he loved Vonnegut.

He knew where I'd gone—and he decided there was nothing for him to do but wait.

I suppose there are all kinds of roommates. Roommates who really are just that—two people who share the same room, moving through the school year together, but neither one sharing anything of consequence. Well, that wasn't us. Somehow, during our freshman year, we'd become genuine friends—two people who trusted one another and always had the other's best interest in mind. I remember I once called him a "real Christian" because of the caring, thoughtful responses he offered whenever I shared a problem. I said it partly to tease him, and partly because I felt it was true. I remember his reaction.

"Yeah," he said, after a moment of thought. "Guess that proves you don't have to be a 'real Christian' to be a real Christian. When you get down to it, Timins, all any of us hope to find in the other person—a college roommate, a best friend, a teacher—is a good person. Loving. Helpful. Thoughtful. With or without God."

As I lay on my bed, he closed his book and walked over to me. "How you feeling, Jack?"

"Like I've lost my favorite uncle in the whole wide world. I can't even begin telling you what a terrific human being my Uncle Ted was, John. Can't even begin. And his piano playing was…joyous…beautiful. His hands moved over the keyboard like cheetahs running across the savannah. Just so effortless. And his laughter was infectious. There's just so much I'm gonna miss."

In a very quiet and gentle voice, John said, "I've never lost anyone this way—so I really don't know how I'd feel. All I can say, Timins, is that I hope my nieces and nephews feel about me someday, the way you feel about him. Your uncle was a lucky man to have a nephew who loved him so deeply."

"And now he's gone."

John grabbed his chair and brought it to my bedside. I could hear him take a deep breath, a habit of his that preceded his saying something really important. So, as he sat down and looked at me, I waited for him to speak.

"Jack, I can see your pain. I really can. But from where I sit, your Uncle Ted is not really gone, He's where all of us end up sooner or later. In the hearts of the people who love us—in the hearts of the people who we loved. He's definitely in you. If he wasn't, the pain wouldn't be so sharp, so acute. There's only one way to help ease that pain."

"I wish I knew what that was."

"You do, Jack, you do. Trust me, you do. Tonight, you're going to spend the night telling me everything you can remember about your Uncle Ted. I want you to bring him to life for me, Jack. Tell me everything you can remember. Where you went, what you saw, what you did, what he said. Tell me everything. I really want to know what a person has to do—how a person has to act—to earn the love and devotion of a man like you."

"Oh, John, I don't even know where to begin."

"Okay," John said, rubbing his chin. "Start here. Tell me what he looked like. Was he tall? Short? Skinny? Was he ruggedly handsome like me?"

I couldn't help but laugh, but I sat up on the edge of my bed. Immediately, I began to see Uncle Ted, getting out of his car, parked in the alley behind my house beneath our sour cherry tree. I saw him running to my dad, and the two of them hugging as if it were years since they'd seen each other. It was always that way. They hugged as if it was the last hug they'd ever share—and then they kissed each other, and ruffled each other's hair. They'd kid one another about their growing baldness—"Getting thin up there, Jack," "Beginning to look like a monk, Ted"—and then they'd laugh. Oh, the way they laughed—from the sheer joy of being together again. After all the kissing, hugging, and laughing, they'd walk into the house, their arms draped across one another's shoulders.

I don't know if I'd ever seen Uncle Ted so clearly—even when he was... here...among us.

"He was way different than your ruggedly handsome self, John. He was wiry. A little shorter than my dad. And he had a broad, impish smile. Whenever we got together with Uncle Ted, Aunt Marian, and my cousin Moira, everyone talked up a storm, like there wasn't enough time for all of us to tell all our stories. What I remember best is the laughter. So much laughter, as if somehow we'd stored it up just for our visits."

"I remember my dad and Uncle Ted sitting together at the piano—together—two brothers laughing and playing the same piano at the same time..."

I told John everything I could remember...everything about everything. The stories piled up as we talked deep into the night...and the ache began to dissipate, even as the gnawing, hollow feeling began filling up with the vivid memories of a wonderful man—memories no one could take away.

That's when I realized that I'd always have my Uncle Ted. My loving uncle.

The wonderful piano player. The delightfully funny man.

I no longer wondered or worried where Uncle Ted was. I knew. I smiled, remembering the words of the poet, e. e. cummings.

i carry your heart with me(i carry it in my heart)

Uncle Ted was right here, with me.

Epilogue
DAMNATION AND REDEMPTION
June 1966 and beyond

I wrote *Frosh: A One-Year Memoir* eons ago.

I started writing it when I left teaching and became a national textbook consultant for McGraw-Hill. People thought my consultant job sounded glamorous, but what it really meant was hundreds, even thousands, of hours spent waiting—in airports, on airplanes, and in hotels far from home. I hate to give you the bad news, but that ain't glamorous.

So, I began writing stories about my adventures on the road to fill those empty hours. Idle hours became writing hours. As I spent more time writing, more and more memories began to bubble up—memories that I'd thought I'd left behind long ago. Those memories included all the events of my life-altering freshman year in college, a year when everything changed.

Writing about that year has permitted me to really look at it, to examine it, to understand it—and to understand myself better. Writing about that year gave me a chance to remember my first love, Katie; to remember the woman, Dr. Monroe, who championed my love of theatre and allowed me to develop talents I never knew I had; to remember Diana, the woman who allowed me to express my sexuality; to remember my roommate, John—a man unique in so many ways; and to remember that, once upon a time, I had an uncle named Ted—the most wonderful uncle a boy could have.

I just reread *Frosh*—and I don't think I gave you the whole year. That's an error I want to correct.

Second semester was over, and I had made dean's list. After I gave my parents this good news, it was virtually impossible for my mother to begin any conversation without saying, "Did I mention that Jack made dean's list this semester?" When the official letter from Kutztown arrived in the mail, that letter landed in her purse, and Mom would proudly pull it out whenever the opportunity arose. Mom had exclusive bragging rights.

I never demurred or tried to stop her.

Kutztown's directors announced they would be doing Ionesco's absurdist drama, *Rhinoceros,* in the fall and *A Man for All Seasons* next year.

I already planned to audition and, before I left campus for the summer, I'd gotten copies of the plays from Dr. Sinclair and Dr. Monroe.

Occasionally, someone would ask me what I learned during my first year of college, and I'd rattle off the names of courses I'd taken: Music Appreciation, Math Concepts, German III, Oral Interpretation, English 101, and Beginning Acting. Sometimes, I'd tell them how much I enjoyed being on stage—and how much I loved stepping outside of myself, becoming somebody else—kind of like trying on a new suit to see how it felt.

Then there were the things I'd learned that I seldom discussed.

I learned how to get rid of a power-hungry, authoritarian dorm counselor.

I learned that it's difficult to find love, and even more difficult to make love stay.

I learned about the mind-bending pleasure of sex—and I began to understand that love and lust were light-years apart.

I learned that God may be in His heaven, but that didn't mean all was right with the world.

I learned that losing someone you love—whether by telling them good-bye or watching their casket being lowered into the earth—was the most painful experience I'd ever known.

I learned that God might not be in His heaven at all.

I learned to doubt so many things that had been certainties when I first stepped across that college threshold nine months earlier.

I was sure my freshman year was filled with enough life lessons to last a lifetime, but the rest of my life would disabuse me of that conclusion. As a frosh, I'd discovered that Alexander Pope's sentient poetic line, *A little learning is a dang'rous thing*, applied to me in so many ways. I thought college would widen and deepen my mind, without ever realizing that it could also widen and deepen my heart. I'd never realized that college might discomfit me with new knowledge or take me down intellectual and emotional paths I had never anticipated.

That's something I learned when I was a frosh.

I returned to Heil Pool—again as assistant manager—and the number one, chart-topping song in the summer of '66 was Frank Sinatra's, *Strangers in the Night*. I'll bet I heard Sinatra croon that tune at least once every day over Heil Pool's PA, and memories of my immediate past invariably caught me unawares.

Just for a moment, I'd wonder where Diana would be teaching this coming September, and how she was doing. But only for a moment. Soon, I'd shake free of my brief reverie and tell myself, *That's enough, Jack. Remember, nobody drowns.* Then the small voice in my head would tease me and ask, *There's more than one way to drown, isn't there?*

During my first week back home, I got a letter from Markowski.

Hey Jack,

As you know, I don't typically write letters. But this is a letter that I've been mulling over for some time, and I believe deep down it's a letter that you have to read.

I want you to know I've been thinking a lot about you as I wait to leave for boot camp. In a lot of ways, it's been a tough year for you, hasn't it? Like every college frosh, it's tough enough leaving home for the first time and living on your own, but then having to live with me—a complete stranger—and an atheist in the bargain...

Timins, your life has been filled with more drama than I've ever seen in one calendar year, and it's only early June. I know you didn't mean to break Katie's heart last Christmas, and I don't think Diane meant to break your heart either this year, but hearts get broken—and it's always bad when one of those hearts is yours. And I watched your heart break all over again when your uncle died. It's difficult when someone you love dies...but suicide is one of those acts that leaves everyone feeling guilty. Always wondering if they might have done something, so it would never have happened.

I'm really sorry about your uncle. I know I've said that before, but I can see how it has affected you. Just remember how much you loved your Uncle Ted and how much he loved you. I know that love was real—deeply felt. That means you've got to honor your uncle by remembering him, out loud. Talk about him. You've got lots of terrific stories to tell—with him as the main character. You spent an entire night spinning tale after incredible tale. Talk about the wonderful person you knew. When we don't talk about the people we've loved and lost—if we don't remember them for the wonderful loving human beings they were—then those people die twice. Don't let that happen.

As you can see, I've been doing a lot of thinking about you. Now about me.

My life's been a different kind of disaster. It took me a while at Kutztown to finally realize I was a fish out of water. I really didn't belong there. Not yet. Maybe not ever. Why the hell did I ever consider becoming an elementary school teacher? Little kids are okay—in the abstract.

I'm not sure why I enlisted in the Army, but I think it's because my life will be pretty well laid out for the next three years—except maybe for the possibility of getting dead. I've got orders to report to Fort Dix on Monday June 27th at 7:00 a.m. The U.S. Army does mornings just like you—early and often. You know how I feel about mornings, but I seriously doubt that the U.S. Army will give a rat's ass.

Despite your struggles with love and loss, Jack, you've already found your niche. You've got your theatre resume started with two productions under your belt, and, because of theatre, you know where you belong. I'm just a little jealous. You're talking about teaching high school, and I know how much you really like going to school—you're a going-to-school kind of guy—so I'm pretty sure you'll love teaching, too.

Someday, I'll finish my college education, and when I do, the Army will pay for it, and I won't be going into education.

We were roommates since last September, and I have to tell you, that having a roommate was the one thing I worried about most when I came to Kutztown, because I pretty much keep to myself. But you're okay. I mean that. I know I'm not the easiest person to live with, but I think we've gotten along pretty well.

Probably the only thing we don't see eye-to-eye about is religion. You're a believer and I'm not. I know that sounds simple, but it's awfully complicated. So here's the one thing I want to tell you before I'm up to my eyeballs in khaki:

You found your niche at Kutztown, but now you've got to find yourself—and sometimes religion really gets in the way and makes everything way more complicated than it has to be. The world is more than do's and don'ts. We still have a responsibility to one another—not because God wants us to be that way—but because that's what it means to be a good, decent human being. One can give up God without giving up any of the good things one is. The only person looking over your shoulder should be you. Or maybe your mom and dad. From what I can tell, they taught you well—you're a good, decent human being.

I'll stop there and say, Good Luck this summer. Don't get burned, by the sun or in any other way. You're gonna have a great three more years, and if you ever make it to

Broadway—on the performing side of the footlights—I expect front row tickets.

As for me, beginning in June, I'll do my best to do it the Army way—even if I think it's...well...dumb. If I don't do it the Army way, the Army will kick my ass, and probably make my life miserable. In case you were wondering, I don't think pennying the colonel in his room would work the way pennying Kervin in his room worked at Kutztown.

I can take the time to write to you because I'm just sittin' and waitin', while you're making the world safe for swimmers. I know you'll be back to school later this year—hopefully with a decent dorm counselor—but I have no idea where I'll be. But wherever I am, I'll send you my address. It'll keep changing as I get moved around. Sooner or later, I'll probably end up in some foreign country. Who knows?

I hope you'll write and tell me what the hell is going on, okay?

You're a good guy, Timins. You'll graduate in another three years and make sure that the world a better place for commas and semi-colons. Make me proud.

Your friend—who's in the Army now,
John

I was tempted to write John, and tell him I was probably less religious than when we met last September—but I think he knew that. I also believe he knew how conflicted that made me. I'd been a rock-solid Catholic for eighteen years—weekly Mass, regular Confession, daily prayers, the whole nine yards—but now doubt was chiseling away at those foundations. Big chunks of belief began to crumble. The certain became uncertain. I prayed, but prayer failed to quell the doubt or restore the certainty.

I continued going to Sunday Mass when I was home—dare I say, religiously?—probably not. I went because Mom and Dad would have been disappointed if I didn't.

Except for the sun, moon, and stars—magnificent as they were—the heavens were empty. No God smiled down. No God frowned from above. I'd pretty much concluded we are on our own—unless we decided that we must reach out to others…and hope they reach out to us. How much evidence did the human race require to dispel the notion of an all-loving, all-merciful, all-just, and almighty God? It occurred to me that World War I, World War II—and my Uncle Ted—were sufficient evidence for me, proving we either had an indifferent God, or none at all.

Questions I'd never previously contemplated became subjects for my curiosity. For instance, how did anyone get to Heaven before Christianity? They couldn't be baptized—so were they ensnared by Original Sin? How could anyone pass through the Pearly Gates? So many questions. So much certainty evaporating into doubt.

The doubts piled up as the years rolled by. I took comfort in Descartes' words, *If you would be a real seeker after truth, it is necessary that at least once in your life you doubt, as far as possible, all things.*

So many priests from so many pulpits had preached that doubting was good, that doubt would strengthen one's faith. Well, maybe for some. As for me, I came to doubt all that I'd been told about God and religion since I was in the cradle.

Once or twice over the decades—when I was on the road—I'd go to Mass, and talk with the pastor while we shared a cup of coffee afterwards. I found that nothing had changed since I attended Catholic school. If I brought up beliefs that I considered conundrums—like the Holy Trinity—I was told, "It's a mystery." When I asked how I could believe in something I found impossible to believe, I was told "to have faith."

I rowed on, a boat against the current.

I never told my parents any of this. I might disappoint God, but I wasn't going to disappoint my parents. If they knew how I felt, they'd worry. And I still believe it's never wise to worry one's parents. It's not enough to be right—and when it comes to matters supernatural, how can anyone ever be sure that they are absolutely right?—one still has to be kind. My doubts grew in silence. I never wanted my parents to blame themselves for my flagging faith, or come to believe that a college education took me down the path to non-belief.

I concluded that being a good human being—helpful, kind, generous, resourceful, and willing—was the most anyone should ever expect. That's the kind of man my Uncle Ted was. And if there are any heavens, he deserves to be there. That's the kind of man my father was. That's the kind of woman my wife, Vivian, is.

I spent much of my life among English teachers—first as a college student, then as an English teacher, and finally as a consultant selling textbooks to English teachers. English teachers wrestle each day with the most important subject in a school's curriculum—the English language. I'm not saying Math and Science aren't important, but the only common denominator—such a wonderful math term—among every subject being taught in school, is English.

English is all about words, and making sense of those words, and drawing conclusions from those words. English teachers are engaged in the task of helping their students—even the most reluctant students—become architects using their language, building ideas, and constructing meaning.

I used to tell my high school seniors that I hoped they could see themselves as carpenters or masons, building something on the page that didn't exist until they put pen to paper.

I'd say, "Words make things real. A good sentence is as real as a house on a hill. It ain't hammers and nails, or bricks and mortar, but it's pretty close."

Some wise guy—or girl—would warn me that "ain't" ain't good usage.

I traveled extensively for a lot of years, and one encounter with one teacher was indelibly inked in my memory. I met a Miss Annabelle Lennox, a teacher working in a tiny district in rural North Carolina—a district so small that she taught every grade level, ninth through twelfth. I was charmed by her mellifluous Southern accent, making it exceptionally easy to listen to her comparison of English and religion.

Over coffee in the faculty lounge, she explained her approach.

"I tell my students that English is a great deal like religion."

I'm sure I had a quizzical look on my face.

"We're in the bible belt here, Mr. Timins. I tell them that because my kids understand religion and so do their parents. I pull out the *Holy Bible*, hold it up, and ask, 'Can anybody tell me what book this is?' Somebody always calls out, 'That's the *Holy Bible*, Miss Lennox.' Then I hold up *Warriner's Grammar*—a book, Mr. Timins, I'm reliably informed, that Moses brought down from the mountain—and I ask, 'Can anyone tell me what book this is?' Usually someone responds, 'Isn't that our grammar book, Miss Lennox?' And I say, 'Yes, it is.'"

I asked her, "Why did you choose those two books?"

She stirred her coffee slowly and said, "Patience, Mr. Timins, I'm headin' there."

Miss Lennox was a suspenseful storyteller. I bet her students loved her.

"I hold up the two books together—the *Holy Bible* and *Warriner's Grammar*—and I ask, 'What's the main difference between these two books?' That always stumps them."

"Well, I'm stumped, too, Miss Lennox. You are going to tell me, aren't you?"

She made a comic circular motion with both hands like a stage magician. She laughed, and said, "Patience, Mr. Timins. All shall be revealed."

I leaned forward in my chair.

"I tell them that the main difference between the *Holy Bible* and *Warriner's Grammar* is this: *Warriner's Grammar* has way more commandments. It's got way more than ten. I tell 'em our English language is filled with commandments aplenty—for spelling, for punctuation, for capitalization, for verb tenses, for pronoun usage, for word order. There's a long list, as I'm sure you know. And I tell 'em that if they break those commandments, they'll have to answer to me, because, in my classroom, I'm God. And they know it. I can't send them to Hell, of course, but for some of them, they'd take Hell over an 'F' grade any day."

We both laughed when I asked her if I should kneel before her.

"Maybe later, Mr. Timins, when we're not in the faculty lounge."

As we walked back to her classroom, she thanked me for coming by and showing her the books my company was selling.

"We're just a tiny school district, Mr. Timins. I know that. But most of my students will be going out into that wide, wide world, and I want them to embrace their language with the same energy and enthusiasm as they embrace their religion. I want them to understand the power of words. I tell them that their words can damn them, or redeem them. They need to understand that."

Her passion was unmistakable.

"They need to understand that words can give us joy—or cause us pain. Every day, we teach books whose worlds are filled with love and hate, laughter and misery, certainty and doubt, comedy and tragedy. We teach books filled with human beings—human beings rejoicing and struggling, human beings at their best and at their worst. We teach them about flawed, but loving, human beings—like me—and probably like you, too. I want them to understand what Carl Sandburg meant when he wrote, *Be careful with your words. Once they are said, they can only be forgiven, not forgotten.*"

As I drove away from her school, I smiled at the wisdom of her comment, *Our words can damn us or redeem us.* Then I remembered when I first learned that lesson.

I learned it when I was a frosh.

Appendix
VITA BREVIS

I'm not sure why Uncle Jack created this timeline. When I opened Box #1 of his personal papers, this timeline sat immediately under the manuscript marked *Frosh: A One-Year Memoir*. Did he want the reader to begin with an overview of his life? I don't really know.

His writings filled six cartons that were numbered, so I read through them in the sequence he'd designed. I could hear Uncle Jack telling me, "Begin at the beginning, Julie. Okay?"

I've always listened to whatever my Uncle Jack told me to do. Why should it be any different just because he's dead?

In case you're wondering, the Latin title preceding the timeline, "*Vita Brevis,*" is Uncle Jack's title. It means "Life is short." His love for Latin was nurtured by his four years in high school studying the language of the Caesars.

I found it curious that the timeline's subtitle—"Three Score Years and Ten"—aligned almost precisely with his own life. Uncle Jack died four days after he celebrated his 70th birthday—two days after Christmas. Perhaps he sensed the end was near.

Jack Timins' Three Score Years and Ten
A Timeline
(in Five Pages—More or Less)

1947: I'm born in Dobbs Ferry, New York, to Jack and Vera Timins. I have one older brother, Will.

1949: I move to Palisades Park, New Jersey. I have a new younger brother, Dennis. I have no memory of living there, except for a few mental snapshots.

1952: I move to Easton, Pennsylvania, and live in the same house on Line St. until college graduation. I begin kindergarten at Webster Elementary School.

1953 –
1961: I attend St. Joseph Elementary School.

- I learn how to ride a bike, swim, hike, bowl, ice skate, play baseball, play football, play basketball, and start a campfire.
- I join the Cub Scouts. Mom is our den mother.
- I play Little League football and baseball for the Fleas, a team sponsored by the Fraternal Order of Fleas.
- I go to see the New York Giants and Willie Mays at the Polo Grounds [1954].
- I make my First Confession and First Communion in 2nd grade [1955].
- The Eagle Scout attached to our den—Richard Bricksus—dies of polio. I see him in an iron lung at Easton Hospital [1955].
- I become an altar boy. Apparently, I'm a quick Latin study, and I teach other altar boys [1956].
- I'm part of St. Joseph's safety patrol at the corner of Davis and Nesquehoning Streets with Bruce Calhoun, Mike Flynn, and Jimmy Welsh.
- I join a bowling league. We bowl at the VFW downtown [1960].

- I get confirmed. My confirmation name is Mark [1961].
- I get a paper route for the *Allentown Morning Call* as I enter 8th grade. I leave my house at 3:45 a.m. 361 days a year. [1960 – 1963].
- I get Mom and Dad Christmas presents with my own money—a Timex wristwatch for Mom and a bowling ball for Dad [1961].

1961 –
1965:   I attend Notre Dame High School.

- I have the highest grade point average of all freshmen my first semester [1961].
- My GPA falls to second place at the end of my second semester [1962].
- I join Glee Club.
- I miss 20 days of school as a sophomore with whooping cough [1962].
- I'm invited into the National Honor Society [1963].
- I discover girls. I fall in love with Richena "Katie" Hindmarch, a fellow lifeguard at Heil Pool [1963].
- I play varsity football my junior and senior years [1963 – 1964].
- Notre Dame's 1963 Football team goes undefeated. I get my varsity letter—a big deal.
- I'm accepted to Kutztown State College for fall 1965—a bigger deal.

1965 –
1969:   I attend Kutztown State College. Earn a B.S. in Education with an English and Drama major.

- I perform in more than a dozen plays over four years. [1965 – 1969]
- I break up with Katie just before Christmas, 1965.
- I lose my virginity.
- My favorite uncle commits suicide.

- I begin losing my faith.
- My older brother, Will, enlists in the United States Marine Corps in May 1966.
- My roommate joins the Army saying, "It's better than staying here."
- I deliver papers in the dorm for two years. Easy cash [1966 – 1968].
- I become Chairman of the Kutztown Reader's Theatre [1967].
- I become the booth announcer for Kutztown's home football games for two years.
- I student teach at Reading HS (Reading, PA) and Parkland HS (Allentown, PA).
- My brother Denny joins the Marine Corps. Both brothers serve in Vietnam.
- Vietnam War continues, but I have a student deferment.

1969 –
1970:   I am hired to teach at Nazareth High School in Nazareth, PA.

- I buy my first car. An Opel Kadett. $1,800 new.
- I am a rookie teacher.
- My department chair, R. Frederick Knecht, offers me inexpensive room and board. He tells me the R in his name stands for "Right."
- I briefly spend time auditioning for roles in NYC. No luck. The threat of the draft keeps me from leaving teaching. I'd prefer not to perform in Army green.
- I direct my first high school production, *Lost Horizon*.
- I have my first automobile accident.
- I apply to graduate school at the University of Washington in Seattle.
- I move to Seattle, much to the dismay of my mother.
- I get a call from a Marine Corps recruiter. I will be reclassified in July and drafted in August unless I find another draft-deferred teaching position. I discover that being a graduate teaching assistant does NOT qualify for a deferment.

- I quickly find another teaching position in the Bellevue Schools in Washington State to maintain my teaching deferment.
- I find an inexpensive apartment on Queen Ann Hill.

1970 –
1972: I am hired to teach HS English in Bellevue School District.

- I'm safe from being drafted.
- I travel to Pennsylvania for Will's wedding to Marg.
- I travel to NYC with 10 students for a Broadway theatre experience.
- Mom and Dad come into NYC to see me.

1972 –
1974: I attend graduate school at the University of Washington.

- I take a leave of absence from Bellevue S.D. for graduate school. I have a teaching assistantship in the Department of Speech.
- I complete my M.A. Speech degree just as the teaching year begins in September 1974.

1974 –
1985: I return to the Bellevue S.D. as a high school teacher.

- I teach English, Speech, Debate, Drama, Acting, as well as Government and U.S. History.
- I direct the fall musicals. *The Sound of Music, Little Mary Sunshine, My Fair Lady*, etc.
- I become a football referee in 1974. I begin working varsity games a year later. I begin working playoff games four years after that.
- I become assistant debate coach and then debate coach, traveling around Washington State to various competitions with the debate team.
- I travel to London over spring break in 1978 and 1979. Go to the Muppet Studio in 1979.
- I resign my teaching position, June 1985.

1985 –
2000:   I become a national sales consultant for a textbook publisher.

- I begin work as national textbook consultant for Harper & Row on July 1, 1985.
- I get training, a company car, and an expense account.
- My extensive, cross-country travel prevents me from refereeing football.
- Macmillan buys Harper & Row, and then I work for Macmillan.
- Macmillan changes textbook division name to Scribner Educational Publishers in late 1985.
- Scribner acquires Laidlaw Brothers in 1986 and becomes Scribner-Laidlaw.
- Everything is reorganized in 1988, and we become Glencoe/Macmillan. Usually referred to as Glencoe.
- I travel nationally to all 50 states and five foreign countries as a national consultant.
- My compensation is significantly higher (probably double) than what I earned as a teacher.
- McGraw-Hill purchases Macmillan in 1991, and Glencoe becomes a division of Macmillan/McGraw-Hill.
- My job allows me to visit all my relatives every year. I visit Mom and Dad at least two or three times each year.
- Dad dies at age 83 in 1999. He is buried on St. Patrick's Day, March 17, 1999.
- Glencoe changes leadership, and the traveling life for consultants becomes increasingly more difficult.
- I meet with my Glencoe boss, telling him no consultant should be expected to work seven days a week. He disagrees.
- I leave Glencoe for Prentice Hall Publishing on June 2nd, 2000, after several disputes with my boss.

2000 –
2014:   I change jobs, working as a consultant for Prentice Hall.

- I join the Prentice Hall Language Arts consultant team. I work in Texas immediately.
- I meet Vivian at Benaroya Hall (Seattle Symphony) during a Pops concert in the fall of 2002. She is one of my former high school students who performed in my musicals. She is an accountant with her own small business.
- I discover that Vivian is the love of my life.
- My mother goes into assisted living in 2003.
- Vivian and I marry in May in a civil ceremony at Vivian's home in 2003. My mother is upset at not being invited. NOTE: No one was invited.
- Vivian and I enjoy life at *Wutherwood*—that's what she calls our home—with our three dogs (Aria, Baloo, and King) and our three cats (Mercedes, Almond Joy, and Nicky).
- Vivian meets Mom Timins on June 25th, 2003. It's Mom's 84th birthday. Vivian is a hit.

2014 –
2016:   Retirement.

- I retire on November 2nd, 2014 with quite a bit of money saved, a small pension, and Social Security. I'd traveled 4.7 million air miles.
- I begin writing. For myself. And for Vivian.

2016 –
2017:   Vivian.

- Vivian is diagnosed with pancreatic cancer on March 15th—beware the Ides of March?—and she dies on September 13th, one day after her 57th birthday. She had said, "I'm going to live to 57 if it kills me."

2017:   Jack.

- I die, two days after Christmas. Four days after my 70th birthday. I am discovered at *Wutherwood* by a neighbor bringing some holiday cheer. I wasn't available to toast the holidays. Ah, well.

Editor's Confession:

 I wrote in the last entry. Uncle Jack wasn't in any position to complete his own timeline.

 This timeline is Uncle Jack's entire life in a few short pages. And *Frosh* is one year of that life in a few hundred pages. Proof of the title Uncle Jack created: *Vita brevis.*

www.ingramcontent.com/pod-product-compliance
Lightning Source LLC
Chambersburg PA
CBHW051339020726
47501CB00007B/2176